Edward Sylvester Ellis

The life and times of Col. Daniel Boone

Hunter, soldier, and pioneer

Edward Sylvester Ellis

The life and times of Col. Daniel Boone
Hunter, soldier, and pioneer

ISBN/EAN: 9783337135126

Printed in Europe, USA, Canada, Australia, Japan

Cover: Foto ©Raphael Reischuk / pixelio.de

More available books at **www.hansebooks.com**

THE LIFE AND TIMES

OF

COL. DANIEL BOONE,

HUNTER, SOLDIER, AND PIONEER.

WITH

SKETCHES OF SIMON KENTON, LEWIS WETZEL, AND OTHER
LEADERS IN THE SETTLEMENT OF THE WEST.

> *"Of all men*
> *Who passes for in life and death most lucky,*
> *Of the great names which in our faces stare,*
> *Is Daniel Boone, backwoodsman of Kentucky.*
>
> *Crime came not near him — she is not the child*
> *Of solitude. Health shrank not from him, for*
> *Her home is in the rarely-trodden wild."*

By EDWARD S. ELLIS,

AUTHOR OF "THE LIFE OF COLONEL DAVID CROCKETT," "NED IN THE
BLOCK-HOUSE," "NED IN THE WOODS," ETC.

PHILADELPHIA:

PORTER & COATES.

INTRODUCTION.

DANIEL BOONE was the ideal of the American pioneer—brave, cool, self-reliant, a dead shot with his rifle, a consummate master of woodcraft, with sturdy frame, hopeful at all times, and never discouraged by disasters which caused many a weaker spirit to faint by the way. All that the pen of romance depicts in the life of one whose lot is cast in the Western forests, marked the career of Boone. In the lonely solitudes he encountered the wild animal and the fiercer wild man; and he stood on the bastions at Boonesborough through the flaming sun or the solemn hours of night, exchanging shots with the treacherous Shawanoe, when every bullet fired was meant to extinguish a human life; he was captured by Indians three times, his companions were shot down at his side, his daughter was carried away by savages and quickly rescued by himself and a few intrepid comrades, his oldest boy was shot dead before he set foot in Kentucky, and another was killed while bravely fighting at Blue Licks; the border town named after him was assaulted and besieged by overwhelming bodies of British and Indians, his brother was slain and he himself underwent all manner of hardship and suffering.

Yet through it all, he preserved his honest simplicity, his unswerving integrity, his prudence and self-possession, and his unfaltering faith in himself, in the future of his country, and in God.

He lived through this crucial period to see all his dreams realized, and Kentucky one of the brightest stars in the grand constellation of the Union.

Such a life cannot be studied too closely by American youth; and in the following pages, we have endeavored to give an accurate description of its opening, its eventful progress and its peaceful close, when, in the fullness of time and in a ripe old age, he was finally laid to rest, honored and revered by the great nation whose possessions stretch from ocean to ocean, and whose " land is the fairest that ever sun shone on ! "

CONTENTS.

CHAPTER VI.

CHAPTER VII.

CHAPTER VIII.

CHAPTER XVII.

CHAPTER XVIII.

CHAPTER XIX.

CHAPTER XX.

CHAPTER XXI.

GENERAL SIMON KENTON.

CHAPTER I.

CHAPTER II.

LEWIS WETZEL.

LIFE AND TIMES

OF

COLONEL DANIEL BOONE.

CHAPTER I.

Birth of Daniel Boone—Fondness for Hunting—An Alarming Absence—A Pedagogue of the Olden Time—Sudden Termination of Young Boone's School Education—Removal to North Carolina—Boone's Marriage—His Children.

DANIEL BOONE was born in Exeter township, Bucks county, Pennsylvania, on the 11th of February, 1735, so that he was just three years the junior of Washington.

Daniel had six brothers and four sisters, he being the fourth child of Squire Boone, whose father landed at Philadelphia from England, October 10, 1717, bringing with him two daughters and nine sons. The township of Exeter, as it is now known in Pennsylvania, was named by the elder Boone after the city in England near which he was born.

There is good authority for believing that the Boone family, when living in the mother country, were attached to the Established Church; but, when they had resided some time amid the peaceful surroundings and gentle influences of the friends and followers of George Fox, they inclined to their religious belief, though it will hardly be claimed that Daniel Boone continued orthodox throughout his adventurous life.

In those days, the educational advantages given youth were very meagre, and frequently none at all. The old-time pedagogue was a man stern and repelling to children, knowing little of the true means of imparting knowledge. About the only branch he handled with any skill was that which came from the nearest tree; and, had he possessed the ability to teach, he lacked, in the generality of cases, the education necessary.

A century and a half ago, Exeter township abounded with game, and the town itself was a pioneer settlement of the most primitive order, consisting of log-houses almost entirely surrounded by forests, in whose depths roamed bears, panthers, deer, and the smaller game so attractive to sportsmen.

It was these which were to educate young Boone more than were the crude means and the tippling teacher in whose charge he was placed. Nothing delighted the lad more than to wander for hours through the woods, gun in hand, stealing among the cool shadows, behind the mossy rocks and along the purling streams, with the soft tread of the Indian, while the keen eyes of the young hunter searched tree-top and bush for the first signs of game, and his ear was ever strained to catch the cautious footstep of the wild beast as it crept faintly over the leaves.

Thus in the grand school of Nature was the great pioneer trained. While yet a small boy, he became noted for his unerring aim with the rifle, and the skill with which he read the "signs" among the trees, that were as closed volumes to others.

The privilege of wandering with gun and dog was all the happiness he asked, and as an inevitable consequence of this mode of life, he grew sturdy, strong, active, and capable of immense exertion without fatigue. It is in just such nurseries as this that the great explorers and pioneers of the world are educated.

One morning, Daniel shouldered his rifle, and whistling to his dog, the two plunged into the woods for one of their usual hunts. The sun was just rising in a clear sky, the air was crisp and invigorating, and the prospect was all that the heart of the young hunter could wish. Those of his relatives who saw him depart thought nothing of it, for the sight was a very common one with him and his brothers, and young as they were, they learned among the rudiments of their training the great fundamental truth to trust in God and themselves.

As the shades of night closed over settlement and forest, the boy Daniel was expected home, though the family had no special misgiving when the hours passed without bringing him, it being supposed that he had penetrated so far into the wilds that he preferred to encamp for the night rather than take the long tramp home.

But, when the second day had passed, and he failed to appear, the parents were in great distress, for it seemed certain that some fatal accident must have overtaken their child. The mature and experienced hunter is always in peril from wild beasts or the wilder human beings who prowl and skulk through the wilderness, and many a man who has braved the dangers of a score of years, has fallen a victim to the treacherous biped or quadruped, who has sought his life with greater cunning than he has done his own work.

It was impossible therefore for them to feel anything but the most painful anxiety for their boy, and, unable to remain idle longer, they called upon their neighbors, and a search-party was organized.

The trail made by the lad was too faint to be followed successfully, and the parties scattered and hunted for traces as best they could.

Hours passed by, every man doing his utmost to discover the fate of the boy, who they hoped was still living somewhere in the depths of the wilderness, though it would seem scarcely possible that, if alive, he was not in a suffering or helpless condition.

But the shouts and reports of their guns remained unanswered, and they pushed forward, hoping against hope. The bonds of sympathy are nowhere stronger than in such frontier settlements, where a common feeling of brotherhood exists, and the men who were searching for the lost Daniel, were hardly less anxious concerning him than were the parents themselves.

Suddenly some one descried a faint, thin column of smoke rising from a nondescript sort of structure, and hurrying toward it, they saw one of the most primitive of cabins, made of limbs and brush and sods of grass piled together. Stealing around to the rude entrance, they peeped in, and saw Daniel himself, looking like an old hunter who had settled down for the season. On the earth-floor of his structure were strewn the skins of the game he had shot, while he was cooking the choicest pieces before the smoking fire. He was only three miles from home, but it might as well have been a hundred, for all the additional comfort it afforded his friends and parents.

The lad looked up with an expression of surprise, wondering what all the excitement was about; and when he found they were hunting for him, it was hard to understand the necessity for doing any such thing.

It was not the first time he had been alone in the woods, and he thought he was as well able to take care of himself as were any of the older pioneers who came to look for him. However, as he was a dutiful son, and had no wish to cause his parents any unnecessary alarm, he gathered up his game and peltries, and went back home with the hunters.

Nothing can be more pleasant to the American boy than just such a life as that followed by Daniel Boone—wandering for hours through the wilderness, on the look-out for game, building the cheery camp-fire deep in some glen or gorge, quaffing the clear icy water from some stream, or lying flat on the back and looking up through the tree-tops at the patches of blue sky, across which the snowy ships of vapor are continually sailing.

But any parent who would allow a child to follow the bewitching pleasures of such a life, would commit a sinful neglect of duty, and would take the surest means of bringing regret, sorrow, and trouble to the boy himself, when he should come to manhood.

The parents of young Boone, though they were poor, and had the charge of a large family, did their utmost to give their children the rudiments of a common school education, with the poor advantages that were at their command.

It is said that about the first thing Daniel's teacher did, after summoning his boys and girls together in the morning, was to send them out again for a recess—one of the most popular proceedings a teacher can take, though it cannot be considered a very great help in their studies.

While the pupils were enjoying themselves to their fullest bent, the master took a stroll into the woods, from which he was always sure to return much more crabbed than when he went, and with his breath smelling very strongly of something stronger than water.

At times he became so mellowed, that he was indulgence itself, and at other times he beat the boys unmercifully. The patrons of the school seemed to think their duty ended with the sending of their children to the school-house, without inquiring what took place after they got there.

One day Daniel asked the teacher for permission to go out-doors, and receiving it, he passed into the clear air just at the moment that a brown squirrel was running along the branch of a fallen tree.

Instantly the athletic lad darted in pursuit, and, when the nimble little animal whisked out of sight among a dense clump of vine and bushes, the boy shoved his hand in, in the hope of catching it. Instead of doing so, he touched something cold and smooth, and bringing it forth, found it was a whiskey bottle with a goodly quantity of the fiery fluid within.

"That's what the teacher comes out here for," thought Daniel, as his eyes sparkled, "and that's why he is so cross when he comes back."

He restored the bottle to its place, and returned to the school-room, saying nothing to any one until after dismissal, when he told his discovery to some of the larger boys, who, like all school-children, were ever ripe for mischief.

When such a group fall into a discussion, it may be set down as among the certainties that something serious to some one is sure to be the result.

The next morning the boys put a good charge of tartar emetic in the whiskey bottle, and shaking it up, restored it to its former place of concealment. Then, full of eager expectation, they hurried into school, where they were more studious than ever—

a suspicious sign which ought to have attracted
the notice of the teacher, though it seems not to
have done so.

The Irish instructor took his walk as usual, and
when he came back and resumed labor, it may be
imagined that the boys were on the tip-toe of expectation.

They had not long to wait. The teacher grew
pale, and gave signs of some revolution going on
internally. But he did not yield to the feeling.
As might have been expected, however, it increased
his fretfulness, and whether he suspected the truth
or not, he punished the boys most cruelly, as
though seeking to work off his illness by exercising
himself with the rod upon the backs of the lads,
whose only consolation was in observing that the
medicine taken unconsciously by the irate teacher
was accomplishing its mission.

Matters became worse and worse, and the whip-
pings of the teacher were so indiscriminate and
brutal, that a rebellion was excited. The crisis
was reached when he assailed Daniel, who struggled desperately, encouraged by the uproar and
shouts of the others, until he finally got the upper
hand of the master, and gave him an unquestion-
able trouncing.

After such a proceeding it was not to be expected
that any sort of discipline could be maintained,
and the rest of the pupils rushed out-doors and
scattered to their homes.

The news of the outbreak quickly spread through
the neighborhood, and Daniel was taken to task

by his father for his insubordination, though the parent now saw that the teacher possessed not the first qualification for his position. And the instructor himself must have felt somewhat the same way, for he made no objections when he was notified of his dismissal, and the school education of Daniel Boone ended.

It was a misfortune to him, as it is to any one, to be deprived of the privilege of storing his mind with the knowledge that is to be acquired from books, and yet, in another sense, it was an advantage to the sturdy boy, who gained the better opportunity for training himself for the great work which lay before him.

In the woods of Exeter he hunted more than ever, educating the eye, ear, and all the senses to that wonderful quickness which seems incredible when simply told of a person. He became a dead shot with his rifle, and laid the foundations of rugged health, strength and endurance, which were to prove so invaluable to him in after years, when he should cross the Ohio, and venture into the perilous depths of the Dark and Bloody Ground.

Boone grew into a natural athlete, with all his faculties educated to the highest point of excellence. He assisted his father as best he could, but he was a Nimrod by nature, instinct and education, and while yet a boy, he became known for miles around the settlement as a most skilled, daring, and successful hunter.

When he had reached young manhood, his father removed to North Carolina, settling near Hol-

man's Ford, on the Yadkin river, some eight
miles from Wilkesboro'. Here, as usual, the boy
assisted his parents, who were gifted with a large
family, as was generally the case with the pioneers,
so that there was rarely anything like affluence at-
tained by those who helped to build up our country.

While the Boones lived on the banks of the
Yadkin, Daniel formed the acquaintance of Rebecca Bryan, whom he married, according to the
best authority attainable, in the year 1755, when
he was about twenty years of age.

There is a legend which has been told many a
time to the effect that Boone, while hunting, mis-
took the bright eyes of a young lady for those of
a deer, and that he came within a hair's-breadth of
sending a ball between them with his unerring
rifle, before he discovered his mistake. But the
legend, like that of Jessie Brown at Lucknow and
many others in which we delight, has no foundation in fact, and so far as known there was no
special romance connected with the marriage of
Boone to the excellent lady who became his
partner for life.

The children born of this marriage were James,
Israel, Jesse, Daniel, Nathan, Susan, Jemima, La-
vinia, and Rebecca.

CHAPTER II.

Social Disturbances in North Carolina—Eve of the American Revolution—Boone's Excursions to the West—Inscription on a Tree—Employed by Henderson and Company—The " Regulators" of North Carolina—Dispersed by Governor Tryon—John Finley—Resolution to go West.

THE early part of Daniel Boone's married life was uneventful, and the years glided by without bringing any incident, event or experience to him worthy the pen of the historian. He toiled faithfully to support his growing family, and spent a goodly portion of his time in the woods, with his rifle and dog, sometimes camping on the bank of the lonely Yadkin, or floating down its smooth waters in the stillness of the delightful afternoon, or through the solemn quiet of the night, when nothing but the stars were to be seen twinkling overhead.

But Daniel Boone was living in stirring times, and there were signs in the political heavens of tremendous changes approaching. There was war between England and France; there was strife along the frontier, where the Indian fought fiercely against the advancing army of civilization, and the spirit of resistance to the tyranny of the mother country was growing rapidly among the sturdy colonists. North Carolina began, through her repre-

sentatives in legislature, those measures of opposi-
tion to the authority of Great Britain, which forecast
the active part the Old Pine Tree State was to
take in the revolutionary struggle for liberty and
independence.

During the few years that followed there was
constant quarreling between the royal governor
and the legislators, and it assumed such propor-
tions that the State was kept in continual ferment.
This unrest and disturbance were anything but
pleasing to Boone, who saw the country settling
rapidly around him, and who began to look toward
the West with the longing which comes over the
bird when it gazes yearningly out from the bars of
its cage at the green fields, cool woods, and enchanting landscapes in which its companions are
singing and reveling with delight.

Boone took long hunting excursions toward the
West, though nothing is known with exact certainty
as to the date when he began them. The Cherokee
war which had caused much trouble along the Carolina frontier was ended, and he and others must
have turned their thoughts many a time to the
boundless forests which stretched for hundreds
and thousands of miles towards the setting sun, in
which roamed countless multitudes of wild animals
and still wilder beings, who were ready to dispute
every foot of advance made by the white settlers.

Such a vast field could not but possess an irresistible attraction to a consummate hunter like
Boone, and the glimpses which the North Carolina
woods gave of the possibilities awaiting him, and

the growth of empire in the West, were sure to produce the result that came when he had been married some fifteen or more years and was in the prime of life.

Previous to this date, the well known abundance of game in Tennessee led many hunters to make incursions into the territory. They sometimes formed large companies, uniting for the prospect of gain and greater protection against the ever-present danger from Indians.

It is mentioned by good authority, that among the parties thus venturing over the Carolina border into the wilderness, was one at the head of which was " Daniel Boone from the Yadkin, in North Carolina, who traveled with them as low as the place where Abingdon now stands, and there left them."

Some years ago the following description could be deciphered upon an old beech-tree standing between Jonesboro and Blountsville:

	D. BOON	
CILLED	A. BAR	ON
IN	THE	TREE
YEAR	1760.	

This inscription is generally considered as proof that Boone made hunting excursions to that region at that early date, though the evidence can hardly be accepted as positive on the point.

It was scarcely a year after the date named, however, that Boone, who was still living on the Yadkin, entered the same section of the country, having been sent thither by Henderson & Company for the purposes of exploration. He was accompanied by Samuel Callaway, a relative, and the ancestor of many of the Callaways of Tennessee, Kentucky, and Missouri. The latter was at the side of Boone when, approaching a spur of the Cumberland mountains, upon whose slopes they saw multitudes of bisons grazing, the great pioneer paused, and surveying the scene for a moment, exclaimed, with kindling eyes :

" I am richer than He who owned the cattle on a thousand hills, for I own the wild beasts of a thousand valleys."

The sight was indeed one which might have stirred the heart of a hunter who could grasp the possibilities of the future of those favored regions.

Daniel Boone may be considered as having undergone a preliminary training from his earliest boyhood for the work which has identified his name indissolubly with the history of Kentucky. He was what may be called a born pioneer, but there were causes at work in North Carolina which led to his departure for the Kentucky wilderness, of which the general reader is apt to lose sight in studying his character.

The approach of the American Revolution in the former State, as in many others, was marked by social disturbances frequently amounting to anarchy. There were many Scotch traders, who had accumulated considerable wealth without having gone through the labor and perils which the natives underwent in providing for their families.

These foreigners adopted an expensive and showy style of living, altogether out of keeping with the severe simplicity that marked that of the colonists.

Nothing was more natural than that this assumption of superiority in the way of social position should roil and excite resentment among those less favored by fortune.

They were not alone in this offensive course: the officers and agents of the Royal Government were equally ostentatious in display and manner of living, and the exasperating snobbishness spread to the magistrates, lawyers, clerks of court, and tax gatherers, who demanded exorbitant fees for their services. The clergymen of the Established Church became oppressive in their exactions, and, as we have stated, society itself was threatened with revolution before the rattle of musketry at Bunker Hill "was heard around the world."

Petitions were sent to the Legislature for relief by the suffering citizens, who were in much the same distressing situation in which Ireland has been many a time since. These prayers were treated with indifference or open contempt, for there are none more reckless and blind than those who are traveling close to the edge of the political volcano rumbling at their feet.

There is a limit beyond which it is always dangerous to tempt the endurance of a people, who now began meeting together, and formed themselves into associations for correcting the evils around them. It was these people who received the name of " Regulators," and who helped to increase the disturbances in that particular section of the country. They deliberately decided "to pay only such taxes as were agreeable to law, and applied to the purpose therein named, and to pay no officer more than his legal fees."

The history of the State records many acts of violence which were inevitable from this condition of affairs. The final collision between the " Regulators " and a strong force of the royal governor Tryon at Alamanance, in which the rebels were badly defeated, occurred in May, 1771, but the disturbances continued with more or less violence until the breaking out of the Revolution, when the mills of God ground so "exceeding fine," that the grievances were removed forever.

It was in such a community as this that Daniel Boone lived, and he and his family were sufferers. What more natural than that he should cast his eyes longingly toward the West, where, though there might be wild beasts and wild men, he and his loved ones could be free from the exasperating annoyances which were all around them?

The perils from Indians were much less alarming to them than were those of the tax-gatherer. Indeed, in all probability, it lent an additional attractiveness to the vast expanse of virgin wilderness, with its splashing streams, its rich soil, its abundance of game and all that is so enchanting to the real sportsman, who finds an additional charm in the knowledge that the pleasure upon which he proposes to enter is spiced with personal danger.

One day a visitor dropped in upon Boone. He

was John Finley, who led a party of hunters to the region adjoining the Louisa River in Kentucky in the winter of 1767, where they spent the season in hunting and trapping. The hunter called upon Boone to tell him about that land in which he knew his friend was so much interested.

We can imagine the young man, with his rifle suspended on the deer-prongs over the fire, with his wife busy about her household duties and his children at play, sitting in his cabin and listening to the glowing narrative of one who knew whereof he was speaking.

Finley told him of the innumerable game, the deer and bison, the myriads of wild turkeys, and everything so highly prized by the sportsman; he pictured the vast stretches of forest in which the hunter could wander for hours and days without striking a clearing; of the numerous streams, some large, some small, and all lovely to the eye, and it needed no very far-seeing vision to forecast the magnificent future which lay before this highly favored region.

It must have been a winsome picture drawn by Finley—aided as it was by the repelling coloring of the scene of his actual surroundings—made so hateful by the oppressive agents of the foreign government which claimed the colonies as her own.

When Finley was through, and he had answered all of his friend's questions, and told him of his many hunting adventures in Kentucky, Boone announced that he would go with him when he should make his next visit. He had already been drawn strongly toward the region, and he wished to see with his own eyes the favored land, before removing his family thither.

The acquisition of such a person was so desirable, that he was sure to be appreciated by those who knew him best, and whether appointed to that position or not, his own matchless resources and natural powers were certain to fix upon him as the leader of the adventurous characters who had decided to explore the dangerous wilderness of Kentucky.

CHAPTER III.

The Party of Exploration—Daniel Boone the Leader—More than a Month on the Journey—On the Border of Kentucky —An Enchanting View—A Site for the Camp—Unsurpassed Hunting—An Impressive Solitude—No Signs of Indians.

DANIEL BOONE now entered upon that epoch in his life, which has interwoven his name with the history of Kentucky, and indeed with the settlement of the West, for though he was not venturing into the wilderness with the intention of remaining there, yet his purpose of "spying out the land " was simply the first step in his career of pioneer of the Dark and Bloody Ground.

The party of exploration, or rather of hunting, numbered a half dozen : John Finley, James Moncey, John Stuart, William Cool, Joseph Holden, and Daniel Boone, who was chosen the leader. It was a strong company, for all the men were experienced hunters, unerring rifle-shots, and well aware of the dangers they were to encounter.

On the first of May, 1769, the party set out for Kentucky in high spirits, and eagerly anticipating the enjoyment that was to be theirs, before they should return from the all-important expedition.

They had selected the most enchanting season of the year, and it is easy to imagine with what glowing anticipation they ventured upon the journey, which was to be more eventful, indeed, than any member of it imagined.

It was a long distance from North Carolina,
across the intervening stretch of stream, forest and
mountain, to Kentucky, with all the temptations
to the hunter to turn aside, temptations which it is
safe to conclude overcame them many a time, for,
when a full month had passed, not one of the
party had stepped within the confines of the Dark
and Bloody Ground.

But, though they were moving slowly, they were
steadily nearing the promised land, and on the 7th
of June the men, bronzed and toughened by the exposure to which they had been subjected, but still
sturdy and resolute, began climbing the precipitous slope of a mountain on the border of Kentucky.

The six who had left North Carolina more than
a month before were there, attired in their rough
hunting costume, and with their ambition and
purpose as strong as ever. Each wore the hunting-
shirt of the forest ranger made of dressed deer-
skins. The leggins were of the same material, and
the feet were protected by strong, comfortably fit-
ting moccasins. There were fringes down the
seams of the leggins, just as seems to be the
favorite custom with many of the red-men in don-
ning their picturesque costumes.

Although these dresses might be attractive to
the eye, yet such a purpose was the last that entered the minds of the wearers, who constructed
them for use only. Their under garments were of
cotton, so coarse that it would have been like sack-
cloth to many a man of modern days; they carried,

as a matter of course, the powder-horn, rifle, hatchet, bullet-pouch, and the other indispensables of a hunter.

It was near the close of the day, and though the party were pretty well. exhausted, yet they pushed on, feeling in many respects like those who, for the first time in their lives, are to gaze upon the land which is more enchanting to them than all the world beside.

Ere the sun sank behind the immense expanse of wilderness, and just when its splendors were illuminating the skies with the glories of the fading day, the hunting party reached the summit of the mountain, and gazed off over Kentucky.

The panorama spread out before them was a most entrancing one, their vision extending over hundreds of square miles, with the rich vales watered by the beautiful streams, the forest alternating with broad natural clearings, with vast stretches of level country upon which the myriads of moving specks were recognized by the experienced eye as bisons, and over which they knew the deer dashed and other wild animals roamed with scarcely a fear of their natural enemy, man. There was many a league in whose solemn depths a human foot had never yet penetrated, and whose echoes had never been awakened by the shot of the rifle. There they lay as silent as at "creation's morn," and the denizens of the woods waxed strong and wandered at will, without fear of the deadly bullet whistling from behind the tree or mossy rock.

True, among these cool woods and within many

of the dark recesses the red Indian ventured, and now and then the sharp whiz of his arrow was heard, and the barbed weapon flashed among the green leaves as it pierced the heart of the unsuspecting natives of the wood.

But where there were such multitudes of wild beasts these deaths were scarcely noticeable, and the white hunters knew that it was a sportsman's paradise that lay spread at their feet.

The picture of these six pioneers who paused on the crest of the mountain as the sun was setting, and looked off over the Kentucky wilderness, is that which has been selected by the artist, who has immortalized the scene on canvas, and a'' will agree that he could not have chosen a more inviting subject.

The surface upon which they looked down was rolling, level far beyond, but quite hilly nearer the base of the mountain, while it all possessed the indescribable charm of variety, and it could not have been more enchanting to the wearied spectators.

Finley had been there before, and, though they may have thought that some of the stories he told were overdrawn, they could well afford to believe them now, when they came to gaze upon the attractive country.

Aye, they stood on the very borders of the land, and they determined that they would venture within it on the morrow. Although they had left home at the most delightful season of the year, yet the spring proved to be a severe one, and their journey had been delayed by stormy weather, so that the glowing panorama at their feet was robed in more roseate colors from its very contrast to that through which they had passed so recently.

Assuming positions of rest, the group feasted their eyes to the full, and we can well imagine the expressions of delight which escaped them, as they constantly caught sight of new and novel scenes and pointed them out to each other.

There lay the region in which they would probably make their future home, whither they would bring their families, and where they would encounter the toil, privation and danger, which invariably attend the pioneers of every country.

Under such circumstances, the time, place and surroundings were invested with a peculiar interest, which could not have been theirs at any other period or under any different conditions.

The sun went down behind the wilderness, and night gradually overspread the scene. The hunters had not caught sight of a single human being beside themselves, and now that darkness had come, they made their preparations to encamp for the night.

They were veterans at this business, as they showed by avoiding such a conspicuous position as they then occupied. The flash of a camp-fire on the mountain-top would have been seen for many miles over the wilderness, and though they had discovered nothing of the red-men, yet it was reasonable to suppose that many of them would look out from the dark recesses at the unwonted spectacle and would suspect the true cause.

And so, from a prudent habit they had formed, they moved down to a neighboring ravine, where they camped for the night.

The spot was favorable in every respect, the gorge being so deep, and surrounded by such a dense thicket, that the glimmer of the camp-fire was not likely to be seen by any one, unless he ventured close enough to hear the murmur of the voices of the hunters as they gathered together for their evening meal.

Near them lay a tree that had been uprooted by some recent storm, and which offered the advantages the hunters could not fail to appreciate at sight. The huge trunk was used for the rear wall of the camp, as it may be termed, while logs and brush were gathered and piled on two sides, leaving the front open, where the fire was kindled against another log. Thus they were secured against any chill during the cold night, while no wild animal was likely to venture across the magic ring of fire, in case he was attracted to the spot.

It was decided not only to make this their resting-place for the night, but their head-quarters during their visit to Kentucky.

Accordingly, their camp was strengthened, as may be said, a roof being made more substantial than ornamental, but sufficient to keep out the rain, and the front was narrowed in, so that no matter how sudden or violent the changes of weather, they were well protected against them.

Their greatest safeguard, however, lay in their own hardy constitutions and rugged health, which they had acquired from their active out-door life long before venturing into this wild region.

This visit to Kentucky was extended all through the summer and autumn until the dead of winter, during which time they made the camp in the gorge their head-quarters.

They had many a glorious hunt, as may well be supposed, and it would be unsafe to estimate the numbers of bisons, deer, wild turkeys, bear and other species of game that fell victims to the unerring marksmen. It is unnecessary to say that they lived like princes, and grew stronger, sturdier, and more hopeful. Although separated from their families to which they were tenderly attached, there was an indescribable charm about this wild out-door life that rendered the social annoyances to which they were subjected at home all the more distasteful.

They felt that if a band of worthy colonists could be gathered, and a venture made into Kentucky, the future was sure to be all they could wish.

Beyond question, this preliminary visit to Kentucky settled the future not only of Boone himself, but of others who were associated with him.

It seems an extraordinary statement to make, and yet it is a fact that, during that entire summer and autumn and a goodly portion of the winter which they spent there, they never once saw an Indian—the very enemy which it was to be supposed they would alone dread, and who would be the most certain to molest them.

When it is remembered that the Indians had

2

made so much trouble on the Carolina frontiers, this is all the more remarkable, until we recollect that Kentucky at that day, and for years after, was regarded by the red-men as a sort of neutral hunting ground, no particular tribe laying claim to it. But it was territory into which each possessed an equal right to venture and wage deadly hand-to-hand encounters—while all united with an undying enmity to drive back any white man who presumed to step foot upon the Dark and Bloody Ground. It must have been, too, that the Indians scattered through the region were not expecting any visitors.

Kentucky at that time belonged to the colony of Virginia. The Shawanoes, Cherokees, and Chickasaws frequently ventured into the region to hunt, but the Iroquois had ceded all their claim to the grounds to Great Britain at Fort Stanwix, in 1768, so that it will be understood that Boone and his companions were not venturing into Indian territory at all, though it is not to be supposed that any estray red-men whom they might encounter in their hunts would be likely to regard the exact status of the matter.

The hunters preferred not to encounter them at all, but were cautious in their movements, and "put their trust in God and kept their powder dry."

Accordingly, as we have stated, they prosecuted their hunting through the sultry summer months, alternating with storm and sunshine, and enjoying themselves to the fullest bent of which such spirits are capable.

Autumn came, cool and invigorating, and winter

with its biting winds and piercing cold followed, making the primitive cabin in the mountain gorge a most inviting spot in which to spend their leisure hours.   They smoked their pipes after the evening meal, and held friendly converse as the hours wore on, when they stretched out and slept through the solemn stillness, broken now and then by the mournful cry of some wild animal, until morning again dawned.

Many of the excursions which they made had led them far into the interior, and, as may be supposed, they kept their eyes and ears open.

They had not only failed to meet an Indian, but failed to catch sight of a wigwam, or the smoke of a camp-fire other than their own; so that, as we have repeated, they were justified, if any one could have been, in believing that the last peril to which they were likely to be exposed, was that from red-men.

And yet it was precisely that danger which was impending over them, and which descended when it was least expected.

CHAPTER IV.

Boone and Stuart start out on a Hunt—Captured by Indians and
Disarmed—Stuart's Despair and Boone's Hope—A Week's
Captivity—The Eventful Night.

ON the morning of December 22, 1769, Daniel
Boone and his friend John Stuart left camp, and
started out on a hunt.

It was the shortest day in the year, so it is to be
supposed that they were desirous of improving it
to the utmost, although they had become so accustomed to such excursions, that there was no special
expectation excited by their venturing forth together for a hunt through the woods.

Experienced as they were in woodcraft, they saw
nothing to cause the slightest misgivings. Their
keen eyes, as they roamed around the horizon, detected no faint wreath of smoke stealing upward
through the tree-tops, telling where the camp of
the treacherous Shawanoe was kindled; the listening ear detected no skillfully disguised bird-call
trembling on the crisp air to warn them of the wily
red-man skulking through the cane, and waiting
until they should come within reach of their bow
or rifle.

After leaving camp, the friends followed one of
the numerous " buffalo paths" through the cane, and
in a few minutes were out of sight of their com-

rades left behind. The air was keen and invigorating, and they traveled carelessly along, admiring
the splendid growth of the timber and cane, showing what an unsurpassed soil awaited the pioneers
who should settle in these valleys, and turn up the
sod for the seed of the harvest.

Where the game was so plentiful, there was no
likelihood of the hunters suffering from lack of
food. The buffaloes were so numerous that they
were able to approach the droves close enough to
reach them with the toss of a stone.

Stuart and Boone enjoyed themselves, as they
had done on many a day before, until the declining
sun warned them that it was time to turn their
faces toward camp, if they expected to spend the
night with their friends in the rude but comfort-
able cabin.

They did so, and the sun had not yet gone down
behind the line of western forest, when they reached
a small hill near the Kentucky River, and began
leisurely moving to the top.

It was at this juncture, that a party of Indians
suddenly sprang up from the cane-brake and rushed
upon them with such fierceness that escape was out
of the question. It was not often that Daniel
Boone was caught at disadvantage, but in this instance he was totally outwitted, and it looked for
the moment as if he and his companion had walked
directly into a trap set for them.

The pioneers were too prudent to attempt anything in the nature of resistance when the result
could but be their almost instant death, for the In-

dians outnumbered them five to one, were fleet as deer, and understood all the turnings and windings of the forest. Accordingly, Boone and Stuart quietly surrendered, hoping for the best, but expecting the worst.

As might be supposed, the Indians disarmed the hunters, and made them prisoners at once. Stuart was terribly alarmed, for he could not see the slightest ground for hope, but Boone, who possessed a most equable temperament, told him to keep up heart.

"As they haven't killed us," said the pioneer, "it shows they intend to spare us for a time, at least."

"Only to torture us to death hereafter," thought his terrified companion.

"I don't doubt that such are their intentions, but between now and the time, we may find our chance. Be obedient and watchful—doing nothing to provoke them, but be ready when the right minute comes."

This was good advice, and Stuart was sensible enough to follow it in spirit and letter.

It might have been expected that if a couple of hunters intended to strike a blow for liberty, they would do so pretty soon after their capture—that is, as soon as the darkness of night was in their favor— but it was only characteristic of Boone that a full week passed before he made the first attempt to escape.

During those seven days they could not fail to catch glimpses, as it were, of freedom, and to be tempted to make a desperate dash, for many a time it is the very boldness of such efforts that succeeds.

But Boone never lost his prudence of mind, which enabled him to abide his time. Stuart, too, acted as he suggested, and they very effectually concealed their eagerness to escape.

However, it was not to be expected that the Indians would be careless enough to allow them to get away, and they maintained a most vigilant watch upon them at all hours of the day and night. When tramping through the wilderness or in camp, when hunting, or sitting around the smoking logs, the suspicious red-men were near them. When the hour came to sleep, the prisoners were placed so as to be surrounded, while a strong and vigilant guard was appointed to watch over them until daylight.

Boone and Stuart affected quite successfully an indifference to their situation, and, inasmuch as they had not sought to take advantage of what might have been intended as traps in the way of opportunities to get away, it was only natural for the captors to conclude that the white men were willing to spend an indefinite time with them.

What the ultimate intentions of these Indians were, can only be conjectured, for they were a long distance from their lodges, but those who ventured upon hunting excursions within the Dark and Bloody Ground were of the fiercest nature, and as merciless as Bengal tigers, as they proved in many

a desperate encounter with the settlers; and it is
no more than reasonable to suppose that they
meant in the end to burn them at the stake, while
they danced about the scene with fiendish glee,
just as they did a few years later with Colonel
Crawford and other prisoners who fell into their
hands.

At last the week ended, and at the close of the
seventh day, the Indians encamped in a thick cane-
brake. They had been hunting since morning,
and no opportunity presented that satisfied Boone,
but he thought the time was close at hand when
their fate was to be decided.

The long-continued indifference as shown by
him and his companion had produced its natural
effect upon the Indians, who showed less vigilance
than at first.

But they knew better than to invite anything
like that which was really contemplated, and, when
the night was advanced, the majority of the warriors stretched out upon the ground in their blankets, with their feet toward the fire.

It had been a severe day with all of them, and
the watchful Boone noticed that the guard appointed over him and his companion were drowsy
and inattentive, while maintaining a semblance of
performing their duty.

"It must be done to-night," was the conclusion
of the pioneer, who was sure the signs were not
likely to be more propitious.

He lay down and pretended slumber, but did
not sleep a wink: his thoughts were fixed too

intently upon the all-important step he had resolved must be taken then or never, and he lay
thus, stretched out at full length before the hostile camp-fire, patiently awaiting the critical moment.

CHAPTER V.

The Escape—The Hunters find the Camp Deserted—Change of Quarters—Boone and Kenton—Welcome Visitors—News from Home—In Union there is Strength—Death of Stuart— Squire Boone returns to North Carolina for Ammunition— Alone in the Wilderness—Danger on Every Hand—Rejoined by his Brother--Hunting along the Cumberland River— Homeward Bound—Arrival in North Carolina—Anarchy and Distress—Boone remains there Two Years—Attention directed towards Kentucky—George Washington—Boone prepared to move Westward.

IT was near midnight when, having satisfied himself that every warrior, including the guard, was sound asleep, Boone cautiously raised his head and looked towards Stuart.

But he was as sound asleep as the Indians themselves, and it was a difficult and dangerous matter to awaken him, for the Indian sleeps as lightly as the watching lioness. The slightest incautious movement or muttering on the part of the man would be sure to rouse their captors.

But Boone managed to tell his companion the situation, and the two with infinite care and caution succeeded in gradually extricating themselves from the ring of drowsy warriors.

"Make not the slightest noise," whispered Boone, placing his mouth close to the ear of Stuart, who scarcely needed the caution.

The camp fire had sunk low, and the dim light

2*

thrown out by the smouldering logs cast grotesque shadows of the two crouching figures as they moved off with the noiselessness of phantoms. Having gained such immense advantage at the very beginning, neither was the one to throw it away, and Stuart followed the instructions of his companion to the letter.

The forms of the Indians in their picturesque positions remained motionless, and it need hardly be said that at the end of a few minutes, which seemed ten times longer than they were, the two pioneers were outside the camp, and stood together beneath the dense shadows of the trees.

It was a clear, starlit night, and the hunters used the twinkling orbs and the barks of the trees to guide them in determining the direction of their camp, towards which they pushed to the utmost, for having been gone so long, they were naturally anxious to learn how their friends had fared while they were away.

Boone and Stuart scarcely halted during the darkness, and when the sun rose, were in a portion of the country which they easily recognized as at no great distance from the gorge in which they had erected their cabin more than six months before.

They pressed on with renewed energy, and a few hours later reached the camp, which to their astonishment they found deserted. The supposition was that the hunters had grown tired or homesick and had gone home, though there is no certainty as to whether they were not all slain by the Indians, who seem to have roused themselves to the danger from the encroachments of the whites upon their hunting-grounds.

It was a great disappointment to Boone and Stuart to find themselves alone, but they determined to stay where they were some time longer, even though their supply of ammunition was running low, and both were anxious to hear from home.

The certainty that the Indians were in the section about them, as the friends had learned from dear experience, rendered it necessary to exercise the utmost caution, for, if they should fall into their hands again, they could not hope for such a fortunate deliverance.

Instead of using the headquarters established so long before, they moved about, selecting the most secret places so as to avoid discovery, while they were constantly on the alert through the day.

But both were masters of woodcraft, and Boone probably had no superior in the lore of the woods. It is said of him that, some years later, he and the great Simon Kenton reached a river from opposite directions at the same moment, and simultaneously discovered, when about to cross, that a stranger was on the other side.

Neither could know of a certainty whether he confronted a friend or enemy, though the supposition was that he was hostile, in which event the slightest advantage gained by one was certain to be fatal to the other.

Immediately the two hunters began maneuvering, like a couple of sparrers, to discover an unguarded point which would betray the truth. It was early morning when this extraordinary duel opened, and it was kept steadily up the entire day. Just at nightfall the two intimate friends succeeded in identifying each other.

A man with such Esquimau-like patience, and such marvelous ingenuity and skill, was sure to take the best care of himself, and during the few days of hunting which followed, he and Stuart kept clear of all " entangling alliances," and did not exchange a hostile shot with the red-men.

In the month of January, they were hunting in the woods, when they caught sight of two hunters in the distance among the trees. Boone called out :

" Hallo, strangers ! who are you? "

" White men and friends," was the astonishing answer.

The parties now hastened towards each other, and what was the amazement and happiness of the pioneers to find that one of the men was Squire Boone, the younger brother of Daniel, accompanied by a neighbor from his home on the far-off Yadkin.

They had set out to learn the fate of the hunting party that left North Carolina early in the spring, and that had now been so long absent that their friends feared the worst, and had sent the two to learn what had become of them, just as in these later days we send an expedition to discover the North Pole, and then wait a little while and send another to discover the expedition.

No one could have been more welcome to the two pioneers, for they brought not only a plentiful supply of ammunition, but, what was best of all, full tidings of the dear ones at home.

Squire Boone and his companion had found the last encampment of their friends the night before, so they were expecting to meet them, though not entirely relieved of their anxiety until they saw each other.

It can be imagined with what delight the four men gathered around their carefully guarded camp-fire that evening, and talked of home and friends, and listened to and told the news and gossip of the neighborhood, where all their most loving associations clustered. It must have been a late hour when they lay down to sleep, and Daniel Boone and Stuart that night could not fail to dream of their friends on the banks of the distant Yadkin.

The strength of the party was doubled, for there were now four skillful hunters, and they had plenty of ammunition, so it was decided to stay where they were some months longer.

It seems strange that they should not have acted upon the principle that in union there is strength, for instead of hunting together, they divided in couples. This may have offered better prospects in the way of securing game, but it exposed them to greater danger, and a frightful tragedy soon resulted.

Boone and Stuart were hunting in company, when they were suddenly fired into by a party of Indians, and Stuart dropped dead. Boone was not struck, and he dashed like a deer into the forest. Casting one terrified glance over his shoulder, he saw poor Stuart scalped as soon as he fell to the earth, pierced through the heart by the fatal bullet.

This left but three of them, and that fearfully small number was soon reduced to two. The hunter who came from North Carolina with Squire Boone was lost in the woods, and did not return to camp. The brothers made a long and careful search, signaling and using every means possible to find him, but there was no response, and despairing and sorrowful they were obliged to give over the hunt. He was never seen again. Years afterward the discovery of a skeleton in the woods was believed to indicate his fate. It is more than probable that the stealthy shot of some treacherous Indian, hidden in the canebrake, had closed the career of the man as that of Stuart was ended.

The subsequent action of Boone was as characteristic as it was remarkable. It is hard to imagine a person, placed in the situation of the two, who would not have made all haste to return to his home; and this would be expected, especially, of the elder brother, who had been absent fully six months longer than the other.

And yet he did exactly the opposite. He had fallen in love with the enchantments of the great Kentucky wilderness, with its streams, rivers and rich soil, and its boundless game, and he concluded to stay where he was, while Squire made the long journey back to North Carolina for more ammunition.

Daniel reasoned that when Squire rejoined his family and acquainted them with his own safety, and assured the wife and children that all was going well with him, the great load of anxiety would be lifted from their minds, and they would be content to allow the two to make a still more extended acquaintance with the peerless land beyond the Cumberland mountains.

Accordingly Squire set out for his home, and it should be borne in mind that his journey was attended by as much danger as was the residence of the elder brother in Kentucky, for he was in peril from Indians all the way.

Daniel Boone was now left entirely alone in the vast forests, with game, wild beasts and ferocious Indians, while his only friend and relative was daily increasing the distance between them, as he journeyed toward the East.

Imagination must be left to picture the life of this comparatively young man during the three months of his brother's absence. Boone was attached to his family, and yet he chose deliberately to stay where he was, rather than accompany his brother on his visit to his home.

But he had little time to spend in gloomy retrospection or apprehensions, for there were plenty of Indians in the woods, and they were continually looking for him.

He changed his camp frequently, and more than once when he lay hidden in the thick cane and

crawled stealthily back to where he had spent the
previous night, the print of moccasins in the earth
told him how hot the hunt had been for him.

Indian trails were all about him, and many a
time the warriors attempted to track him through
the forest and canebrakes, but the lithe, active
pioneer was as thorough a master of woodcraft
as they, and he kept out of their way with as much
skill as Tecumseh himself ever showed in eluding
those who thirsted for his life.

He read the signs with the same unerring accuracy he showed in bringing down the wild
turkey, or in barking the squirrel on the topmost
limb. Often he lay in the canebrake, and heard
the signals of the Indians as they pushed their
search for the white man who, as may be said,
dared to defy them on their own ground.

Boone could tell from these carefully guarded
calls how dangerous the hunt was becoming, and
when he thought the warriors were getting too close
to his hiding-place, he carefully stole out and located
somewhere else until perhaps the peril passed.

There must have been times when, stretched
beneath the trees and looking up at the twinkling
stars, with the murmur of the distant river or the
soughing of the night-wind through the branches,
his thoughts wandered over the hundreds of miles
of intervening wilderness to the humble home on
the bank of the Yadkin, where the loved wife and
little ones looked longingly toward the western sun
and wondered when the husband and father would
come back to them.

And yet Boone has said, while admitting these
gloomy moments, when he was weighed down by
the deepest depression, that some of the most en-
joyable hours of his life were those spent in solitude, without a human being, excepting a deadly
enemy, within hail.

The perils which followed every step under the
arches of the trees, but rendered them the more
attractive, and the pioneer determined to remove
his family, and to make their home in the sylvan
land of enchantment just so soon as he could complete the necessary arrangements for doing so.

On the 27th of July, 1770, Squire Boone returned
and rejoined his brother, who was glad beyond description to receive him, and to hear so directly
from his beloved home. During the absence of
the younger, the other had explored pretty much
all of the central portion of Kentucky, and the result was that he formed a greater attachment than
ever for the new territory.

When Squire came back, Daniel said that he
deemed it imprudent to stay where they were any
longer. The Indians were so numerous and vigilant that it seemed impossible to keep out of their
way; accordingly they proceeded to the Cumberland River, where they spent the time in hunting
and exploration until the early spring of 1771.

They gave names to numerous streams, and,
having enjoyed a most extraordinary hunting jaunt,
were now ready to go back to North Carolina and
rejoin their families.

But they set out for their homes with not the

slightest purpose of staying there. They had seen too much of the pleasures of the wood, for either to be willing to give them up. In North Carolina there was the most exasperating trouble. The tax-gatherer was omnipresent and unbearably oppressive; the social lines between the different classes was drawn as if with a two-edged sword; there were murmurs and mutterings of anger in every quarter; Governor Tryon, instead of pacifying, was only fanning the flames; ominous signs were in the skies, and anarchy, red war and appalling disaster seemed to loom up in the near future.

What wonder, therefore, that Daniel Boone turned his eyes with a longing such as comes over the weary traveler who, after climbing a precipitous mountain, looks beyond and sees the smiling verdure of the promised land.

He had determined to emigrate long before, and he now made what might be called the first move in that direction. He and his brother pushed steadily forward without any incident worth noting, and reached their homes in North Carolina, where, as may well be supposed, they were welcomed like those who had risen from the dead. They had been gone many months, and in the case of Daniel, two years had passed since he clasped his loved wife and children in his arms.

The neighbors, too, had feared the worst, despite the return of Squire Boone with the good news of the pioneer, and they were entertained as were those at court when Columbus, coming back from his first voyage across the unknown seas, related his marvelous stories of the new world beyond.

Daniel Boone found his family well, and, as his mind was fixed upon his future course, he began his preparations for removal to Kentucky.

This was a most important matter, for there was a great deal to do before the removal could be effected. It was necessary to dispose of the little place upon which they had lived so long and bestowed so much labor, and his wife could not be expected to feel enthusiastic over the prospect of burying herself in the wilderness, beyond all thought of returning to her native State.

Then again Boone was not the one to entertain such a rash scheme as that of removing to Kentucky, without taking with him a strong company, able to hold its own against the Indians, who were certain to dispute their progress.

It is easy to understand the work which lay before Boone, and it may be well believed that months passed without any start being made, though the great pioneer never faltered or wavered in his purpose.

Matters were not improving about him. The trouble, distress, and difficulties between the authorities and the people were continually aggravated, and the Revolution was close at hand.

At the end of two years, however, Boone was prepared to make the momentous move, and it was done. The farm on the Yadkin was sold, and he had gathered together a goodly company for the purpose of forming the first real settlement in Kentucky.

During the few years immediately preceding, the territory was visited by other hunters, while Boone himself was alone in the solitude. A company numbering forty, and led by Colonel James Knox, gathered for a grand buffalo hunt in the valleys of the Clinch, New River, and Holston. A number of them skirted along the borders of Tennessee and Kentucky.

While they were thus engaged, others penetrated the valleys from Virginia and Pennsylvania, and among them was a young man named George Washington.

As is well known, his attention had been directed some time before to the lands along the Ohio, and he owned a number of large claims. He clearly foresaw the teeming future of the vast West, and he was especially desirous of informing himself concerning the lands lying in the neighborhood of the mouth of the Kanawha.

At that particular date, the Virginians were converging toward the country south of the river, and there were many difficulties with the Indians, who then as now are ready to resist entrance upon their hunting-grounds, even though the immigrants are backed by the stipulations of a recently signed treaty.

CHAPTER VI.

Leaving North Carolina—Joined by a Large Company at Powell's Valley—Glowing Anticipations—Attacked by Indians in Cumberland Gap—Daniel Boone's Eldest Son Killed—Discouragement—Return to Clinch River Settlement—The Check Providential—Boone acts as a Guide to a Party of Surveyors—Commissioned Captain by Governor Dunmore, and takes command of Three Garrisons — Battle of Point Pleasant — Attends the making of a Treaty with the Indians at Wataga—Employed by Colonel Richard Henderson—Kentucky claimed by the Cherokees—James Harrod—The First Settlement in Kentucky—Boone leads a Company into Kentucky—Attacked by Indians—Erection of the Fort at Boonesborough—Colonel Richard Henderson takes Possession of Kentucky — The Republic of Transylvania — His Scheme receives its Death-blow—Perils of the Frontier—A Permanent Settlement made on Kentucky Soil.

On the 25th of September, 1774, Daniel Boone and his family started to make their settlement in Kentucky.

He had as his company his brother Squire, who had spent several months with him in the wilderness, and they took with them quite a number of cattle and swine with which to stock their farms when they should reach their destination, while their luggage was carried on pack-horses.

At Powell's Valley, not very far distant, they were joined by another party, numbering five families and forty able-bodied men, all armed and provided with plenty of ammunition. This made the force a formidable one, and they pushed on in high spirits.

When night came they improvised tents with poles and their blankets, and the abundance of game around them removed all danger of suffering from the lack of food, for it was but sport to bring down enough of it to keep the entire company well supplied.

The experience of the Boones, when they passed through this region previously, taught them to be on their guard constantly, for the most likely time for the Indians to come is when they are least expected, and the leaders saw to it that no precaution was neglected.

And yet it is easy to see that such a large company, moving slowly, and encumbered by women and children and so much luggage and live-stock, was peculiarly exposed to danger from the dreaded Indians.

On the 10th of October they approached Cumberland Gap. The cattle had fallen to the rear, where they were plodding leisurely along, with several miles separating them from their friends in front, when the latter suddenly heard the reports of guns coming to them through the woods. They iustantly paused and, looking in each other's pale faces, listened.

There could be no mistaking their meaning, for the reports were from the direction of the cattle in the rear, and the shouts and whoops came from the brazen throats of Indians, who had attacked the weak guard of the live-stock.

Boone and his friends, leaving a sufficient guard

for the women and children, hurried back to the assistance of the young men, who were in such imminent peril.

There was sore need of their help indeed, for the attack, like the generality of those made by Indians, was sudden, unexpected, and of deadly fierceness. When the panting hunters reached the spot, they found the cattle had been stampeded and scattered irrecoverably in the woods, while of the seven men who had the kine in charge, only one escaped alive, and he was badly wounded.

Among the six who lay stretched in death, was the oldest son of Daniel Boone, slain, as may be said, just as he was about entering upon the promised land.

The disaster was an appalling one, and it spread gloom and sorrow among the emigrants, who might well ask themselves whether, if they were forced to run the gauntlet in that fearful fashion, they would be able to hold their own if spared to reach Kentucky?

A council was called, and the question was discussed most seriously. Daniel Boone, who had suffered such an affliction in the loss of his child, strenuously favored pushing on, as did his brother and a number of the other emigrants, but the majority were disheartened by the disaster, and insisted on going back to their homes, where, though the annoyances might be many, no such calamity was to be dreaded.

The sentiment for return was so strong that the Boones were compelled to yield, and turning about, they made their way slowly and sadly to Clinch River settlement, in the southwestern part of Virginia, a distance of perhaps forty miles from where they were attacked by Indians.

It would be difficult to look upon this occurrence in any other light than a most serious check and misfortune, as certainly was the case, so far as the loss of the half dozen men was concerned, but the turning back of the rest of the party was unquestionably a providential thing.

It was a short time previous to this, that the historical Logan episode took place. The family of that noted chief and orator were massacred, and the fierce Dunmore War was the consequence. This was impending at the very time Boone and the others were journeying toward Kentucky, and breaking out shortly afterwards, extended to the very section in which the emigrants expected to settle, and where in all probability they would have suffered much more severely had they not turned back for the time.

Nothing could change the purpose of Boone to enter into Kentucky, and to make his home there. Although obliged from the sentiment of his friends to withdraw for a time, he looked upon the check as only a temporary one, and was confident that before long he would be firmly fixed in what he called the " land of promise."

Boone was not to be an idle spectator of the famous Dunmore War going on around him. In the month of June, 1774, he and Michael Stoner were requested by Governor Dunmore of Virginia

3

to go to the falls of the Ohio, for the purpose of guiding into the settlement a party of surveyors, sent cut some months before.

Boone and his friend promptly complied, and conducted the surveyors through the difficult and dangerous section without accident, completing a tour of eight hundred miles in a couple of months.

Shortly afterward Boone rejoined his family on Clinch river, and was there when Governor Dunmore sent him a commission as captain, and ordered him to take command of three contiguous garrisons on the frontier, during the prosecution of the war against the Indians.

Boone, who had proven his coolness and intrepidity many a time, was equally prompt in discharging the responsible duty with which the governor honored him. It is believed that the pioneer was present at the famous battle of Point Pleasant, which perhaps was the most furious contest ever waged with the Indians on Virginia soil.

The Shawanoes, Delawares, Mingoes, Wyandots and Cayugas, to the number of 1500, and under the leadership of such famous chiefs as Logan, Cornstock, Elenipsico, Red-Eagle and others, made a fight against General Lewis and his brave Virginians, not only with bravery, but with a skill which came within a hair's-breadth of annihilating the entire force of whites as utterly as was that of General Custer more than a century later.

Finally, however, the sanguinary fight terminated in favor of the Virginians, by a skillful maneuvre at the proper moment, and the savages were completely routed. Not long afterward a treaty of peace was made in which the Indians surrendered all claim to Kentucky. As the Six Nations had done the same six years before, it may be said that all the aboriginal title to Kentucky was extinguished when Boone settled there.

Dunmore's War having terminated with the utter overthrow of the combined tribes, the militia that had been called into service were discharged, and Boone returned to his family on Clinch River.

He had already become known as a hunter and explorer possessing great daring and shrewdness, and those were the days when such men were needed in wresting the Western wilderness from the grasp of the wild Indian, who was sure to fight the advancing hosts of civilization with the treacherous fierceness which the barbarian always displays in defending its young.

Boone, therefore, had been home but a short time, when he received a request from a company of North Carolinians, who proposed purchasing a large tract of land lying to the south of Kentucky River from the Cherokee Indians, to attend their treaty to be held at Wataga in March, 1775, with a view of negotiating with them, and determining the boundaries of the purchase.

This association was known as Colonel Richard Henderson's Company, and it was one of the most extraordinary that was engaged at any time in opening up our Western territory.

When the Boones returned from their first visit to Kentucky, it is scarcely necessary to say that they gave glowing descriptions of its wonderful attractiveness for the hunter and settler. These accounts spread over North Carolina and created great excitement, one of the direct results being the formation of Colonel Henderson's Company. The originator was a man of education, wealth and energy, and he displayed such ability and daring in its management, that he frightened off most of his rivals, or led them to enlist under his banner.

At that time the entire country lying within the natural lines formed by the Ohio, Kentucky and Cumberland rivers was claimed by the Cherokee Indians, who lived within the boundaries of North Carolina. Previously, however, Virginia had given an impetus to the exploration and adventure in Kentucky, by presenting to her officers and soldiers Western lands by way of bounties for their services in the British army, in the old war between France and England. It was required that these lands should be surveyed by the claimants, who were also given a large discretion in locating their claims.

The first of these was made upon the Kanawha in the year 1772, and the second was on the south side of the Ohio the following year.

The business having begun it was pressed vigorously forward. Extensive tracts were surveyed on the north fork of the Licking and numerous salt-licks, and other especially desirable spots were taken up.

The year 1774 was notable for arrivals in Kentucky of those who were entitled to lands, besides scores of others who went to indulge in speculation, and to secure the most valuable sections before they could be taken by others.

Among those daring explorers and hunters was James Harrod, at the head of a party of Kentuckians from the shores of the Monongahela. They followed the Kentucky River into the interior, and left it at a place afterwards known as "Harrod's Landing." Moving further westward they located themselves in a beautiful and attractive section, where they erected the first log-cabin ever built in Kentucky.

This was near the present town of Harrodsburg, in the spring of 1774, and this place, therefore, may claim to be the oldest settlement in Kentucky. Harrodsburg is now the capital of Mercer county, and is thirty miles south of Frankfort, with a population of about 2,500. It is an attractive summer retreat, and enjoys a fine reputation for its mineral waters.

As we have stated, the most remarkable of the many associations formed for the settlement of Kentucky was that organized by Colonel Richard Henderson of North Carolina.

It was intended to obtain by purchase from the Cherokee Indians their right to the same, and then to take possession of the immense area. As soon as the organization of the company was effected, Daniel Boone was fixed upon to conduct the negotiations with the Cherokees. As might have been anticipated, he met with perfect success, and Colo-

nel Henderson went to Wataga, a small place on
the Holston River, where, in solemn council, on
the 17th of March, 1775, he delivered to them a
consideration in merchandise, for which he received
in return a deed to Kentucky, signed by all the
leading chiefs.

This was a most important step indeed, but another of no less importance remained to be taken,
and that was to assume possession of the territory
claimed by Colonel Henderson.

This gentleman was too energetic and clear-
sighted to delay such a necessary measure, and his
wisdom was further shown by fixing upon Captain
Daniel Boone for the carrying out of his intentions.

A small company of brave and trustworthy men
were at once selected, who were sent to Kentucky
under the direction of Boone, with instructions to
open a road from the Holston to the Kentucky
River, and to erect a station at the mouth of Otter
Creek, on the latter stream.

This was serious business, and none appreciated
it more than Boone and his companions, who knew
that the treaty signed with the chiefs would not
afford them the slightest protection against the
treacherous Indians. They proceeded with the
greatest care and caution, keeping their most vigilant sentinels on the lookout at night, while every
man, it may be said, was on guard through the
day.

They pushed steadily forward, until they reached
a point about fifteen miles from where Boonesborough stands, using all the dispatch possible, and

escaping molestation up to that time. But at the place named, they were suddenly fired upon by Indians, who, springing up from their ambush, attacked them with great ferocity. Two of the whites were killed and two wounded, but they repulsed their assailants a few minutes later.

Boone and his friends lost no time in pressing ahead; but three days later, they were fired upon by Indians again, and two of their number were killed and three wounded. Well might Kentucky be named the Dark and Bloody Ground, for its soil has been crimsoned with the life-current of its earliest pioneers, from the very hour they first placed foot within its borders.

The settlers, however, had no thought of turning back, but fought their way, as may be said, to the Kentucky River, which they reached on the 1st of April, 1775, and began the erection of the fort of Boonesborough at a salt lick, about two hundred feet from the south bank of the river.

A few days later, the Indians shot one of the men, but the others paused in their work only long enough to give their late comrade a respectful burial, and to shed a few tears of sympathy over his loss, when they resumed cutting and hewing the logs and placing them in position.

They continued steadily at work, and the fort was finished by the middle of June following, when, having satisfactorily discharged his duty, Boone returned to his family at the Clinch River settlement.

Kentucky was formally taken possession of on

the 20th of April, 1775, which, it may be stated, was on the very day that Colonel Richard Henderson reached the age of forty years, there being about two months difference between his age and that of Daniel Boone.

Henderson was a native Virginian, who had been a judge in the Superior Court of the Colonial Government of North Carolina; but the halls of justice were shut up by the anarchy occasioned by the Regulators, and he engaged a number of the most influential of North Carolinians in the Utopian scheme of founding the Republic of Transylvania. It was with this grandiloquent project in their mind, that Kentucky was taken possession of on the date named, and everything considered necessary was done for laying the foundation stones of the model republic in the heart of American territory.

The death-blow of the grand scheme was received before it was fairly born. Governor Martin of North Carolina issued a proclamation, declaring the purchase of the lands by Colonel Henderson and his association from the Cherokees illegal; but, as a matter of equity, the State subsequently granted 200,000 acres to the company.

Virginia did the same thing, granting them an equal number of acres bounded by the Ohio and Green Rivers. Tennessee claimed this tract, but gave in compensation therefor the same number of acres in Powell's Valley. Thus ended the attempt to found the Transylvania Republic, but the original projectors of the movement acquired individual fortunes, and Colonel Henderson himself, when he died, ten years later, was the possessor of immense wealth, and was loved and respected throughout the entire territory.

The old fort at Boonesborough, being the first real foothold gained by the pioneers, was sure to become most prominently identified with the Indian troubles that were inevitable. It was to be a haven of safety to many a settler and his family, when the whoop of the vengeful Shawanoe or Miami rang through the forest arches, and the sharp crack of the warrior's rifle sent the whizzing bullet to the heart of the white man who had ventured and trusted his all in the wilderness.

It was to be the lighthouse on the coast of danger, warning of the peril that lay around and beyond, but offering protection to those who fled to its rude shelter, as the cities of the olden times received and spread their arms over the panting fugitive escaping from his pursuers.

The old fort was a most notable figure in the history of the West, a hundred years ago. There have been gathered in the structure of logs and slabs, the bravest men who ever trailed the red Indian through the wilderness. There those mighty giants of the border, Boone, Kenton, Wells, M'Clelland, the Wetzel and McAfee Brothers, M'Arthur, and scores of others converged from their long journeyings in the service of the Government; and, closing about the fire, as they smoked their pipes, they told of the hand-to-hand encounter in the silent depths of the woods, of the

manœuvering on the banks of the lonely mountain
stream, of the panther-like creeping through the
canebrake on the trail of the Indian, of the camps
at night, when the Shawanoes were so plentiful that
they did not dare close their eyes through fear that
their breathing would betray them, of the smoking
cabin with the mutilated forms of husband, wife,
and babe showing that the aboriginal tigers had been
there, of the death-shots, the races for life, and the
days of perils which followed the daring scout up
to the very stockades of Boonesborough.

Sometimes one of the rangers of the wilderness
would fail to come into the fort when expected.
There would be mutual inquiries on the part of
those who had been accustomed to meet him.
Perhaps some one would say he was scouting for
the Government, but nothing would be known with
certainty, and a suspicion would begin to shape
itself that he had "lain down," never to rise again.

Perhaps some ranger in threading his way
through the long leagues of trackless forests would
stop to camp from the snow which was whirling
and eddying about him, while the wintry wind
moaned and soughed through the swaying
branches overhead; and mayhap, as he cautiously
struck flint and steel in the hidden gorge, he saw
dimly outlined in the gathering gloom the form of
a man, shrunk to that of a skeleton, in which the
spark of life had been extinguished long before.

The bullet-hole in the chest, or the cleft made
in the skull by the fiercely-driven tomahawk,
showed why it was the scout had been missing so

long, and why his cheery voice and ringing laugh would never be heard again.

Boonesborough, as we have stated, stood about 200 feet from the Kentucky River, one of its angles resting on its banks near the water, and extending from it in the form of a parallelogram. The length of the fort, allowing twenty feet for each cabin and opening, was 260 with a breadth of 150 feet. The houses were built of rough logs, and were bullet-proof. They were square in form, one of the cabins projecting from each corner, the remaining spaces along the sides being filled with cabins, constructed more with an eye to strength than beauty.

On the side facing the river was a large strong gate moving on wooden hinges, and a similar one was placed on the opposite side.

The cabins along the four sides were connected by pickets, which consisted of slabs, sharpened at one end and driven deep into the ground. Such forts would be of little account in these days, but they were effective against the Indians who followed such desultory warfare, and who were thus compelled, as may be said, to transfer the advantage which they naturally sought to their enemies.

A frontier fort like Boonesborough did not afford that absolute protection which would allow the garrison to lie down and slumber in peace, certain that all danger was removed. The Indian was wily and catlike by nature; he knew the advantage of mining, and took naturally to the most insidious methods of warfare; but the whites, if vigilant, were sure to detect snch demonstrations, and they possessed the power to countermine, and defeat any and every movement of the savages. Besides this, and above all, the garrison possessed a shelter from which to aim their deadly rifles, and they might well scorn the attempt of any force of warriors that could be gathered together.

The fort with its cabins was completed in the early summer of 1774, including also the cabins and buildings intended for the friends and families who were expected to join them a few months later. Colonel Henderson and a couple of the proprietors visited the place, and gave it its name in honor of the great pioneer who had built it.

These leaders took with them some forty new settlers, a large number of pack-horses, and a goodly supply of such articles as were needed at a frontier-post like Boonesborough. And now it will be admitted that Boone and his employers were fully warranted in believing that at last a permanent settlement had been planted on Kentucky soil.

CHAPTER VII.

Boone Rejoins his Family at the Clinch River Settlement—
Leads a Company of Immigrants into Kentucky—Insecurity
of Settlers—Dawn of the American Revolution—British
Agents Incite the Indians to Revolt against the Settlements.

DANIEL BOONE showed his faith in the success
of the enterprise, by announcing his intention of
bringing his family into Kentucky to stay as long
as they lived.

Accordingly he proceeded to the Clinch River
settlement, where he gave more glowing accounts
than ever of the beauties and attraction of the new
country.

The result was inevitable. The stories of foreign
lands never lose any of their brilliant coloring
when they come from the mouth of one who has
passed through the enchanting experiences of
which he tells us.

What though he speaks of the deadly peril
which lingers around the footsteps of the explorer,
is it not one of the laws of this strange nature of
ours that the attraction is thereby rendered the
greater? is it not a sad fact that the forbidden
pleasure is the one that tastes the sweeter?

Boone set his neighbors to talking, and by the
time his family was ready to move to Kentucky, a
number were fully as eager as he to go to the new
country.

The pioneer was chosen to lead them. They turned their backs forever upon North Carolina in the autumn of 1775, and facing westward, set out for their destination.

When they reached Powell's valley, several other families were awaiting them, and, thus re-enforced, the company numbered twenty-six men, four women, five boys and girls—quite a formidable force, when it is remembered they were under the leadership of Daniel Boone, to whom the trail had become so familiar during the preceding years.

This little calvacade wound its way through Cumberland Gap, all in high spirits, though sensible of the dangers which, it may be said, hovered about them from the very hour they left Clinch River.

Good fortune attended the venture, and for the first time of which we have record, the entire journey was made without the loss of any of their number at the hands of the Indians.

Never forgetting that the utmost vigilance was necessary to insure this exemption, if such insurance be considered possible, Boone permitted nothing like negligence, either when on the march or in camp.

But, in recalling those first expeditions to the West, one cannot help wondering at their success. Had the Indians shown a realizing sense of the strength in union, which they displayed at the battle of Point Pleasant, the Thames, and in the defeats of St Clair, Crawford and others, they could have crushed out these attempts at settle-

ment, and postponed the opening up of the country
for many years. What more easy than to have
concentrated several hundred of their warriors,
and, waiting until the little companies of settlers
had penetrated too far into their territory to withdraw, led them into ambush and annihilated every
man, woman and child?

But they chose, when not engaged in their rare
movements on a large scale, to fight in a desultory
fashion, firing from behind the tree or from the
covert, or watching for the unsuspecting settler
to appear at the door of his cabin.

This manner of fighting made the feeling of un-
certainty general, for no man could know when
the peril threatened his wife and little ones, nor
when the spiteful attack would be made by some
small band of warriors, venturing from the main
body and relying upon their own celerity of movement to escape before the settlers could rally in
time to strike back.

This species of warfare, we say, was extremely
perilous to the settlers and pioneers, but it could
never become an effective check to the advancing
hosts of civilization, which were beginning to con-
verge from a dozen different directions upon the
fair forests and fertile plains of Kentucky.

When Boone and his party reached the headwaters of Dick's River, a halt was made, and a division took place. Several of the families preferred
to settle at Harrodsburg—the cabin of Harrod having been erected there the year previous. With
mutual good wishes, therefore, they separated from

the main company, and pushing resolutely forward, reached their destination in safety.

As a matter of course, there was but the one haven which loomed up invitingly before Daniel Boone,—that was the station named after himself, and which was now at no great distance away. He and the main body reached it without molestation, and they helped to swell the numbers that were already making Boonesborough the strongest post in the West.

It is one of the facts of which the pioneer was proud throughout his long, eventful life, that his wife and daughter were the first white women who ever "stood upon the banks of the wild and beautiful Kentucky."

But, as we have stated, settlers, speculators, surveyors, and adventurers were converging to the Dark and Bloody Ground, which was receiving an influx almost daily—the most of the new-comers being of a character desirable and useful to a new country. The latter part of 1775 was specially noteworthy for the number of settlers who entered Kentucky. The majority of these made their rendezvous at Boonesborough, which soon became what might be called the headquarters of the pioneers. Many attached themselves to Boone's colony, others went to Harrodsburg, while some, having completed the survey of their lands, returned home.

It was during these stirring days that Boone received visits from Kenton, the McAfees and other men, who became so noted afterward as scouts and border rangers.

Those were momentous times in the Colonies, for, as the reader will observe, our forefathers were on the very verge of the American Revolution. The country was trembling with excitement from one end to the other. In the spring of the year occurred the battle of Lexington, when was fired the shot that was "heard around the world," and the war opened between Great Britain and the Colonies. Men left the plow in the furrow, the shop and their homes, and hastened to arms, while Boone and his brother colonists were planting their homes hundreds of miles beyond the frontiers of the Carolinas. Many believed the treaties previously made with the Indians would protect them from molestation at their hands, but in this expectation the pioneers were wofully disappointed.

It was necessary for the mother country to put forth the most gigantic efforts to subdue her American colonies, or she would be confronted with rebellions among her colonial possessions all around the globe.

Despite the treaties with the aborigines, English emissaries were soon at work, inciting the Indians to revolt against the intruders upon their soil. There is good reason to believe that more than this was done, and Great Britain furnished the tribes with guns and ammunition, with which to give practical expression to their enmity toward the white settlers in Kentucky and Tennessee.

The American Indian, as a rule, does not require much persuasion to begin the work of rapine and massacre, as we have found from dealing with him ourselves. When they have received their supplies from our Government agents, and have had their usual "palaver" with the peace agents, they are fully prepared to enter upon the war-path.

The student of Western history will recognize the date named as the beginning of the most troublous times on the Kentucky frontier. The settlers had planted themselves on the soil with the purpose of remaining, and they were prepared to defend their homes against all comers. But the most resolute bravery and consummate woodcraft cannot give absolute protection from such a foe as the original American.

The sturdy settler who plunged into the woods, with his glittering axe in hand, was not secure against the shot from behind the tree which bordered his path, and the plowman who slowly guided his team to the opposite end of the clearing, could have no guarantee that one of the painted warriors had not been crouching there for hours, waiting with his serpent-like eyes fixed upon him, until he should reach the spot in order to send a bullet through his heart; the mother, busy with her household duties, was not sure that the leaden messenger would not be aimed, with unerring skill, the moment she showed herself at the door, nor could she be assured that when her little ones ventured from her sight, they would not be caught up and spirited away, or that the tomahawk would not be sent crashing into their brain.

The sounds of what seemed the hooting of owls in the dead of night were the signals which the

Indians were exchanging as they crept like pan-thers from different directions upon the doomed cabin ; the faint caw of crows, apparently from the tops of the trees, were the signals of the vengeful warriors, as they approached the house which they had fixed upon as the one that should be burned and its inmates massacred.

There was the fort known as Harrod's Old Cabin and Boonesborough, while other rude structures were reared in the clearings with the intention of being used as a protection against the red-men. These served their good purpose, and many a time saved the settlers from the peril which stole upon them like the insidious advance of the pestilence that smites at noonday,—but they could give no security to the lonely cabins with the stretches of forest between and the faint trail connecting them with the fort.

When the Shawanoes and Miamis came, it was like the whirlwind, and many a time they delivered their frightful blows, withdrew, and were miles away in the recesses of the woods, where pursuit was impossible, before the garrison at the station could answer the call for help.

But, as we have said, these frightful atrocities and dangers could not turn back the tide of emigra-tion that was pouring westward. The trail which Boone had marked from Holston to Boonesborough was distinct enough for the passage of pack-horses, and the long files which plodded over the perilous path always had their heads turned to the west-ward.

The flat-boats that swung slowly with the current down the Ohio were pierced with bullets from the shores, and, in some instances, nearly all the occupants were picked off by the Indian marksmen ; but had it been in the power of these cumbrous craft to turn back, they would not have done so.

The American pioneer is daunted by no danger, baffled by no difficulty, and discouraged by no adversity. The time had come for opening up the western wilds, and nothing but the hand of Providence himself could stop or delay the work.

CHAPTER VIII.

Comparative Quiet on the Frontier—Capture of Boone's Daughter and the Misses Callaway by Indians—Pursued by Boone and Seven Companions—Their Rescue and Return to their Homes.

IT was the summer of 1776, and the colonies were aflame with war. Those were the days which tried men's souls, and the skies were dark with discouragement and coming disaster. There were many hearts that could only see overwhelming failure in the momentous struggle in which the country was engaged.

For a time, comparative quiet reigned in the neighborhood of Boonesborough. The settlers improved the time to the utmost. While some hunted and fished, others cleared the land, and a promising crop of corn had been put in the rich soil. Only one of the colony had been shot by Indians during the preceding winter, the band which did it having withdrawn before any retaliatory measures could be taken.

On the afternoon of the seventh of July, Miss Betsey Callaway, her sister Frances, and a daughter of Daniel Boone entered a canoe under the bank of the river, as children would naturally do to amuse themselves. Betsey was a young lady, but the other two were about thirteen years of age,—

all bright, joyous girls, who had no thought of danger, as they paddled about the rock where the frail boat had been moored.

They were laughing and paddling, when suddenly a rustling among the overhanging bushes arrested their attention, and, turning their gaze, they saw with consternation the painted face of an Indian warrior.

The girls were almost paralyzed with terror. The savage warned them by signs to make no outcry, through penalty of being brained with the tomahawk griped in his hand. They could only huddle together in terror and await his pleasure, whatever it might be.

The sinewy Indian then stepped cautiously into the canoe, and took up the paddle, which he handled with the skill peculiar to his people. With scarcely the slightest plash, he silently forced it out from the undergrowth and started for the other shore.

The terrified girls looked appealingly in the direction of the stockades, but they dare make no outcry. The stalwart savage dipped the paddle first on one side and then on the other, and the canoe rapidly neared the shore, beneath whose overhanging bushes it glided the next moment like an arrow.

Turning toward the girls, the Indian signified that they were to leave the boat, and the poor girls could do nothing less. Several other warriors who were in waiting, joined them, and the journey was instantly begun toward the interior.

No more unfavorable time for the captives could have been selected. It was late in the afternoon, and before anything like pursuit could be organized it would be night, and the trail invisible. The Indians would use all the woodcraft at their command, and doubtless the morning would see them many miles removed from the settlement.

The captors took the very precautions of which we have spoken, directing their steps toward the thickest cane, where they separated and made their way through it with the utmost caution, with a view of rendering their footprints so faint that pursuit would be out of the question.

Having assured themselves, so far as they could, that their trail was hidden from the scrutiny of the settlers, the Indians with the three girls made another turn, and striking a buffalo path, pushed forward without delay.

The girls had been reared in a society where out-door life and exercise were a part of their creed, and they stood the unwonted task forced upon them with much greater fortitude than would have been supposed. They walked nimbly along, taking great consolation in each other's company, though they were almost heartbroken at the thought that every mile through the gloomy forest was taking them so much further away from their loved ones, and lessened in the same degree their chances of rescue by their friends at Boonesborough.

It being midsummer, they did not suffer from cold, and but for their terror of their ultimate fate, they would have cared nothing for the jaunt.   Still, as children will feel under such circumstances, they had strong hopes that their parents and friends would soon be in close pursuit of the Indians.

And such indeed was the case.   For it was not long before the girls were missed at Boonesborough, and search made for them.   Some one had seen them in the canoe, and when it was discovered that the boat was left on the opposite side of the river, and when the keen eyes of the pioneers were able to detect the imprint of moccasins along the shore where the craft had been moored on their side, there could be no doubt of what it meant.

The girls had been captured and carried away by Indians.

It can be well understood that great excitement spread among the families of Boonesborough, all of whom were drawn together by the closest ties of friendship, and who shared in each other's joys and woes.   The whole male force were ready to start at a moment's notice to the rescue.

But that was not the way in which to secure them, for it would have been equally effective for a hunting party to go in search of the timid antelope with drums and banners.   What was needed was a small company of hunters, brave, swift of foot, clear-headed and skilled in the ways of the woods.

They should be men who could trail the red Indian where the imprints of his moccasined feet were invisible to ordinary eyes, and who, when the critical emergency should come, were sure to do just the right thing at the right time.

There were plenty such in Boonesborough, and there could be no difficulty in finding them. At the head, of course, stood Daniel Boone himself, and he selected seven others who could be relied on in any emergency; but, by the time the pursuit could be begun, the shades of night were settling over wood and river, and it was out of the question to attempt anything like an intelligent search for the girls.

In such a case there is no basis for reasoning, for though it may seem certain to the veteran hunter that his enemy has taken a certain course in order to reach his distant lodge, yet the morning is likely to show that he has gone on a different route altogether.

The American Indian, who is educated from his infancy in cunning and treachery, is likely to do that which is least expected and provided against; and Boone, therefore, did not make the mistake of acting upon any theory of his own which was likely to cause him to lose many precious hours of pursuit.

But it was the season when the days were longest, and at the earliest streakings of the morning light, the eight pioneers were on the other side of the river, looking for the trail of the Indians.

The delicate imprints were discovered almost instantly by the keen-eyed hunters, who started on the scent like bloodhounds, eager to spring at the throats of the savages.

But the pursuit was scarcely begun, when they were confronted by the very difficulty which they anticipated.

The Indians, as we have shown, had separated and made their way through the thickest cane with such extreme care, that they succeeded in hiding their trail from the lynx eyes of even Boone himself.

In such an emergency, the pursuers could only fall back on their own resources of calculation and observation.

They noticed that the tracks all pointed in one general direction, and there was, therefore, a basis for deciding the side of the cane where they emerged. Acting upon this theory, they made a circuitous journey of fully thirty miles, and sure enough, struck the trail just as they hoped rather than expected.

Boone showed his woodcraft now by forming a reasonable theory and acting promptly upon it, for, though he may have been right, still he would have lost all the advantage by a failure to follow it up instantly.

Recalling the unusual precautions taken by the Indians to throw their pursuers off their trail, Boone was convinced that the savages would believe that these precautions had accomplished their purpose, and they would therefore relax their vigilance. Their course, as a consequence, would be followed more easily.

Accordingly, Boone and his comrades changed the route they were following, with the idea of crossing the path of the Indians. They had not gone far when they discovered it in a buffalo path, where it was quite evident that, from the careless manner in which the red-men were traveling, they had no suspicion of their pursuers being anywhere in the vicinity.

This was favorable to Boone and his companions, but they understood the delicacy and danger of the situation, which was of that character that they might well tremble for its success, even with the great advantage gained.

None knew better than they the sanguinary character of the American Indian. The very moment the captors should see that it was impossible to retain the prisoners, they would sink their tomahawks in their brains, even though the act increased their own personal peril tenfold.

It was all important that the pursuit should be vigorously pressed, and at the same time it was equally important that the savages should be kept in ignorance of the men who were trailing them so closely.

As silently, therefore, as shadows, the pioneers, with their guns at a trail, threaded their way through the forest and dense cane-brakes. Their keen and trained vision told them they were gaining rapidly upon the Indians, who were proceeding at that leisurely gait which was proof that they held no suspicion of danger.

The settlers had already traveled a long distance, and even their iron limbs must have felt the effects of journeying full forty miles through the wilderness, —but they pushed on with renewed vigor, and, as the day advanced, observed signs which showed unmistakably that they were close upon the captors.

The pursuers slackened their gait and advanced with the extremest caution, for only by doing so could they hope to succeed in the rescue of the young girls.

Suddenly the figures of the warriors were discerned through the trees a short distance ahead. They had stopped, and were in the act of kindling a fire, evidently meaning to encamp for the night. The Indians were startled at the same moment by sight of the whites hurrying toward them, and not one of the dusky red-skins could misunderstand what it meant. Had it been possible for such a misunderstanding, they were undeceived the next instant.

The pursuers showed their earnestness by not waiting a moment for the warriors to rally, but four bringing their rifles to their shoulders, took a quick aim and fired into the party. The smoke of the powder had scarcely time to curl upward from the muzzles of the guns, when the whole eight charged straight into camp on a dead run, and with the fury of tigers.

When the Indians saw those figures coming, they had no time to slay the amazed captives, but, snatching up only one of their guns, they scattered pell-mell for the wood. As they went at headlong haste, Boone and one of his men fired, while still on a dead run. Each fugitive was "hit hard," but he managed to get away in the gathering darkness, and it may safely be concluded that none of the survivors looked upon that particular expedition against the settlers at Boonesborough in any other light than a failure.

The joy of the three girls over the rescue must
be left to the imagination of the reader. They
were terrified almost out of their senses when captured, but they knew they would soon be missed
from home, and their friends would be on the trail,
but they were old enough to understand the vast
disadvantages under which they would be placed,
knowing that no pursuit could be instituted until
the morrow.

And then, too, they knew the meaning of the
extreme precaution taken by the Indians in separating and walking so carefully through the densest
of the canebrakes. And, as mile after mile was
placed behind them, and the warm summer day
drew to a close, many a misgiving must have sad-
dened their hearts, as they looked through the
gathering shadows and failed to see anything of the
loved forms.

But they had come, bursting into camp like
thunderbolts,—the Indians had fled in terror, and
the girls were restored to their friends without a
hair of their heads being harmed.

The place where the recapture took place was
thick with cane, and some of the pursuers would
have been glad to keep on and inflict further
chastisement upon the Indians,—but that was im-
practicable, and, as the girls were out of danger,
the party turned about and started back toward
Boonesborough, where they arrived without mishap or further adventure, and where, as may well
be supposed, their return created joy and thanks-
giving throughout the entire settlement.

This incident, one of the most romantic of the innumerable occurrences of the border, possessed a significance which some of the settlers failed to see. The presence of the Indians so near Boonesborough and the daring abduction was not done by what may be called an irresponsible company of warriors. On the contrary, they were one of the many scouting parties sent out to make observations of all the settlements along the border, with a view of organizing a combined movement against them.

The agents of England, who had been so industriously at work for months with the Indians of the West, used means which at last accomplished their purpose, and, while hostilities were being pushed with such vigor in the East against the struggling colonies, it threatened to assume a more desperate and sanguinary character in the West.

The red men had been aroused to action, and their manner of warfare was as fierce and merciless as that prosecuted by the East India Sepoys, nearly a century later, against Great Britain. It was not long before the danger was plainly seen, and so profound was the fear excited by the surety of the coming war, attended, as it was certain to be, by the most atrocious massacres, that hundreds of speculators made all haste to leave the imperiled country and return to their former homes in the East.

CHAPTER IX.

General Uprising of the Indians—The Border Rangers—Attack
upon Boonesborough — Repulse of the Assailants—Second
Attack by a Larger Force and its Failure—Arrival of Forty-five
Men—Investment of Logan's Fort—Timely Arrival of Colonel
Bowman with Reinforcements—Attack upon Harrodsburg.

THERE was a deliberation and completeness in
the preparations of the Indians against the settlements along the western border which, if possible,
lent additional terrors to the danger that was soon
to break upon them.

The scouts who came in to Boonesborough, Harrodsburg, and other points, from their long jour-
neys through the forest, reported the tribes everywhere making ready for the warpath. There were
gatherings at their towns, councils, turbulent assem-
blies, throwing of the tomahawk, shooting matches,
running races, and that general excitement which
to the experienced forest ranger can mean but the
one thing.

The months passed, the breaking out of hostilities was delayed, and immigrants kept dropping in,
as may be said, until the month of July, 1777,
when nearly fifty men came in one company and
settled in the immediate vicinity of Boonesborough.

This was a most welcome addition indeed, for it
was evident to all that the hour was at hand when

every arm would be needed in the defence of their homes and firesides.

Boone knew what was going on among the surrounding tribes, and he threw away no chances and neglected no precautions. His vigilant sentinels were always on duty, day and night, and nothing was more certain than that the garrison could not be taken by surprise.

Besides this, Kenton, Brady, M'Clelland, the McAfee Brothers, and other rangers, were constantly moving over the long stretches of forest, making tours of observation to the Indian villages and gathering points, so that no excuse existed for the whites being surprised.

In the month of April, 1777, the sentinels at Boonesborough discovered suspicious signs in the woods immediately surrounding them. The signals and moving figures showed that a large body of Indians were gathering in front of the stockades, and there could be no doubt that an attack was intended upon the station.

The settlers were ready, and when the red men opened fire, they received such a fierce fusillade in return, that no doubt could exist as to the injury inflicted. The Indian fights from the bushes and hidden places, and is at disadvantage when he is forced to attack a foe who is equally protected.

From behind the trees the warriors aimed their rifles, and the flashes of flame here, there, and everywhere among the green vegetation, showed where they stood, with their black eyes sighting along the barrels, waiting to fire at whatever point showed any probability of exposing a white enemy to their accurate aim.

But beyond the stockades and in the blockhouses were the Kentucky riflemen, whose unerring aim, whose steady nerve and cool courage have never been surpassed, and whose skill in the use of their favorite weapon has made them renowned throughout the world.

Their guns were thrust out of the loopholes, and the pioneers seized the first chance offered, no matter how slight.

Perhaps the jet of fire behind some tree or among some dense bushes disclosed nothing of the warrior who caused it, but an instant later, maybe, the bronzed face of the Indian was cautiously exposed for a single instant, as he peered out to see the result of his carefully-aimed shot.

That second was enough, for the half dozen Kentuckians watched for just such an opportunity, and like lightning the sharp, whiplike crack of as many rifles broke the stillness, and the red skin rolled over backward, his skull riddled by bullets, while the smoke of his own gun was curling upward from its muzzle, and the death-yell trembled half uttered on his coppery lips.

The Indians killed one settler and wounded four others, while it was never known how many of their own number were shot. They fought bravely, but soon saw they had attempted an impossibility and withdrew.

Boone knew better than to believe this was the end. On the contrary, he and his comrades were convinced it presaged more serious danger to the settlement.

In this supposition he was right, for on the great national anniversary following, the Indians reappeared with fully double their former force, and began what was intended as a regular siege of Boonesborough.

It is not to be supposed the red-men knew or had any idea of the associations connected with that particular date, for the Declaration of Independence was just a year old; but the fourth of July is not a fortunate day for a foe to assail an American force, and so it proved in this instance, for the whole attack and its result was but a repetition of that of three months previous.

The Indians fought with great courage, accepting every chance offered, and killing one man and wounding four, precisely as they did in April.

The vigilant Kentuckians saw seven of the warriors drop before their fire, and it is not improbable that others were slain or at least wounded. The fight was kept up with little intermission for two days and nights, at the expiration of which time the assailants became convinced that no hope of success remained to them, and they drew off as before.

Thus it came to pass that Boonesborough, while in its very infancy, underwent two fierce attacks from the Indians.

Immediately after the second, came the forty-five men from the East, and no further disturbance or molestation took place during that year, which was one of great material advancement on the part of the settlement. Those who joined it continued to be of the right material, and they came with the ambition to rear themselves homes in the western wilderness, where their families could live in comfort and safety.

The first step necessary, and in fact about all the steps necessary, could be summed up in the single word—*work*.

And they put forth all their energies toward clearing broad spaces of the surrounding forest, and putting the rich virgin soil under cultivation. It was of that fertile, vigorous nature that it but needed the opportunity to bring forth, some a sixty and some a hundred fold.

It was like that of the famous Green Isle of the sea,—"Tickle it with a straw, and it would laugh a harvest."

Meantime the other stations and settlements were given a taste of Indian warfare and peril. Logan's Fort was invested by a large force of Indians in the month of May, 1777, and it was placed in imminent danger, for it was not so strong as Harrodsburg or Boonesborough, and the investing red-skins were overwhelming in numbers.

The siege continued for several days and nights, during which it became plainer and plainer that the warriors were certain to subdue it, in which case the garrison would be put to death.

But at the very hour when despair was settling over the hearts of the brave defenders, Colonel

Bowman appeared with a re-enforcement, and the Indians were scattered like chaff in the wind.

Two months previous the fort at Harrodsburg was attacked, but the savages were bravely resisted, and they retired with a slight loss, having wounded four of the whites, one of whom afterward died.

CHAPTER X.

A Diner out—The "Hannibal of the West"—Election of General Clark and Gabriel Jones as Delegates to the Virginia Legislature—Their Journey to the Capital—General Clark obtains the Loan of a Large Supply of Ammunition—Erection of the County of Kentucky—General Clark attacked and pursued by Indians on his Voyage down the Ohio—Conceals the Ammunition and delivers it safely at the Border Stations—General Clark marches upon Kaskaskia and captures the obnoxious Governor Rocheblave—Governor Hamilton of Detroit organizes an Expedition against the Settlements—General Clark captures Fort St. Vincent and takes Governor Hamilton a Prisoner—Captures a Valuable Convoy from Canada and Forty Prisoners—Secures the Erection of Important Fortifications by Virginia.

ONE day a boy sixteen years old, who lived four miles above Harrodsburg, went out in the woods to hunt game. The name of the lad was Ray, and he afterward became the General of that name who is so closely identified with the settlement of the West.

Like all boys in Kentucky he was a good shot, and he was not out long before he brought down a small blue-wing duck, which he picked, dressed, and roasted to a rich, juicy brown, building his fire on the brow of a hill, a few rods east of his home.

Just as young Ray had gotten the bird in a shape to delight the palate of an epicure, a fine, soldierly-looking man came out of the woods and called in a cheery voice:

" How do you do, my young man ? "

The boy looked up in surprise and said—

" I am very well, sir, thank you."

" What is your name ? "

" Ray, and I live in the house down yonder."

" Ain't you afraid to hunt alone in the woods, when the Indians are making so much trouble ? "

" Well, I try to be careful, but there is danger in these times everywhere, as it seems to me ; but won't you help me eat this duck which is now ready for the table ? "

" I'm obliged to you, for I am quite hungry."

Accordingly he sat down and attacked the duck, which he remarked was very toothsome, especially when a person was so a-hungered as he, and complimenting the boy upon his culinary skill, he kept at work until there wasn't a particle left for young Ray, who was somewhat astonished and not altogether enthusiastic over the style in which his visitor disposed of the bird.

" But," said General Ray afterward, " he would have been welcome to all the game I could have killed, when I afterward became acquainted with his noble and gallant soul."

When the meal was finished, the visitor thanked the lad for his hospitality and said :

" My name is Clark, and I have come out to see what you brave fellows are doing in Kentucky, and to give you a helping hand if necessary."

Young Ray conducted him to Harrodsburg, where he spent some time in carefully noting the capacity of the station in the way of defence against the attacks that were pretty certain to be made very soon.

The gentleman was General George Rogers Clark, who at the time was a Major in the Army, and was engaged in forming his grand scheme for the conquest of the British posts in the Northwest. He was one of the most conspicuous figures of the times, and is known in history as the " Hannibal of the West."

The first visit which he made to the frontier was in 1775, when he spent several days at Harrodsburg. His military genius was so well known that the command of the irregular troops in Kentucky was given him. He remained in the West until autumn, when he went back to Virginia, but returned to Kentucky the succeeding year, which was the occasion of his introduction to the embryo General Ray, as we have just related.

At a public meeting of the settlers at Harrodsburg, held on the 6th of June, 1775, General George Rogers Clark and Gabriel Jones were chosen to represent the territory in the Colony of Virginia. The all-important point at that critical juncture was whether Virginia would consider the colony under her protection and render her the assistance she needed against the combinations of the Indians.

It will be borne in mind that Colonel Henderson claimed Kentucky by virtue of purchase from the Cherokees, and if such claim was recognized, then no protection could be demanded from Virginia, no more than from Pennsylvania. In General

Clark's judgment the wiser course was for the people to appoint agents with the power to negotiate with Virginia, and in the event of the State refusing to acknowledge the claim of the colony upon her, then General Clark proposed to use the lands of Kentucky as a fund with which to obtain settlers and establish an independent State. The sovereign people had determined otherwise, and with many misgivings as to their recognition, General Clark and his colleague set out for the capital of Virginia.

The way was long, and there were no public conveyances of which to take advantage. When they reached Williamsburg, the legislature had adjourned *sine die*. Thereupon Gabriel Jones made his way to the settlements on the Holston, while General Clark, with the resolution to accomplish something for the imperiled settlers on the frontier, proceeded to the home of Governor Henry, who was lying sick in his room.

The Governor was so impressed by the statements of Clark, that he gave him a letter to the Executive Council of the State, and, with this document, the officer hastened to that body, and briefly but graphically depicting the needs of the colony, asked the Council to loan him five hundred-weight of powder to be used in the defence of the several stations.

The members of the Council expressed themselves as anxious to do everything in their power for the endangered colonists, but there was a threatened legal entanglement, which prevented them from making the loan in the manner desired. On account of the efforts of Colonel Henderson and Company, the inhabitants of Kentucky had not yet been recognized as citizens, and until that important question was settled, the utmost that could be done was to loan the ammunition to the Kentuckians as friends, at the same time holding General Clark personally responsible, in case of the failure of the State to give citizenship to the colonists.

General Clark lost his patience with this proposition. He had made his way to Virginia at great personal risk, to obtain the gunpowder, and he was ready to give his utmost services in defending the colony, but he could not admit the justice of becoming responsible for the value of the ammunition so sorely needed by the settlements, and he therefore declined to receive it upon such terms. Rather than do so, he announced that he would go back to Kentucky, put in operation his original scheme, and use all the resources of the territory to erect it into an independent and sovereign State.

This determination General Clark declared in a letter to the Council, after taking time to deliberate fully over the proposition. Its reception produced a result which he hardly dared hope. The Council called him before it, reconsidered their action, and ordered that the powder be sent to Pittsburg at once, where it was to be turned over to General Clark to be used in the defence of the settlements of Kentucky.

This took place in the latter part of August, and in the autumn of the same year the memorial was laid before the Virginia Legislature. The delegates could not be admitted to seats, but, before the session was over, they secured legislative action that marked an epoch in the history of the colony, which was its erection into the county of Kentucky, by which it was entitled to a separate county court, two justices of the peace, a sheriff, constables, coroners, and militia officers. Thus to General Clark must be given the credit of securing the first political organization of Kentucky, by which it was entitled to representation in the Virginia Assembly, and to a separate judicial and military establishment.

Having accomplished this important purpose, General Clark and Gabriel Jones made ready to start to Kentucky again. The powder and a large quantity of lead were still at Pittsburg, awaiting them, and they proceeded to that point and took charge of the supplies. With seven boatmen they started on their voyage down the Ohio.

General Clark felt the importance of making all possible haste in the matter, for the Indians were sure to attempt its capture if they knew of the prize passing through their country.

By some means or other they learned the truth, and the boat, with its small crew, was scarcely out of sight of Pittsburg, when the Indians appeared along the banks and began firing upon it with the hope of disabling the crew. Then they entered their canoes and began a pursuit of the boat containing the ammunition.

Without offering resistance, General Clark devoted his energies to flight, and his men plied their oars with such success that they held the advance all the way to the mouth of Limestone Creek, where General Clark resorted to stratagem to save the valuable property in his hands.

His men had rowed with such unremitting energy that they could not hold out much longer. The boat was therefore turned up Limestone Creek, speeding along between the banks with such swiftness, that it kept out of sight of the Indians for a long time.

At the proper point, the craft was run ashore, the men sprang out, and the powder was concealed in the bushes. Then the boat was turned adrift, and the little party started overland for Harrodsburg, where they arrived without mishap. A few days later, the General returned with a strong force, recovered all the ammunition, delivered it at Harrodsburg, without the loss of a pound, and shortly after it was distributed among all the stations, which were thus provided with the indispensable means of defending themselves against the impending assaults.

It will be admitted that General George Rogers Clark did a most important service for Kentucky in thus furnishing her with ammunition, and in securing her erection into the County of Kentucky ; but this did not end his services, and when it was least expected by his enemies, he assumed the offensive.

General Clark possessed rare military gifts, as he demonstrated on more than one important occasion.

The Governor of the Canadian settlements in the
the Illinois country was using his utmost endeavor
to incite the Indians to devastate the American
frontier. This being established beyond question,
the Governor of Virginia placed two hundred and
fifty men under Clark, with permission to march
against the settlements. He descended the Ohio,
landed and hid his boats, and then started overland
for his destination, his soldiers carrying the small
amount of provisions they had on their backs.
These were soon exhausted, and, for two days,
they ate nothing but roots and a few berries, but
all the time pushed vigorously forward.

As silently as phantoms, and as totally unexpected, it may be said, they appeared before Kaskaskia in the dead of night. The place was captured before anything like resistance could be
thought of. This was a noteworthy exploit, for
Kaskaskia but a short time before had resisted a
much larger force.

General Clark understood the value of prompt-
ness and celerity in military movements, and without an hour's unnecessary delay he sent out detachments against three other towns, which in
every instance were captured, the obnoxious Governor Rocheblave himself being one of the prisoners.
He was sent to Virginia, there being found among
the papers on his person instructions from Quebec
to do his utmost to rouse the Indians against the
settlers, and even to go to the extent of offering
bounties for the scalps of Americans.

The Illinois settlers transferred their allegiance

to Virginia, which owned the territory by right of charter and conquest, and, in the autumn of 1778, erected it into the County of Illinois—thus sealing an act of brilliant generalship on the part of Clark, which has few parallels in the history of the West.

The danger, instead of being over, only deepened, for Hamilton, the Governor of Detroit, was a resolute official, and, burning under the smart inflicted by the audacious American officer, began the organization of an overwhelming force of British and Indians, with which to move up the Ohio, to Fort Pitt, capturing all the settlements on the way, purposing also to lay siege to Fort Kaskaskia itself.

This was alarming tidings to Clark, who saw no probability of being able to hold the country, though he resolved to make its re-conquest dear to the invaders. The forces which Governor Hamilton was gathering far outnumbered his and were equally experienced, and their march up the country promised to be practically irresistible. Besides this, the Governor gathered hundreds of Indians, who were thirsting for the opportunity for massacre and plunder. Thus, never in the history of the frontier did a more portentous cloud gather in its sky.

In this hour of gloom and almost despair, General Clark learned that Governor Hamilton, who had reached Fort St. Vincent—now known as Vincennes—had divided his force, by sending most of the Indians against the adjoining settlements.

This opportunity was similar to those the great Napoleon was so quick to perceive, nearly a half

century later, and which did so much to establish
his marvelous military genius in the eyes of the
world.

It was in the dead of winter, being February,
1779, and yet the runner had scarcely come into
Kaskaskia with the important tidings, when General
Clark, with one hundred and fifty picked men, was
threading his way through the wilderness in the
direction of Vincennes. Fortunately the weather
was unusually mild, but when within nine miles of
the enemy, they reached the drowned lands of the
Wabash, where they were compelled to wade to
their armpits for a long distance, and to use so
much caution in advancing, that it was five days
before the entire body got safely across.

On the 23rd of February, the American force
appeared before the fort, and General Clark demanded its surrender. This was promptly refused,
and Clark made his preparations to take it. As
the garrison had not expected them, he began a
siege, carefully investing it as best he could, and
confident that it could not hold out long.

So it proved. At the end of eighteen hours it
was surrendered by Governor Hamilton, the Americans not losing a man. The governor was sent
a prisoner to Williamsburg, and a large quantity of
stores fell into the hands of General Clark.

This was a brilliant achievement indeed, but it
was not all. General Clark captured a convoy
from Canada on its way to the post which had just
surrendered, and secured the mail, $45,000, and
forty prisoners. Shortly after an express arrived

from Virginia, thanking him and his gallant companions for the reduction of the Kaskaskia country; and not long after, Virginia, through the
agency of General Clark, extended her western
establishments and erected a number of fortifications.

CHAPTER XI.

Boone leads a Party to the Blue Licks to make Salt—Capture of Boone and Surrender of the Entire Party—Conducted to Detroit—His Captors Refuse to Exchange him—He is Adopted by the Shawanoes—He discovers a Formidable Expedition is to move against Boonesborough—His Escape and Arrival at Boonesborough—The Attack Postponed—Boone leads a Party against an Indian Town on the Sciota—Encounter with a War Party—Returns to Boonesborough—The State Invested by Captain Duquesne and a Large Force—Boone and the Garrison determine to Defend it to the Last——Better Terms Offered—Treachery Suspected—The Attack—The Siege Raised.

WE have been compelled, in the preceding chapter, to carry forward for a few years the history of the military and political movements connected with the earlier history of Kentucky in order to give an intelligent idea of the work performed by its great pioneer Daniel Boone.

During the exciting military occurrences to which we have referred, Boonesborough was stirred by a startling disaster.

The settlement was greatly in need of salt, and, as it was a work of extreme difficulty and danger to secure its importation from the Atlantic States, the much simpler method was resorted to of having it manufactured at the Blue Licks, where there was such an abundance of brackish water that the work was easily done.

Collecting some thirty men, Boone set out for

the Blue Licks which were at no great distance, and they began immediately the process of evaporating the water and collecting the saline deposit. Salt is one of the prime necessities of life, and they were desirous of making enough of it to last them for a long time to come.

The operation of salt-making is not a complicated one, even in these modern days, and there was scarcely the work to keep the whole thirty men busy all the time. As might be supposed, Boone spent many hours in hunting.

It is probable that the Indians, learning of the weakened condition of Boonesborough, had determined on attacking it with a force which promised to insure its capture. For this purpose they gathered two hundred warriors and started for the settlement, without Boone or any of his party suspecting the danger that was moving down upon their friends.

Still further, knowing that the unsuspicious white men were engaged at the Licks, the large force of Indians turned in that direction and advanced with the noiselessness of so many shadows.

Daniel Boone, at that juncture, was alone, hunting in the woods, when he came face to face with the two hundred warriors, who appeared as suddenly as if cast up by the earth.

Without stopping to parley, Boone whirled about and started on a dead run, darting in and out among the trees, doing his utmost to dodge the bullets that he expected would be sent after him, and to place himself beyond sight of the Indians, who were desirous of securing so renowned a man as he.

But Boone was not so young as when he had his former desperate encounters with the red men, and the dozen warriors who instantly sped after him were among the fleetest of their tribe.

The pioneer made good progress, but as he glanced furtively over his shoulder every few seconds, he saw that the savages were gaining rapidly upon him, and his capture was certain. He held out as long as there was the slightest hope, but soon abruptly halted and surrendered.

There is something singular in the consideration which the Indians showed Boone on more than one occasion. It will be remembered that when he and Stuart were captured, they were kept day after day, until they gained a chance to escape; and, in the present instance, the captors conducted him back to the main body, where he was still held a prisoner, no harm being offered him.

This was at a time when the fury of the savages was stirred to the highest point against the settlers, and when the treacherous bullet, the crashing tomahawk, the deadly knife and the smoke of the burning cabin were more typical of the manner of warfare, than were any of the amenities of civilized, contending forces.

It may have been the Indians recognized the importance of the capture they had made in the person of the great Daniel Boone, for they treated him kindly and conducted him back to the Blue Licks, where the rest of the settlers were encamped.

There, upon the solemn promise of the Indians to spare their lives and give them good treatment, Boone surrendered the entire command to them.

Boone was court-martialed for this act, and, whether he deserved credit for it or not, is hard to determine. Such a daring officer as General Clark never would have surrendered under such circumstances, and thirty frontiersmen of to-day would give a good account of themselves against an aboriginal force of ten times their number.

On the other hand, the partisans of the pioneer plead that he saw that it was unquestionably the best thing to be done, inasmuch as the majority of the Indians would turn back with their prisoners, and thus Boonesborough would be saved from an attack, which, in its weakened condition, it would scarcely be able to resist.

It will be seen that this is not a conclusive argument by any means, for if the war party had appeared before the stockades with the thirty prisoners and threatened to put them to the torture, before the eyes of their families, they could have secured any terms they chose. On the other hand, the two hundred savages could have exterminated the little band in the woods as utterly as did Sitting Bull and his warriors the forces of General Custer nearly a hundred years later. It may be set down, therefore, that the court-martial which acquitted Boone, voiced the sober second thought of his friends in this much disputed matter.

There is reason to believe that the Indians felt a genuine admiration for the pioneer, for they kept in spirit and letter the agreement they made respecting the treatment of himself and comrades. The capture of so large a force, including the leader himself, was an achievement on the part of the Indians calling for great self-congratulation, as they started with their captives for old Chillicothe, on the Miami.

Old Chillicothe was the principal town of the Shawanoes who had taken Boone, and as it was in the depth of winter, the march through the wilderness occupying three days was very severe. On this journey the Indians treated the whites well, sharing their food with them, and only showing by their unremitting vigilance that they regarded them in the light of prisoners.

They were kept at the Shawanoe village several weeks, and then the pioneer and ten of his men were conducted to Detroit (which at that time was a British garrison), and, with the exception of Boone, were presented to the commandant, who showed them much consideration.

The commandant was desirous of securing Boone, and requested the Indians to bring him in, but they refused. A number of prominent gentlemen in Detroit, who knew of the pioneer, joined with the officer in offering a large reward for Boone, with the purpose of exchange, or of sending him back to his family at Boonesborough.

The Shawanoes were deaf to the proffers, and, to end the annoyance, started for their villages on the Miami, taking the leader with them.

The truth was, the red-men had formed a feeling

of strong friendship for their famous prisoner, and were determined to adopt him. It was with such an intention that they left Detroit and made their way through the woods to their own towns, occupying more than two weeks in the journey.

Reaching their destination at last, Boone was formally adopted into the Shawanoe tribe. Respecting this novel ceremony, Peck, the biographer of Boone, says:

"The forms of the ceremony of adoption were often severe and ludicrous. The hair of the head is plucked out by a painful and tedious operation, leaving a tuft some three or four inches in diameter on the crown for the scalp-lock, which is cut and dressed up with ribbons and feathers. The candidate is then taken into the river in a state of nudity, and there thoroughly washed and rubbed, 'to take all his white blood out.' This ablution is usually performed by females. He is then taken to the council-house, where the chief makes a speech, in which he expatiates upon the distinguished honors conferred on him. His head and face are painted in the most approved and fashionable style, and the ceremony is concluded with a grand feast and smoking."

Boone had now been changed from a white to a red man; that is, in the eyes of the red-men themselves, and his native shrewdness and cunning told him that his true course was so to conduct himself as to give the Shawanoes the impression that he shared their opinion with them.

Having received the ceremony of adoption, and

well aware of the strong friendship the members of the tribe felt for him, he knew he was in no personal danger, so long as he chose to remain one of them.

But nothing could be further from his intentions than that of spending any considerable time with the Shawanoes, but he was well aware that but one opportunity of escape would be offered him; should he fail, no second chance would present itself. It will therefore be seen that no precaution was to be neglected that promised to add to the prospect of success.

He could not but feel anxious concerning his wife and children, and he was uneasy over the situation of Boonesborough; so much so, that he resolved to seize the first opportunity of leaving, and to press his efforts with such vigor that he could scarcely fail.

He adopted his old custom of pretending to be satisfied with his condition, and of holding no thought of running away. Although little else was left for him to do, it was not to be expected that it would deceive the Indians or lead them to relax their vigilance to any perceptible extent. They must have known it was the very stratagem he had adopted successfully a few years before with their people, besides being the one which would naturally occur to a prisoner.

In the month of June, 1778, a company of Shawanoes went to the Sciota Licks to make salt, taking Boone with them. He thought the chance promised to be a good one for getting away, and he was on the alert.

But the Indians were equally so, and they kept him so busy over the kettles that he dared not make the attempt. Finally, having secured all they wished of salt, they started homeward again, and reaching old Chillicothe, Boone's heart was filled with consternation at the sight of 450 warriors in their paint, fully armed and ready to march upon Boonesborough.

This was a formidable force indeed, more than double that against which the garrison had ever been forced to defend themselves, and it seemed to the pioneer as if the settlement, his family and all his friends were doomed to destruction.

It was now or never with Boone: if his escape was to prove of any benefit to others than himself, it would not do to delay it any longer. The settlers were unaware of their danger and unless duly warned, were likely to fall victims to Shawanoe cunning and atrocity.

Boone determined to leave within the succeeding twenty-four hours, no matter how desperate the chance, and once beyond sight of his captors, he would push forward night and day until he could reach Boonesborough.

But eager as he was to go, no opportunity presented itself that day or evening. His active brain continued busily at work, and, before he closed his eyes in snatches of fitful slumber, he had decided on the course to pursue.

He rose early the next morning, and started out for a short hunt, as he had frequently done, for such a stratagem promised to give him more chance of getting a good start of his pursuers, it being naturally supposed that the hour of a hunter's return is one of the most uncertain occurrences in this world.

The pioneer was one hundred and sixty miles from Boonesborough, but he was scarcely out of sight of the Indians, when he headed straight for the settlement, and ran like a man who realizes it is a case of life and death. It was a long distance to tramp, where the need was so urgent, but the fugitive was spurred on by the strongest of all incentives.

He did not spare himself. He had concealed enough for one meal about his person before starting, and this was all he ate while making the long journey occupying five days. He did not dare to stop long enough to shoot any game, for fear his pursuers would be upon him. He took many precautions to conceal his trail, but was fearful that the piercing eyes of the Shawanoes would not be deceived. He was apprehensive, too, that if he should fire his gun, the report would bring his vengeful captors upon him.

Climbing some elevation, he looked searchingly back over the route traveled, for sight of the smoke of the tell-tale camp-fire, or that of the moving figures close on his trail.

But he saw none, and at the close of the fifth day, tired, hungry, and worn, he made his appearance in front of the Boonesborough stockade and was admitted with amazement and delight by his friends, who believed he had been killed long before. So general, indeed, was this belief in his death that his wife and family had moved back to their home in North Carolina some time previous.

Just as he had feared, he found the station in the very condition to fall a prey to the Indians. Its immunity from attack for months previous had induced carelessness and indifference, and had the immense war party of Shawanoes appeared at the same time with the pioneer, the fort could not have held out an hour before a vigorous attack.

But Boone's presence inspired courage, and the garrison and settlers set to work instantly. Everything was done to put the station in the best possible state for defence. There was not an hour to lose, for it was supposed the savages would be directly upon the heels of the pioneer, and a constant and vigilant lookout was maintained.

But the hours passed, and no Indians appeared: in fact, the escape of Boone proved the salvation of the settlement named after him, in a manner altogether unsuspected.

Shortly after the flight of the pioneer, another of his friends succeeded in getting away, and he came into the station with the gratifying news that the march against Boonesborough had been postponed for three weeks on account of the flight of Boone, whose purpose was divined at once by the Indians.

This postponement was a most providential thing, not only for Boonesborough itself, but for all the stations along the frontier, for it gave them time in which to make every preparation for the attacks which were foreshadowed by the Indian spies that were encountered in every direction.

Finally Boone determined to make an offensive movement, with a view of striking something like fear into the hearts of the Indians who were meditating these attacks, and exciting a corresponding degree of confidence among his friends.

On a bright morning early in August, with nineteen picked men, he left the station and started for one of the Indian towns on the Sciota, intending to effect its capture before anything like an effective resistance could be made.

To accomplish such a work in an Indian country, requires the utmost secrecy and celerity of movement. No time, therefore, was lost on the road, when once the start was made, and, threading their way rapidly through the forest, they advanced straight toward the Indian town, and were within a few miles, when, to their astonishment, they encountered thirty of its warriors who were hurrying to join the main body that at that moment was marching against Boonesborough.

The instant the forces caught sight of each other, a regular bushwhacking fire began, lasting only a few minutes, when the Indians broke and fled, having one brave killed and two wounded. None of the whites were hurt, and they captured several horses and such property as the Indians could not take away with them.

Two of the swiftest runners were instantly sent

to the Indian town, and they came back with news that it was evacuated. The flank movement, therefore, of the settlers had accomplished nothing.

Only one thing remained to be done: the Indians were moving upon Boonesborough, but there was a possibility of Boone and his men getting there ahead of them. They turned about and the race began.

On the sixth day, Boone found himself at the same distance from Boonesborough as was the main body; by the exercise of great care, he and his men avoided observation and got ahead of them, reaching the station on the seventh day, while the formidable enemy made their appearance before the town on the eighth day.

The war party was a large one, indeed, and looked irresistible. It had the British banners flying, and was commanded by Captain Duquesne, with eleven other Canadian Frenchmen and a number of the most prominent Indian chiefs, while the woods seemed to be literally alive with warriors. Many a settler, as he looked out upon the scene, felt that resistance to such a force was useless and the end of Boonesborough was close at hand.

Captain Duquesne, with great confidence in his ability to capture the place, sent in a demand to Captain Boone to surrender it at once in the name of his Britannic Majesty. Boone, in reply, asked to be allowed two days in which to consider the summons, and Duquesne granted the request.

Boone at once summoned his friends to council, and found, when they were gathered, that there were only fifty; but, after a full interchange of views, they decided to defend the station to the last man. The investing force numbered at the least calculation fully ten times as many as they, and a prolonged resistance would be sure to excite them to the highest degree of fury; but the resolution was unanimous, and there was no faltering on the part of the intrepid commander or any of his comrades.

At the expiration of the two days, Boone appeared at one of the bastions and announced his intention of defending the place, at the same time thanking the French commander for his courtesy in giving him the forty-eight hours in which to make his preparations against attack.

Captain Duquesne was surprised and disappointed over this decision, for he seems to have been confident that the settlers, after soberly thinking over and discussing the matter, would see not only the uselessness, but the suicidal folly of a resistance, which would exasperate the Indians, who would be irrestrainable in their vengeance, after the fall of the station.

The British commander was so anxious to secure the surrender of Boonesborough, that he immediately proposed more advantageous terms, making them so liberal, indeed, that Boone and eight of his companions accepted the invitation to go outside with a view of holding a conference.

Boone and his escort went forth in good faith, but they had not been in the clearing long when it became evident that a trap was set and treachery intended.

By a sudden concerted movement, the whites escaped from the Shawanoes, who were seeking to surround them, and dashing into the gates, closed them and hastened to the bastions, where they stood ready to answer the British captain at the muzzle of the rifle.

The fight commenced at once, a hot fire being opened from every direction upon the fort, but the pioneers returned it so sharply, and with such precision, that the Indians were forced to shelter themselves behind stumps and trees, from which they could discharge their guns with less certainty of aim.

Captain Duquesne gained a more appreciative idea of the skill of the Kentucky marksmen than he had ever held before, for the station was not only well guarded on every side, but it seemed impossible for a warrior to show himself for a second without being perforated by some settler, whose rifle sent out its sharp, whiplike crack, whenever an " opening " presented itself.

So ceaseless was the vigilance of the whites, and so accurate and deadly their aim, that Captain Duquesne quickly perceived that despite the overwhelming numbers at his command, he would have to try some other method other than the desultory firing, which promised to accomplish absolutely nothing at all.

He therefore determined to undermine and blow up the garrison.

It was not quite two hundred feet from the fort to the bank of the river, where the Canadians and Indians at once began digging in the direction of the stockades.

But the dangerous work of mining is always open to defeat by countermining, as was proven by the gallant defenders of Fort Presq'Isle, when they were so sorely pressed, and Boone instantly set his men at work.

As the dirt was cast up, it was also thrown over the pickets, the purpose being that Captain Duquesne should be apprised that his scheme was discovered, and the settlers were engaged in the same proceedings.

Boone learned what the besiegers were doing, by observing that the water below the fort was muddy, while it was clear above.

Captain Duquesne saw that it was idle to prosecute this method of attack, when the enemy were countermining, and he gave it over.

But he had with him, as we have shown, the most formidable force that in all the history of Boonesborough was ever gathered before it, and he doubted not that it must fall before a regular siege.

Accordingly he invested it, intending to starve the garrison into submission, if no other method presented itself, for there was nothing to be feared in the way of re-enforcements coming to the assistance of the defenders.

The siege lasted nine days. During this time, the settlers had only two men killed, while some of the besiegers were constantly falling before their deadly rifles. They could accomplish nothing, and Captain Duquesne decided to raise the siege.

CHAPTER XII.

The Peculiar Position of Boonesborough—Boone rejoins his
Family in North Carolina — Returns to Boonesborough—
Robbed of a Large Amount of Money—Increased Emigra-
tion to the West—Colonel Rogers and his Party almost Annihilated—Captain Denham's Strange Adventure.

IT must have caused Captain Duquesne great
mortification to come to this conclusion, after setting out with a force ten times as great as that
against which he contended, and with every reason
to count upon success; but his provisions were
almost exhausted, and nearly every time he heard
the sharp crack of a rifle from the defences it
meant that he had one less warrior than before.
The prospect of his triumph was diminishing
slowly, but none the less steadily, day by day.

Under such circumstances there was but one
thing to do, and that was to raise the siege. This
was done at the close of the ninth day after the
attack, having lost, as is stated, thirty-seven men,
with a much larger number wounded.

Boonesborough was never again subjected to a
formidable assault by Indians. It had gone through
its crucial period, and there was many a day and
hour when it seemed certain that the advanced
station in the wilderness must succumb to the
hordes of Indians who, like so many fierce blood-
hounds, were bounding against the stockades.

A peculiar condition of the settlement of the West now acted as a shield to Boonesborough. Between the site of the station and the Ohio River were continually springing up smaller stations, and many of these were so weak as to invite attack, while Boonesborough had proved her powers of resistance.

The Indians were too wise to pass beyond the weaker stations with a view of attacking one further away and much stronger. It therefore came to pass, as already stated, that the siege of which we have made mention was the last danger to which Boonesborough was subjected.

Something like peace and quietness came to the station, where every stockade was pierced with bullets, and the settlers began more earnestly the work of clearing the land for cultivation.

The opportunity having presented itself for the first time, Boone set out for North Carolina to join his family. As they were mourning him for dead, their excitement and delight possibly may be imagined, when the hardy hunter came smilingly out of the woods, and, catching up his little ones in his arms, kissed them over and over again and pressed his happy wife to his heart.

He had a strange story to tell them of his captivity among the Indians—his escape, his tramp through the forest, the attack upon Boonesborough and the repulse of the British and Indians, and finally his long journey over mountain and wood to rejoin them.

Boone stayed in North Carolina all winter with

his family, who doubtless would have been glad to
remain there still longer ; but the fires of the Revolution were flaming and bringing great suffering and
privation, and the pioneer showed that Boonesborough could never again be placed in serious
peril.

The following summer, therefore, Boone and his
family went back to the station, where he set the
good example of devoting his energies to the cultivation of the tract of land which belonged to him,
and to assisting other immigrants that were pouring into the country. This was a work as substantial in its way as roaming the woods in search of
game, as was his favorite custom in his earlier
days.

And yet, while thus engaged, he was subjected
to a great annoyance if not humiliation. He was
openly accused of cowardice for his surrender of his
party at the Blue Licks the preceding year. Colonel
Richard Callaway and Colonel Benjamin Logan
brought charges against him, which, as hinted in
another place, led to his trial by court-martial.
His two friends were induced to do this as an act
of justice to Boone, and with a view of setting at
rest the accusations continually made in certain
quarters.

Without giving the particulars of the court-
martial, it is sufficient to mention as its direct result, Captain Boone's promotion to the rank of
major and his increased popularity with all his
citizens.

A misfortune, however, overtook the pioneer,

which probably caused him more mental suffering than anything that took place during his long, eventful life.

A commission having been appointed by legislature to settle Kentucky land claims, Major Boone attested his faith in the future of the young State by gathering all his funds, with which he started for Richmond, with the intention of investing the entire amount in lands.

On the road he was robbed of every dollar. Boone makes no mention of the distressing circumstance in his autobiography, and none of the particulars are known; but, as he had a great many sums entrusted to him by friends, it will be understood that this misfortune amounted in reality to a public calamity.

However, the robbery did not impair the confidence which was generally felt in Boone's integrity. Those who knew him best, knew he was the soul of honor,—one who would undergo privation and suffering at any time rather than inflict it upon others.

The opinion of the people is best shown in the following letter written by Colonel Thomas Hart, of Lexington, Kentucky, dated Grayfields, August 3, 1780:

" I observe what you say respecting our losses by Daniel Boone. (Boone had been robbed of funds in part belonging to T. and N. Hart). I had heard of the misfortune soon after it happened, but not of my being partaker before now. I feel for the poor people who, perhaps, are to lose their preemptions; but I must say, I feel more for Boone, whose character I am told suffers by it. Much degenerated must the people of this age be, when among them are to be found men to censure and blast the reputation of a person so just and upright, and in whose breast is a seat of virtue too pure to admit of a thought so base and dishonorable. I have known Boone in times of old, when poverty and distress had him fast by the hand; and in these wretched circumstances, I have ever found him of a noble and generous soul, despising every thing mean; and therefore I will freely grant him a discharge for whatever sums of mine he might have been possessed of at the time."

There was general peace, so to speak, along the frontier, and that part of our country took immense strides in the march of civilization; and yet the year 1779 is noted for the occurrence of one of the bloodiest battles that ever was fought in that portion of the West.

In the autumn of the year, Colonel Rogers, who had been to New Orleans to procure supplies for the posts on the upper Mississippi, made his way back until he came opposite the present site of Cincinnati.

As he reached that point he discovered the Indians coming out of the mouth of the Little Miami, in a large number of canoes, and crossing to the Kentucky side of the Ohio. He determined at once to attempt a surprise, with a view of cutting them off, as they effected a landing.

The Ohio was quite low at that season, and was

very shallow on the southern shore, a long sand-bar extending along the bank. Colonel Rogers landed his men, some seventy in number, upon this bar, and started them for a point a short distance away, where he hoped to effect the capture of the entire party of Indians.

But Rogers had made a most fearful miscalculation.

They had scarcely started toward the spot, when they were fiercely attacked by a large force of Indians, numbering fully two hundred. They first poured in a terrible volley and then springing to their feet, rushed upon the panic-stricken whites, with their knives and tomahawks. Before this hurricane-like charge, Colonel Rogers and more than forty of his men were almost instantly killed. Those who were not shot down, made a frenzied flight to the river, with the warriors at their heels.

But the guards left in charge of the boats were so terrified by the disaster, that they hurriedly rowed out in the river again, without waiting to take their imperiled comrades aboard.

Caught thus between two fires, the remnants turned about, and, making a desperate charge upon their enemies, succeeded in forcing their way through the furious warriors, and those who survived managed to reach Harrodsburg.

In this battle, or massacre, as it may well be called, sixty whites, including the commander, Colonel Rogers, were killed, a loss only equaled by that of the Blue Licks some time previous. The disaster spread a gloom over the frontier, and awakened a dread in some quarters that the Indians would be roused to combined action against the settlements, and that a long series of disasters were likely to follow.

It was at this battle that an incident took place, almost too incredible for belief, but it is established upon the best authority.

Among those who were wounded by the terrific volley poured into the whites was Captain Denham, who was shot through both hips in such a manner that the bones were broken, and he was deprived of the use of his legs. Nevertheless he managed to drag himself to the top of a fallen tree hard by, where he hid himself until the battle was over and the Indians gone.

His condition was deplorable, for as his friends had fled, he could not expect any assistance, and it looked indeed as if it would have been a mercy had he been killed outright.

However, he kept up a brave heart and was able to reach the side of the river to drink, when his consuming thirst came upon him. Thus he lived until the close of the second day, when he discovered that some one else was hiding near him. Whoever he was, the captain concluded it must be a wounded person and most likely one of his own race, inasmuch as the Indians always take off their wounded when the opportunity is presented them.

Accordingly the captain hailed him, and sure enough found it was a comrade, who was wounded in both arms, so as to make them useless. Both were plucky soldiers, and as there seemed to be a man " between them," they formed a strange partnership.

The captain did the shooting, while his friend carried him about on his shoulders, from place to place.

In this manner they existed until the 27th of September, when they hailed a passing flat-boat, which took them to Louisville, where they eventually recovered and lived many years afterward.

CHAPTER XIII.

Colonel Bowman's Expedition—Its Disastrous Failure—Death of Boone's Son—Escape of Boone—Colonel Byrd's Invasion—Capture of Ruddell's and Martin's Station—Daring Escape of Captain Hinkston.

AN invasion of the Indian country is always popular on the frontier, and when Colonel Bowman, known to be a good soldier, issued his call for volunteers, shortly after the massacre of Colonel Rogers and his command, there was no lack of responses.

He requested them to meet at Harrodsburg, for the purpose of moving against the Indian town of Chillicothe, and there in a short time were gathered three hundred men, among them being the veteran Indian fighters, Harrod and Logan, each holding rank as Captain, but Boone was not a member of the expedition.

The company was a formidable one, and it started from Harrodsburg in the month of July, pressing forward through the woods with such celerity and skill that it reached the neighborhood of the Indian towns at nightfall without its approach being suspected.

Here a consultation was held, and it was decided to attack the place at the favorite hour of the savages—just before the break of day—and the plan of assault was agreed upon.

Advancing close to the Indian town, the little army separated into two equal divisions, Colonel Bowman retaining command of one, while Captain Logan led the other. The latter officer was to move half way round the town, while the Colonel was to go the other way, until they met, when the superior officer would give the signal for an attack "all along the line."

Captain Logan obeyed his orders promptly, and, reaching the point agreed upon, halted and awaited his superior. But unaccountably Colonel Bowman did not appear.

Logan remained motionless until his impatience gave way to uneasiness, as he saw the minutes slipping by, and he determined to find out the cause of the delay. His men were concealed in the long grass, when the light of day broke over the woods, but Logan, moving here and there, could learn nothing of his superior.

Several of his own men, in shifting their positions, the better to hide themselves, attracted the attention of some Indian dogs, which instantly set up a barking. This brought out a warrior, who moved cautiously in the direction where the object that alarmed the canine seemed to be. He probably had no thought that white men were near at hand, and he might have been made prisoner, but, as is often the case, and as seems to have been the rule on the frontier, at the very crisis the whites committed a fatal piece of carelessness. One of the hunters fired his gun.

As quick as lightning the truth flashed upon the

6

warrior, and whirling about, he ran like a deer to his cabin. In an incredibly short space of time, the entire village was alarmed. Logan plainly heard the Shawanoes hurrying the women and children to the woods, through the cover of a ridge stretching between them and the other division of soldiers.

Meantime the warriors prepared themselves for the attack, by gathering with their guns in a strong cabin, doubtless intended as a fort or means of defence, while Logan and his men took possession of a number of lodges from which the savages had withdrawn.

He determined upon using the material of these simple structures as shields in reaching the stronghold of the Shawanoes, and his men were about to make the advance, confident of success, when orders came from Colonel Bowman to retreat at once.

The Colonel discovered that the Indians had not been completely surprised, as was intended, and he thought it too dangerous to venture upon an attack under such conditions—hence the order to Captain Logan to extricate his force while there was opportunity of doing so.

The order was received with amazement, but there was no choice but to obey, "though they knew some one had blundered." The position of the assailants was such that an orderly retreat was difficult, and it soon became impossible; the men felt that each must look out for himself, and they broke and scattered for the wood, running the gauntlet of the destructive fire of the warriors, who shot, as may be said, at their leisure.

After the loss of several lives Logan's force got out of its dangerous advanced position, joined the other division under command of Colonel Bowman, and the retreat was continued in the direction of Harrodsburg with some semblance of order.

But nothing gives a foe greater courage than the sight of a retreating opponent, and when the Shawanoes saw the strong force of volunteers hurrying away, they too rushed from their fort and assailed them. There were less than fifty warriors, while the whites numbered almost six times as many, and yet the retreat was continued in the face of the insignificant number of savages, who fired upon them from every point of vantage, the settlers continually falling back, as did the British before the galling shots of the volunteers at Lexington.

There have been those who defended the course of Colonel Bowman in this distressing affair, and who insist that his only course was to retreat before the attack of a much more numerous force than his own, but it seems clear he lost his head from the moment he came in sight of the village. He failed to comply with his share of the movement as arranged by himself, and when the Shawanoes rallied and pursued his men, instead of turning about and scattering them, he continued retreating in a disorderly fashion, giving no orders, but allowing every one to do as he thought best.

But some of his subordinates were better officers

than he, and when the Colonel halted his force in the worst possible position, Logan, Harrod, and several others mounted the pack-horses and dashed through the woods in the direction of the galling shots. The noted Blackfish was leading the warriors, and unless checked, the indications were that the whites would be cut off to a man.

Captains Logan and Harrod, with their brave comrades, charged wherever they caught sight of Indians, or whenever the flash of a gun was seen, and after some vigorous work, they killed the chief Blackfish and dispersed the rest of his warriors.

The road thus cleared, Colonel Bowman's crippled command continued its retreat, and finally reached Harrodsburg without further molestation.

The expedition had proven itself one of that long list of failures and disasters which mark the history of military expeditions against the Indians on the frontier from the earliest settlement down to the massacre of Custer and his command.

The Revolution was approaching its close, it being the year 1780, and hundreds of settlers from the East had swarmed into Kentucky and taken up land. In their eagerness to acquire possession, they almost forgot the danger which hung over them, laying themselves so invitingly open to attack, that the British and Indians took up the gauntlet which, it may be said, was thus thrown in their faces.

The conquest of Kentucky was a favorite scheme with the British, and in the summer of 1780, a formidable invasion was made under the direction of Colonel Byrd, at the head of six hundred Indians and Canadians, and with six pieces of artillery.

His first demonstration was against Ruddell's station, on the Licking. This had a weak garrison, and when Captain Ruddell was confronted with the formidable force and summoned to surrender, he saw that it would be folly to refuse. The artillery at the command of his foe could speedily batter the fort to pieces, and he agreed to capitulate on condition that his garrison should be under the protection of the British. Colonel Byrd readily agreed to this reasonable stipulation, and the gates were thrown open.

The instant this was done, the Indians poured tumultuously in, and laying hold of the soldiers claimed them as prisoners. Captain Ruddell remonstrated indignantly with Colonel Byrd at this violation of his agreement, but the British colonel, although he did his best to restrain his Indians, was unable to do so.

Colonel Byrd seems to have been a gentleman, and, when the Indians proposed to attack Martin's Station, a short distance off, and which they were confident of capturing, he refused to move and threatened to withdraw from Kentucky altogether, unless the chiefs and sachems should pledge themselves that in every case the prisoners taken should be given in charge of him, the Indians confining themselves entirely to the plunder and booty obtained.

The agreement was made on the part of the

leaders, and then Colonel Byrd marched against Martin's Station. The artillery he took along undoubtedly proved irresistibly persuasive in almost every instance, for he captured the station with little difficulty, and the Indian chiefs compelled their warriors to adhere to the pledge they had given.

The Indians now became eager to attack Bryant's Station, but Colonel Byrd did not seem to have much enthusiasm over the invasion of Kentucky, and he declined to go further. He collected his stores, and, placing them upon boats, retreated to Licking Forks, where his Indians withdrew, taking with them the prisoners captured at Ruddell's Station.

Among the captives was Captain John Hinkston, a noted Indian fighter, who, as may be supposed, was on the alert for a chance to get away from his captors, knowing, as he did, that he was liable to suffer torture at their hands.

On the second night, succeeding the separation of the Indians from the command of Colonel Byrd, the warriors halted close to the river. When they started to build a camp-fire, the fuel was found to be so wet that it was fully dark before they could get the flames going, and so many of the guard were called upon to assist in the difficult work that Captain Hinkston made a sudden dash, broke through the lines, and amid a storm of hastily aimed bullets succeeded in reaching the shelter of the woods.

As night had just settled, Hinkston felt secure

in his escape, though the Indians immediately scattered and began such a vigorous search that he heard them moving in all directions about him, sometimes so close that he could almost touch them, and was forced to stand as motionless as the tree trunks beside him, lest they should detect his cautious movements.

But he gradually worked away from the Indian camp, when the vigor of the hunt had relaxed somewhat, and, starting in the direction of Lexington, kept going all night; for, as he was confident the Shawanoes would take his trail at daylight, it was important that he should make all progress while the opportunity was his.

His hopes rose as hour after hour passed, and he was congratulating himself on the goodly distance made, when to his consternation he came directly up to the very Indian camp from which he fled long before. He had committed that error which people lost in the woods are so prone to commit, that of walking in a circle instead of in a straight line.

As may be supposed, Hinkston was startled, and he did not stand long surveying the smoking camp-fires, with the grim warriors gathered about them; but turning once more, he re-entered the woods, making his way with so much caution, that whatever might happen, he was sure of not repeating the blunder committed.

The night was so cloudy and dark, that he was deprived of the compass of the hunter, the stars in the sky, and he wet his finger and held it over

his head. This enabled him to tell the direction
of the wind which was gently blowing, and by repeating the act, he was enabled to pursue substan-
tially the same direction through the night, so that
when daylight came, he was sure of one thing, he
had placed a goodly number of miles between him
and his enemies.

He was so worn out that he crept close to a
fallen tree, where he slept several hours. When he
awoke he found he was surrounded by a dense fog,
which shut out objects a dozen feet distant. The
moisture was dripping from the leaves, and the day
was as dismal as can be imagined; but such
weather served to help conceal his trail, and he
was hopeful that none of the keen-eyed Indians
would succeed in tracing him to his resting-place.

But the Shawanoes were prosecuting a most vigorous search, and he stepped along with the greatest
care, glancing to the right and left, expecting every
minute to see some brawny warrior suddenly spring
out of the fog upon him.

On the right he would hear the call of a turkey,
answered a moment by another on the left, followed perhaps by a general chorus from all points
of the compass. ~

Those wild turkeys were Indians signaling to
each other, and they frequently approached so
close, that more than once Hinkston felt it impossible to break through the fiery ring that was
closing about him.

Sometimes the pursuers varied their signals by
imitating the howling of wolves, or the bleating of

fawns, and they were often so close that discovery would have been inevitable but for the London-like vapor which enveloped the trembling fugitive.

But good fortune waited on Captain Hinkston, and he finally extricated himself from the perilous vicinity and reached Lexington without harm.

CHAPTER XIV.

Colonel Clark's Invasion of the Indian Country—Boone is Pro-
moted to the Rank of Colonel—His Brother Killed at Blue
Licks and Boone narrowly Escapes Capture—Attack upon
the Shelbyville Garrison—News of the Surrender of Cornwallis—Attack upon Estill's Station—Simon Girty the Renegade—He Appears before Bryant's Station, but Withdraws.

THIS same year 1780 was noteworthy for two
memorable incidents in the history of Kentucky.
The first was Colonel Byrd's invasion, and the
other was the retaliatory invasion of the Indian
country by the gallant Colonel Clark, and his attack upon the Shawanoe towns.

The prisoners taken by the Indians at Ruddell's
Station were kept by their captors, who released
a few after the expiration of several years, but a
great many perished by the tomahawk and knife.

Byrd's invasion created great excitement, and
the proposed retaliatory measure of Colonel Clark
was received with enthusiasm. The brave settlers
rallied to his standard from every direction, and in
a short time he had a full thousand men under his
command.

Such a force, composed of such material, might
well be considered invincible, for no combination
of Indians could have been formed on the frontier
capable of checking its march.

Colonel Clark, at the head, marched directly into the Indian country, spreading devastation wherever he went. The towns were burned and the corn-fields laid waste—a piece of cruelty, but war is always cruel—and by destroying their crops, the warriors were given something else to do besides forming expeditions against the frontier settlements. No attempt was made to check the advance of Colonel Clark, and his force having inflicted an incalculable amount of injury, withdrew and disbanded.

Only one skirmish had taken place; that was at an Indian village where about twenty men were killed on each side.

In the same year the organization of the militia of Kentucky was perfected. Colonel Clark was appointed brigadier-general and commander-in-chief of all the militia. Major Daniel Boone was advanced to the rank of colonel, and with Pope and Trigg held second rank, Floyd, Logan and Todd holding first.

A singular fatality seemed to attach itself to Blue Licks, already the scene of several disasters to the whites. In October, 1780, Boone and his brother visited the place, and had scarcely reached it when they were fired upon by a number of Indians in ambush, and the brother fell dead.

Boone himself dashed into the woods and fled for life, the Indians pursuing with the help of a dog. The latter clung so close to the heels of the fugitive, that, when he got a safe distance, he turned about and shot him, then resuming his flight, he soon placed himself beyond all danger from the savages.

In March, 1781, a number of straggling Indians entered Jefferson county at different points, and hiding along the paths, treacherously shot down several settlers. This served as a reminder to the pioneers that it was too soon to count upon any degree of safety from the red men.

In fact there was a state of continual unrest along the border. Among those killed in the manner mentioned, was Colonel William Linn. Captain Whitaker, with the resolve to punish the assassins, started in hot pursuit of them.

Striking their trail, he followed it rapidly to the Ohio, where he entered several canoes purposing to cross and continue the pursuit. He supposed that the warriors had already gone over, but such was not the case, the Indians being concealed on the Kentucky shore.

Just as Captain Whitaker and his men were pushing off, the savages fired, killing and wounding nine of them, but the others turned with such fierceness, that the Indians were put to flight, several of their number being left dead.

In the succeeding month a small station near Shelbyville, which had been founded by Boone, became so alarmed that the settlers determined to remove to Bear's Creek. While engaged in doing so, they were attacked by Indians and many killed.

Colonel Floyd hastily gathered twenty-five men and started in pursuit, but he was ambushed, half his party killed, and he himself would have been tomahawked, but for the assistance of the noted scout, Captain Wells, who helped him off the ground.

Toward the close of 1781, news reached Kentucky that Lord Cornwallis had surrendered at Yorktown, that the war was ended, and the Independence of the American colonies secured forever. It is impossible to imagine the delight which thrilled the country at this joyful tidings. America now took her place among the nations, and began that career of progress, advancement and civilization which has made her people the foremost of the world.

The settlers along the frontier believed their day of security and safety had come at last, and that now they might give their whole attention to the development of the country.

But the hope was an unsubstantial one. The American Indians, as a rule, are as regardless of treaties as are we, and they showed no disposition to recognize the fact that the war was over and the dawn of universal peace had come.

In May, 1782, twenty-five Wyandots suddenly appeared in front of Estill's Station, and after killing one man, and taking a prisoner, retreated. Captain Estill, with an equal force, started in pursuit, and overtook them at Hinkston's, where he savagely attacked them. His lieutenant, Miller, showed the white feather, failed to carry out instructions, and Captain Estill and nine of his men were killed and scalped, the Indians also losing their leader and half their warriors.

Simon Girty the renegade figures as an actor in the darkest deeds in the history of the West. He was a soldier at the fierce battle of Point Pleasant, but was so maltreated by his Commander, General Lewis, after the battle, that he forswore his race, and became one of the leaders of the Indians and the most merciless enemy of the settlers.

In the month of August, a runner arrived at Bryant's Station with news that Girty, at the head of a large force of Indians, was pushing through the woods with the intention of capturing the station. Immediate preparations were made to receive them, and when the Indians appeared, on the 14th of August, everything possible had been done to put the place in the best form of defence.

Girty was at their head, as had been announced, and he at once advanced to the clearing and summoned the settlers to surrender, telling them that no other course was left, for, besides the large force under him he had a number of re-enforcements marching to join him with artillery.

The sound of the last word was alarming to most of the settlers, but Reynolds, one of their number, took upon himself to answer Girty, who had assured them of honorable treatment in case of capitulation, and the tomahawk in the event of their failure to accept the terms.

The answer of Reynolds to this demand was of the most insulting nature. He laughed at the threats of Girty and challenged him to make them good; he said he was the owner of one of the mangiest and most worthless curs ever seen, and that he put the last crowning disgrace upon the poor dog by naming him "Girty;" that if he had military artillery or re-enforcements, he was invited to exhibit them, and that, finally, if Girty remained two hours longer before the fort, they would go out and scalp him and all the warriors he had with him.

This was an emphatic reply to the question, and Girty expressed in turn his regret that the settlers were so blind to the fate of themselves and those dependent upon them ; but he had given them fair warning, and their blood must be on their own heads.

They had deliberately chosen to disregard the proffer of peace and safety, and the world could not blame him now for carrying out his threat— that of putting every one to death with the toma-hawk.

The resistance which they had determined to offer would only excite the Indians to the highest point of fury, and they would now be irrestrain-able.

Thereupon Simon Girty went back to where his Indian allies were awaiting him, placed himself at their head, and then deliberately turned about and marched away, without firing a shot at the station !

CHAPTER XV.

Arrival of Boone with Re-enforcements—Pursuit of the Indian
Force—Boone's Counsel Disregarded—A Frightful Disaster—
Reynold's Noble and Heroic Act—His Escape.

ON the morning succeeding the departure of
Girty and his Indians from the front of Bryant's
Station, Boone reached the place with re-enforcements, among them being his son Israel and his
brother Samuel. Before the day closed, Colonel
Trigg came in from Harrodstown, and Colonel
Todd from Lexington, each with a similar force, so
that the retreat of the noted renegade was the best
thing that could have taken place for his own personal safety.

The company that gathered within the station
was a curious one—numbering about two hundred,
one-fourth of whom were commissioned officers.
A noisy consultation was held, and amid much uproar and wrangling, it was resolved to pursue the
Indians at once, without awaiting the arrival of
Colonel Logan, who was known to be approaching
with a large force, and was certain to arrive within
the succeeding twenty-four hours.

Accordingly the pursuit was begun without
delay, and it proved most easy to keep up, for the
retreat of Girty and his Indians was marked by
such a broad and plain trail that there could be no
mistaking it.

The bushes had been bent down, the bark was hacked off the trees with tomahawks, and articles were strewn along the way with most remarkable prodigality.

Indeed there was so much pains taken to show the trail that Boone and his older companions were alarmed. They believed Girty had caused it to be done for the very purpose of drawing them in pursuit, and Boone spoke to many of the officers. But they laughed at his fears and pressed forward with the ardor of Kentuckians who see the certainty of a fierce struggle close at hand, where the victory is likely to be on their side.

When the settlers reached Blue Licks—an ominous name for them—they discovered several Indians on the other side of the Licking, who leisurely retreated into the woods, without showing any special alarm over the pursuit of the Kentuckians.

As it was certain that Girty and his whole force were immediately in front, another consultation was held; for the pursuers began to feel the need of care and caution in their movements. After a long discussion, all turned to Boone, who they felt was the best qualified to advise them in the emergency.

The grave face and manner of the great pioneer showed that he appreciated the danger.

"Our situation is a critical one," said he; "you know nothing of the nature of the country on the other side of the Licking, and the Indians have acted in such a manner that I'm satisfied they have laid an ambush for us. In my opinion, we

have the choice of two courses: the first is to
divide our men and send one half up the river to
cross it at the Rapids and attack in the rear, while
the rest make a simultaneous assault in front. But
the other course and the one which I most earnestly
urge is to await the coming of Colonel Logan and
his re-enforcements. We have a strong body in
front of us, and we have been taught more than
one lesson by the disasters of the past few years,
which we cannot afford to forget to-day. At any
rate, we ought not to try to cross the river until we
have sent forward spies to learn the number and
disposition of the troops."

These were the words of wisdom and prudence,
but they fell upon unwilling ears, and the majority
bitterly opposed the advice of the old pioneer.
They insisted that the Indians were fleeing in
alarm, and that such delay would give them time
to get away unscathed, while the proposal to
divide the settlers would so weaken them that the
Indians would fall upon the detachments separately
and destroy them. It may be said there was
reason in the last objection, but none in the
former.

It is probable there was little discipline in this
wrangling assemblage which was engaged in discussing a most momentous question, for while the
arguments were going on, Major McGary sprang
upon his horse, spurred him at full gallop toward
the river, calling upon all those who were not
cowards to follow him.

The next instant he was plunging through the

stream, and the whole shouting rabble rushed tumultuously after him. There was no semblance of order as they shouted, struggled, and hurried pell-mell to their doom. Simon Girty, the renegade, from the woods on the other side, must have smiled grimly, as he saw his victims doing everything in their power to hasten their own destruction, just as the majority of the expeditions against the Indians did before and have done since.

The soldiers hastened forward, until they reached the point against which Boone had warned them— the heading of two ravines. They had scarcely halted, when a party of Indians appeared and opened fire upon them. McGary returned the fire, but his position was disadvantageous, being on an exposed ridge, while, as usual, the Shawanoes were in a ravine with plenty of opportunity to conceal themselves, while picking off the whites.

The majority of the settlers had not yet come up, but they were hurrying forward in the same wild disorder, and continued rushing up the ridge, in time to meet the fire from the Indians which grew hotter and more destructive every minute.

Although placed at such disadvantage, the whites fought with great bravery, loading and shooting rapidly, though without any attempt at discipline and regularity. The fact was, the whites saw they were entrapped, and each and all were fighting for their very lives.

Had the warriors been given their choice of ground, they would have selected in all probability that taken by the respective combatants, for nothing

could have been more in favor of Girty and his
savages.

The Indians gradually closed in around the
whites, loading and firing with great rapidity,
while the settlers fell fast before the bullets rained
in upon them from every quarter.

Among the officers, Todd, Trigg, Harland and
McBride were soon killed, and Daniel Boone's son
Israel, while gallantly doing his duty, fell pierced
by bullets. The savages gaining confidence from
their success continued to extend their line, so as
to turn the right of the Kentuckians, until they
got in their rear and cut off their retreat to the
river.

The soldiers saw what the Indians were doing,
for the heavy fire indicated it, and they became
panic-stricken. At once every one thought of
saving only himself, and a tumultuous, headlong
rush was made for the river. As a matter of
course, the savages did not allow the invitation to
pass unaccepted, and they swarmed down upon
the demoralized whites, tomahawking them without
mercy.

Most of the horsemen escaped, but the slaughter
of the foot soldiers was terrible. Nearly all of
those who were in Major McGary's party were
killed, and at the river the scene became appalling.
Horsemen, foot soldiers, and painted Indians were
mingled in fierce confusion, fighting desperately in
the water, which was crowded from shore to shore.

A score of soldiers, having got across, halted and
poured a volley into the red men, which checked

them for a few minutes; but they quickly rallied and resumed the massacre and pursuit, the latter continuing for fully twenty miles. More than sixty Kentuckians were killed, a number made prisoners; and another disaster was added to the long roll of those which mark the history of the attempts at civilization in the West.

Daniel Boone bore himself in this fight with his usual intrepidity and coolness, doing his utmost to check the hurricane-like rush of the Indians, and endeavoring to rally those around him into something like organized resistance. Could this have been done, the renegade Girty and his merciless horde would have been routed, for some of those who fought on his side admitted years afterward that they were once on the very point of breaking and fleeing in disorder.

But Boone saw his son and many of his closest friends shot dead, and himself almost surrounded by Indians, before he comprehended his imminent personal peril.

The ford which was looked upon by most of the settlers as the only door of escape was crowded with fugitives, and several hundred warriors were between him and the river. Instead of seeking to reach the stream, he turned toward the ravine from which the Shawanoes themselves had emerged, and, with several comrades, made a desperate dash for it.

There was firing all along the line at the few who took this exceptional means, and several small parties sprang after them. Boone and his companions were fleet of foot, but he succeeded in eluding their enemies more by strategy than speed, and finally brought his friends to the river bank at a point so far below the ford that they were invisible to the Indians.

Here they swam across and then started for Bryant's Station, which they reached without further molestation.

Such an utter rout and irretrievable disaster is always marked by some extraordinary incidents. Reynolds, who made the insulting reply to Simon Girty, when he demanded the surrender of Bryant's Station, was in the battle and fought furiously against the renegade and his allies, but was forced back by the turbulent tide which, once set in motion, swept everything before it.

Reynolds was making for the river, when he overtook an officer on foot who was so weak from wounds received in a former engagement with the Indians, that he could not keep up with the fugitives, and, indeed, was so exhausted, that he was ready to fall fainting to the ground.

Reynolds sprang from his horse and helped the officer upon it, and then told him to do the best he could. The captain did so and saved himself.

Reynolds was now placed in great peril, but he made a plunge into the river, and soon carried himself by powerful strokes to the other side, where he was immediately made prisoner.

The Shawanoes, at this juncture, were so engaged in capturing and killing the fugitives, that they could not leave very large guards to keep those who fell into their hands. .

Thus it came about that the guard placed over Reynolds was a single Indian, but he was tall and muscular, and would have preferred to tomahawk his prisoner and join in the general massacre.

Reynolds did not give him time to debate the matter, but, turning quickly upon the warrior, dealt him a blow which felled him like an ox, and then, before he could rise, Reynolds was in the woods, speeding for life.

One of the first men whom he encountered, after reaching the settlement, was the officer to whom he had given his horse, when there was no other means by which he could be saved.

The officer appreciated the favor, and showed it by making Reynolds a present of two hundred acres of land.

CHAPTER XVI.

General Clark's Expedition—A Dark Page in American History
—Colonel Crawford's Disastrous Failure and his own Terrible
Fate—Simon Girty.

KENTUCKY now approached an eventful period
in her history. As we have stated, the career of
Daniel Boone is woven in the very warp and woof
of the narrative of the early days of the West, and
in order to reach a proper understanding of the life
and character of the great pioneer, it is necessary
to carry the two along together.

The defeat and massacre at Blue Licks excited a
profound shock and indignation along the frontier,
and the feeling was general that necessity demanded the chastisement of the Indians, who
would be likely otherwise to continue their depredations.

The gallant and clear-headed officer, General
George Rogers Clark, the " Hannibal of the West,"
issued a call for volunteers to assemble at Bryant's
Station. The General was so popular, and the confidence in him so universal, that hundreds flocked
to the rendezvous, where, in a brief time, he placed
himself at the head of one of the most formidable
forces ever raised in that portion of the country
during its early days.

The Indians were too wise to meet this army in

anything like open battle. They carefully kept out of its way, expending their energies in picking off stragglers, and occasionally sending in a stray shot from some point, from which they could flee before it could be reached by the infuriated soldiers.

General Clark pushed forward, burned several Indian towns, and laid waste many fields. A few prisoners were taken, and a few killed, when the expedition returned and disbanded.

This was the only enterprise of the kind that was set on foot by Kentucky during the year 1782, which, however, was marked by one of the darkest deeds on the part of white men, which blacken the pages of our history.

On the 8th of March, Colonel Daniel Williamson, with a body of men, marched to the Moravian town of Gnadenhutten, where he obtained possession of the arms of the Christian Indians through treachery, and then massacred one hundred of them in as cruel and atrocious manner as that shown by Nana Sahib at Cawnpore. The harvest of such an appalling crime was rapine and death along the frontier, as it has been demonstrated many a time since.

These outrages became so numerous that Colonel William Crawford organized an expedition in Western Pennsylvania, numbering 450 men, with which he started against the Wyandot towns on the Sandusky.

His force in fact was nothing but an undisciplined rabble, and no one could predict anything but disaster, when it should penetrate the Indian

7

country. It was this lack of discipline that had given the death-blow to so many expeditions against the tribes on the frontier, and which is the strongest ally an enemy can have.

Early in June, Colonel Crawford's force reached the plains of Sandusky, straggling along like the remnants of a defeated army, and so mutinous that numbers were continually straying back, deserting openly and caring nothing for the wishes or commands of their leader.

Colonel Crawford saw that a crisis was approaching, and calling a council, it was agreed that if a large force of Indians was not encountered within the succeeding twenty-four hours, they would withdraw altogether from the country.

A thousandfold better would it have been had they done so at once.

Within the succeeding hour, scouts came in with the news that a large body of savages were marching against them, and at that moment were almost within rifle-shot.

The proximity of danger impressed itself upon the soldiers and officers, who made hurried preparations to receive the warriors that appeared shortly after, swarming through and filling the woods by the hundred.

The whites were eager for battle and they opened upon them at once, keeping up a hot galling fire until dark, when the Indians drew off. The soldiers slept on their arms.

At daylight the fight was renewed, but it assumed the nature of a skirmish more than that of a regular battle. The Indians had suffered severely, and they were more careful of exposing themselves. They took advantage of the trees and bushes, firing rapidly and doing considerable damage.

But the soldiers were accustomed to such warfare, and they not only held their own ground, but maintained a destructive, though desultory fire which was more effective than that of the enemy.

The most alarming fact was that the Indians were not only waiting for re-enforcements but were receiving them all through the day. The spies of Colonel Crawford reported that other warriors were continually coming in, it being evident that runners had been sent out by the chiefs to summon all the help they could command.

This caused a great deal of uneasiness on the part of the whites, who saw the probability of an overwhelming force gathering in front of them, with the awful sequel of massacre, which had marked so many expeditions into the Indian country.

At sunset, when the second day's battle ceased, an anxious consultation was held by the officers of Crawford's command, at which the momentous question was discussed as to what was to be done.

The conviction was so general that they would be attacked by a resistless force, if they remained on the ground another day, that it was agreed to retreat during the night. As the savage force was already very large and was hourly increasing, it will be understood a withdrawal could only be accomplished by the utmost secrecy, and amid the most profound silence.

It was decided, therefore, that the march should begin at midnight, in perfect silence, and preparations were made to carry out the decision of the council of officers.

At a late hour the troops were arranged in good order, and the retreat was begun. A few minutes after, some confusion and the firing of guns were noticed in the rear and threatened a panic, but the soldiers were speedily quieted, and the withdrawal resumed in an orderly manner.

Probably it would have been continued as intended, but, at the critical moment, some terrified soldier called out that the Indians had discovered what they were doing and were coming down upon them in full force.

The retreat at once became a rout, every man feeling that scarcely a hope of escape remained. The cavalry broke and scattered in the woods, and the desperate efforts of Colonel Crawford, who galloped back and forth, shouting and seeking to encourage them to stand firm, were thrown away.

As if it was decreed that nothing should be lacking in this grotesque tragedy, the men shouted and yelled like crazy persons, so that the impression went to the astounded Indians that "the white men had routed themselves and they had nothing to do but to pick up the stragglers."

The sequel can be imagined. The warriors sprang to the pursuit and kept it up with the ferocious tenacity of blood-hounds, all through the night and into the succeeding day. The massacre went on hour after hour, until over a hundred of the soldiers had been killed or captured, and still another frightful disaster was added to those which already marked the history of the development of the West.

Among the prisoners captured were two—Dr. Knight, the surgeon of the company, and Colonel Crawford himself.

Dr. Knight and the Colonel were taken at the close of the second day, the latter having incurred unusual danger from his anxiety respecting the fate of his son. Their captors were a small party of Delawares, who carried them to the old Wyandot town. Just before reaching it, a halt was made, and the celebrated chief, Captain Pipe, painted Dr. Knight and Colonel Crawford black. This meant they had already been doomed to death by being burned at the stake!

Their immediate experience did not tend to lessen their terrors. As they moved along, they continually passed bodies of their friends that had been frightfully mangled by their captors, who were evidently determined that the massacre of the Christian Indians should be fully avenged.

When near the Indian town, they overtook five prisoners who were surrounded by a mob that were tormenting them by beating and taunting. Suddenly the Indians sprang upon them with a yell, and every one was tomahawked. Colonel Crawford was turned over to a Shawanoe doctor, and Surgeon Knight went along with them.

A few minutes previous, Simon Girty, the renegade, rode up beside them and became more fiendish in his taunts than the Indians. He had been acquainted with Colonel Crawford years before, and had special cause for enmity, because the Colonel had used his efforts to defeat Girty for some military office he was eager to obtain.

He now commented upon their appearance (being painted black and of course in great distress of mind), and he assured them that their death at the stake was one of the certainties of the immediate future. He laughed and swore and was in high spirits, as well he might be; for, inspired as he was by the most rancorous hatred of his own race, he had been gratified that day by assisting in one of the most dreadful disasters to the settlers that had ever occurred on the frontier.

When the village was reached, Colonel Crawford seized a forlorn hope of escaping by appealing to a Shawanoe chief named Wingenund, who had frequently visited his house, and between whom quite a strong friendship existed.

When the chief learned that Colonel Crawford was painted black, he knew that nothing could save him, and he withdrew to his own lodge that he might not witness his sufferings; but Crawford sent for him, and the chief could not refuse to go to his friend.

Their meeting was quite affecting, the chief showing some embarrassment and pretending to be uncertain of the identity of the prisoner, through his paint.

"You are Colonel Crawford, I believe."

"Yes, Wingenund, you must remember me."

"Yes, I have not forgotten you; we have often drank and eaten together, and you have been kind to me many times."

"I hope that friendship remains, Wingenund."

"It would remain forever, if you were in any place but this, and were what you ought to be."

"I have been engaged only in honorable warfare, and when we take your warriors prisoners we treat them right."

The chief looked meaningly at the poor captive and said,

"I would do the most I can for you, and I might do something, had you not joined Colonel Williamson, who murdered the Moravian Indians, knowing they were innocent of all wrong and that he ran no risk in killing them with their squaws and children."

"That was a bad act—a very bad act, Wingenund, and had I been with him, I never would have permitted it. I abhor the deed as do all good white men, no matter where they are."

"That may all be true," said the chief," but Colonel Williamson went a second time and killed more of the Moravians."

"But I went out and did all I could to stop him."

"That may be true, too, but you cannot make the Indians believe it, and then, Colonel Crawford, when you were on the march here, you turned aside with your soldiers and went to the Moravian towns, but found them deserted. Our spies were watching you and saw you do this. Had you been looking for warriors, you would not have gone there, for you know the Moravians are foolish and will not fight."

"We have done nothing, and your spies saw nothing that your own people would not have done had they been in our situation."

"I have no wish to see you die, though you have forfeited your life, and had we Colonel Williamson, we might spare you; but that man has taken good care to keep out of our reach, and you will have to take his place. I can do nothing for you."

Colonel Crawford begged the chief to try and save him from the impending fate, but Wingenund assured him it was useless, and took his departure.

Shortly afterward the Indians began their preparations for the frightful execution.

A large stake was driven into the ground, and wood carefully placed around it. Then Crawford's hands were tied behind his back, and he was led out and securely fastened to the stake.

At this time, Simon Girty was sitting on his horse near by, taking no part in the proceedings, but showing by his looks and manner that he enjoyed them fully as much as did the executioners themselves.

Happening to catch the eye of the renegade, Colonel Crawford asked him whether the Indians really intended to burn him at the stake. Girty answered with a laugh that there could be no doubt of it, and Crawford said no more. He knew that it was useless to appeal to him who was of his own race, for his heart was blacker and more merciless than those of the savages who were kindling the fagots at his feet.

The particulars of the burning of Colonel Crawford have been given by Dr. Knight, his comrade, who succeeded in escaping, when he, too, had been condemned to the same fate. These particulars are too frightful to present in full, for they could only horrify the reader.

Colonel Crawford was subjected to the most dreadful form of torture, the fire burning slowly, while the Indians amused themselves by firing charges of powder into his body. He bore it for a long time with fortitude, but finally ran round and round the stake, when his thongs were burned in two, in the instinctive effort to escape his tormentors.

The squaws were among the most fiendish of the tormentors, until the miserable captive was driven so frantic by his sufferings that he appealed to Girty to shoot him and thus end his awful sufferings.

This dying request was refused, and at the end of two hours nature gave out and the poor Colonel died.

Simon Girty assured Dr. Knight that a similar fate was awaiting him, and Knight himself had little hope of its being averted. A son of Colonel Crawford was subjected to the same torture, but, as we have stated, Dr. Knight effected his escape shortly afterward.

Simon Girty, the most notorious renegade of the West, remained with the Indians until his death. He became a great drunkard, but took part in the defeat and massacre of St. Clair's army in 1791, and was at the battle of the Fallen Timbers, three years later. Fearful of returning to his own kindred at the end of hostilities, he went to Canada, where he became something of a trader, until the breaking out of the war of 1812, when he once more joined the Indians and was killed at the battle of the Thames.

CHAPTER XVII.

Adventure of the Spies White and M'Clelland—Daring Defence of her Home by Mrs. Merrill—Exploits of Kennan the Ranger.

THE block-house garrison at the mouth of Hocking River was thrown into considerable alarm on one occasion by the discovery that an unusual number of Indians were swarming in their town in the valley. Such a state of affairs, as a rule, means that the savages are making, or have made, preparations for a serious movement against the whites.

To ascertain the cause of the presence of so many warriors in that section, two of the most skillful and daring rangers of the West were sent out to spy their movements. These scouts were White and McClelland, and the season on which they ventured upon their dangerous expedition was one of the balmy days in Indian summer.

The scouts made their way leisurely to the top of the well-known prominence near Lancaster, Ohio, from whose rocky summit they looked off over the plain spreading far to the west, and through which the Hocking River winds like a stream of silver.

From this elevation, the keen-eyed scouts gazed down upon a curious picture—one which told them of the certain coming of the greatest danger which can break upon the frontier settlement. What they saw, and the singular adventures that befell them, are told by the Reverend J. B. Finley, the well-known missionary of the West.

Day by day the spies witnessed the horse-racing of the assembled thousands. The old sachems looked on with their Indian indifference, the squaws engaged in their usual drudgery, while the children indulged unrestrainedly in their playful gambols. The arrival of a new war party was greeted with loud shouts, which, striking the stony face of Mount Pleasant, were driven back in the various indentations of the surrounding hills, producing reverberations and echoes as if so many fiends were gathered in universal levee. On several occasions, small parties left the prairie and ascended the mount from its low and grassy eastern slope. At such times, the spies would hide in the deep fissures of the rocks on the west, and again leave their hiding-places when their unwelcome visitors had disappeared. For food, they depended on jerked venison and corn-bread, with which their knapsacks were well stored. They dare not kindle a fire, and the report of one of their rifles would have brought upon them the entire force of Indians. For drink, they resorted to the rain-water which still stood in the hollows of the rocks; but, in a short time, this source was exhausted, and McClelland and White were forced to abandon their enterprise, or find a new supply. To accomplish this, M'Clelland, being the oldest, resolved to make the attempt. With his trusty rifle in hand and two canteens slung over his shoulders, he cautiously descended, by a circuitous route, to the prairie skirting the hills on the north.

Under cover of the hazel thicket, he reached the river, and turning the bold point of a hill, found a beautiful spring within a few feet of the stream now known by the name of Cold Spring. Filling his canteens, he returned in safety to his watchful companion. It was now determined to have a fresh supply of water every day, and the duty was performed alternately.

On one of these occasions, after White had filled his canteens, he sat watching the water as it came gurgling out of the earth, when the light sound of footsteps fell on his ear. Upon turning around he saw two squaws within a few feet of him. The eldest gave one of those far-reaching whoops peculiar to Indians.

White at once comprehended his perilous situation. If the alarm should reach the camps or town, he and his companion must inevitably perish. Self-preservation compelled him to inflict a noiseless death on the squaws, and in such a manner as, if possible, to leave no trace behind. Ever rapid in thought and prompt in action, he sprang upon his victims with the rapidity and power of the lion, and grasping the throat of each, sprang into the river. He thrust the head of the eldest under the water, and while making strong efforts to submerge the younger (who, however, powerfully resisted him), to his astonishment, she addressed him in his own language, though in almost inarticulate sounds. Releasing his hold, she informed him she had been a prisoner ten years, and was taken from below Wheeling; that the Indians had killed all the family; that her brother and herself were taken prisoners, but he succeeded, on the second night, in making his escape.   During this narrative, White had drowned the elder squaw, and had let the body float off down the current, where it was not likely soon to be found. He now directed the girl to follow him, and, with his usual speed and energy, pushed for the mount.

They had scarcely gone half way, when they heard the alarm-cry, some quarter of a mile down the stream.   It was supposed some party of Indians, returning from hunting, struck the river just as the body of the squaw floated past.   White and the girl succeeded in reaching the mount, where M'Clelland had been no indifferent spectator to the sudden commotion among the Indians.   Parties of warriors were seen immediately to strike off in every direction, and White and the girl had scarcely arrived before a company of some twenty warriors had reached the eastern slope of the mount, and were cautiously and carefully keeping under cover. Soon the spies saw their foes, as they glided from tree to tree and rock to rock, till their position was surrounded, except on the west perpendicular side, and all hope of escape was cut off.   In this perilous position, nothing was left but to sell their lives as dearly as possible.

This they resolved to do, and advised the girl to escape to the Indians and tell them she had been taken prisoner.   She said, "No! Death in the presence of my own people is a thousand times better than captivity and slavery.   Furnish me with a gun, and I will show I know how to die.   This place I will not leave. Here my bones shall lie bleaching with yours, and, should either of you escape, you will carry the tidings of my death to my few relatives.

Remonstrance proved fruitless. The two spies quickly matured their means of defence, and vigorously commenced the attack from the front, where, from the very narrow backbone of the mount, the savages had to advance in single file, and without any covert. Beyond this neck, the warriors availed themselves of the rocks and trees in advancing, but, in passing from one to the other, they must be exposed for a short time, and a moment's exposure of their swarthy forms was enough for the unerring rifles of the spies. The Indians, being entirely ignorant of how many were in ambuscade, grew very cautious as they advanced.

After bravely maintaining the fight in front, and keeping the enemy in check, the scouts discovered a new danger threatening them. The foe made preparation to attack them on the flank, which could be most successfully done by reaching an isolated rock, lying in one of the projections on the southern hill-side. This rock once gained by the Indians, they could bring the whites under point-blank range without the possibility of escape. The spies saw the hopelessness of their situation, which it appeared nothing could change.

With this impending fate resting over them, they continued calm and calculating, and as unwearied as the strongest desire of life could produce. Soon M'Clelland saw a tall, swarthy figure preparing to spring from a covert, so near to the fatal rock that a bound or two would reach it, and all hope of life would then be gone. He felt that everything depended on one single advantageous shot; and, although but an inch or two of the warrior's body was exposed, and that at the distance of eighty or a hundred yards, he resolved to fire.

Coolly raising his rifle, shading the sight with his hand, he drew a bead so sure that he felt conscious it would do the deed. He touched the trigger with his finger; the hammer came down, but, in place of striking fire, it broke his flint into many pieces! He now felt sure that the Indian must reach the rock before he could adjust another flint, yet he proceeded to the task with the utmost composure. Casting his eye toward the fearful point, suddenly he saw the warrior stretch every muscle for the leap, and with the agility of a panther he made the spring, but, instead of reaching the rock, he uttered a yell and his dark body fell, rolling down the steep to the valley below.

Some unknown hand had slain him, and a hundred voices from the valley below echoed his death cry. The warrior killed, it was evident, was a prominent one of the tribe, and there was great disappointment over the failure of the movement, which, it was considered, would seal the doom of the daring scouts.

Only a few minutes passed, when a second warrior was seen stealthily advancing to the covert, which had cost the other Indian his life in attempting to reach. At the same moment the attack in front was renewed with great fierceness, so as to require

the constant loading and firing of the spies to prevent their foes from gaining the eminence. Still
the whites kept continually glancing at the warrior,
who seemed assured of the coveted position.

Suddenly he gathered his muscles and made the
spring. His body was seen to bound outward, but
instead of reaching the shelf, for which it started,
it gathered itself like a ball and rolled down the
hill after his predecessor.

The unknown friend had fired a second shot!

This caused consternation among the Shawanoes,
and brave as they unquestionably were, there was
no one else who tried to do that which had cost
the others their lives. Feeling that they had no
ordinary foe to combat on the hill, the savages
withdrew a short distance to consult over some
new method of attack.

The respite came most opportunely to the spies,
who had been fighting and watching for hours and
needed the rest.

It suddenly occurred to M'Clelland that the girl
was not with them, and they concluded that she
had fled through terror and most probably had
fallen into the hands of the Indians again, or what
was equally probable, she had been killed during
the fight.

But the conclusion was scarcely formed, when she
was seen to come from behind a rock, with a smoking
rifle in her hand. Rejoining the astonished and
delighted spies, she quickly explained that she was
the unsuspected friend who shot the two warriors
when in the very act of leaping to the point from

which they expected to command the position of the defenders.

While the fight was at its height, she saw a warrior advance some distance beyond the others, when a rifle-ball from the scouts stretched him lifeless. Without being seen, the girl ran quickly out to where he lay and possessed herself of his gun and ammunition.

Subsequent events showed what good use she made of the weapon. Her life among the Indians taught her to see on the instant the point which the warriors would strive to secure, and, which secured, would place the spies at their mercy. She crawled under some brush, and carefully loading the rifle, held it ready for the critical moment.

It was a singular coincidence, in which the girl must have perceived the hand of Providence, that the second warrior who advanced to the spot was recognized by her as the identical wretch who led the company which killed nearly all her family and who carried her away a prisoner. She made sure, when she pulled trigger upon him, that the bullet should go straight to the mark!

M'Clelland and White appreciated the value of the ally who had joined them, for, without those well-aimed shots of hers, the two must have fallen before the rifles of the Shawanoes. They congratulated her on her nerve and skill, and assured her, that her achievements alone had placed them in a position in which they could feel there was some hope of escape.

As night approached, dark and tumultuous clouds

rolled up from the horizon, and overspreading the skies rendered the night like that of Egypt. As the spies felt that their withdrawal from the dangerous spot must be effected, if effected at all, before the rise of the morning's sun, they saw how much the inky blackness of sky and earth was likely to embarrass them.

However, as the girl was intimately acquainted with the topography of the country immediately surrounding them, it was decided that she should take the lead, the others following close after her.

The great advantage likely to accrue from such an arrangement was that, if they encountered any Indians, as they were more than likely to do, her knowledge of their tongue would enable her to deceive them. They had not gone a hundred yards when the wisdom of this course was demonstrated.

A low "whist" from the guide admonished the spies of danger, and, as agreed beforehand, they sank flat upon their faces and waited for the signal that all was right, before going further. Peering cautiously through the dense gloom, they became aware that the girl was missing, and she was gone so long that they were filled with serious misgivings.

Finally her shadowy figure came out of the gloom, and she told them she had succeeded in having two sentinels removed whose position was such that it would have been impossible for them to get by undiscovered.

In the same noiseless manner the flight was resumed, and the three phantoms moved along through the gloom for a half hour, when they were startled by the barking of a dog close to them. Instantly White and M'Clelland cocked their guns, but their guide whispered that they were now in the very middle of the village, and their lives depended on the utmost silence and secrecy. They needed hardly to be assured of that, and they signified that her directions would be followed implicitly.

A minute later they were accosted by a squaw from an opening in her wigwam ; the guide made appropriate reply, in the Indian tongue, and without pause, moved on. Her voice and manner disarmed suspicion, and the three were not disturbed.

Only a short distance further was passed, when the girl assured them they were beyond the limits of the village, and the great danger was ended. She had shown extraordinary wisdom and shrewdness in leading the spies out of their great peril. She knew the Shawanoes had their sentinels stationed at every avenue of escape, and instead of taking those which it would seem most natural to follow under the circumstances, she adopted the bold plan of disarming all these precautions by passing directly through the center of the village. The very boldness of the plan proved its success.

The fugitives now made for the Ohio River, and, at the end of three days' hard travel, they safely reached the block-house. Their escape prevented the contemplated attack by the Indians, and the adventure itself is certainly one of the most remarkable of the many told of the early days of Ohio and Kentucky.

Among the members of Mr. Finley's church was a quiet, plain-looking woman who was mild, gentle, and consistent in her talk and conversation. And yet this Mrs. Merril was the heroine of the following wonderful exploit:

In 1791, the house of Mr. Merril, in Nelson county, was assaulted by Indians. He was fired upon and fell wounded into the room. The savages attempted to rush in after him, but Mrs. Merril and her daughter succeeded in closing the door. The assailants began to hew a passage through it with their tomahawks; and, having made a hole large enough, one of them attempted to squeeze into the room. Undismayed, the courageous woman seized an axe, gave the ruffian a fatal blow as he sprang through, and he sunk quietly to the floor. Another, and still another, followed till four of their number met the same fate. The silence within induced one of them to pause and look through the crevice in the door. Discovering the fate of those who had entered, the savages resolved upon another mode of attack. Two of their number clambered to the top of the house, and prepared to descend the broad wooden chimney. This new danger was promptly met. Mrs. Merril did not desert her post ; but directed her little son to cut open the feather bed, and pour the feathers upon the fire. This the little fellow did with excellent effect. The two savages, scorched and suffocated, fell down into the fire, and were soon dispatched by the children and the wounded husband. At that moment a fifth savage attempted to enter the door; but he received a salute upon the head from the axe held by Mrs. Merril, that sent him howling away. Thus seven of the savages were destroyed by the courage and energy of this heroic woman. When the sole survivor reached the town, and was asked, " What news?" a prisoner heard his reply: " Bad news! The squaws fight worse than long knives."

William Kennan, a noted scout and ranger, was the hero of many extraordinary incidents.

He had long been remarkable for strength and activity. In the course of the march from Fort Washington, he had repeated opportunities of testing his astonishing powers in those respects, and was admitted to be the swiftest runner of the light corps. On the evening preceding the action, his corps had been advanced in front of the first line of infantry, to give seasonable notice of the enemy's approach.

As day was dawning, he observed about thirty Indians within one hundred yards of the guard-fire, approaching cautiously toward the spot where he stood, in company with twenty other rangers, the rest being considerably in the rear. Supposing it to be a mere scouting party, and not superior in number to the rangers, he sprang forward a few paces in order to shelter himself in a spot of peculiarly rank grass, and, after firing with a quick aim at the foremost Indian, fell flat upon his face, and proceeded with all possible rapidity to reload his gun, not doubting for a moment that his companions would maintain their position and support him.

The Indians, however, rushed forward in such overwhelming masses, that the rangers were compelled to flee with precipitation, leaving young Kennan in total ignorance of his danger. Fortunately, the captain of his company had observed him, when he threw himself in the grass, and suddenly shouted aloud: "Run, Kennan, or you are a dead man!" He instantly sprang to his feet, and beheld the Indians within ten feet of him, while his company were more than one hundred yards in front.

Not a moment was to be lost. He darted off, with every muscle strained to the utmost, and was pursued by a dozen of the enemy with loud yells. He at first pressed straight forward to the usual fording-place in the creek, which ran between the rangers and the main army; but several Indians, who had passed him before he arose from the grass, threw themselves in his way and completely cut him off from the rest.

By the most powerful exertions, he had thrown the whole body of pursuers behind him, with the exception of one young chief, probably Meeshawa, who displayed a swiftness and perseverance equal to his own. In the circuit which Kennan was was obliged to make, the race continued for more than four hundred yards. The distance between them was about eighteen feet, which Kennan could not increase, nor his adversary diminish. Each for the time put his whole soul in the race.

Kennan, as far as he was able, kept his eye upon

the motions of his pursuer, lest he should throw the tomahawk, which he held aloft in a menacing attitude, and, at length, finding that no other Indian was at hand, he determined to try the mettle of his pursuer in a different manner, and felt for his knife in order to turn at bay. It had escaped from its sheath, however, while he lay in the grass, and his hair almost lifted the cap from his head when he found himself wholly unarmed.

As he had slackened his space for a moment, the Indian was almost within reach of him when he started ahead again ; but the idea of being without arms lent wings to his flight, and for the first time he saw himself gaining ground. He had watched the motions of his pursuer too closely to pay proper attention to the nature of the ground before him, and suddenly found himself in front of a large tree, which had been blown down, and upon which had been heaped brush and other impediments to the height of eight or nine feet.

The Indian, heretofore silent, now gave utterance to an exultant shout, for he must have felt sure of his victim. Not a second was given to Kennan to deliberate. He must clear the obstacle in front or it was all over with him. Putting his whole soul into the effort, he bounded into the air with a power which astonished himself, and, clearing limbs, brush, and everything else, alighted in perfect safety on the other side. An exclamation of amazement burst from the band of pursuers bringing up the rear, not one of whom had the hardihood to attempt the same feat.

Kennan, however, had no leisure to enjoy his triumph. Dashing into the creek, where the high banks would protect him from the fire of the enemy, he ran up the edge of the stream until he found a convenient crossing place, and rejoined the rangers in the rear of the encampment, panting from the fatigue of exertions which had seldom been surpassed. But little breathing time was allowed him. The attack instantly commenced, and was maintained for three hours with unabated fury.

When the retreat took place, Kennan was attached to Major Clark's battalion, which had the dangerous service of protecting the rear. The corps quickly lost its commander, and was completely disorganized. Kennan was among the hindmost when the flight commenced, but exerting those same powers which had saved him in the morning, he quickly gained the front, passing several horsemen in his flight.

Here he beheld a private in his own company, lying upon the ground with his thigh broken, who, in tones of distress, implored each horseman as he hurried by to take him up behind. As soon as he beheld Kennan coming up on foot, he stretched out his hands and entreated him to save him. Notwithstanding the imminent peril of the moment, his friend could not reject such an appeal, but, seizing him in his arms, placed him upon his back, and ran in this manner several hundred yards.

At length the enemy was gaining upon them so fast, that Kennan saw their death was certain

8

unless he relinquished his burden. He accordingly told his friend that he had used every exertion possible to save his life, but in vain; that he must relax his hold about his neck, or they would both perish. The unhappy man, heedless of every remonstrance, still clung convulsively to Kennan's back, until the foremost of the enemy, armed with tomahawks alone, were within twenty yards of them. Kennan then drew his knife from its sheath, and cut the fingers of his companion, thus compelling him to relinquish his hold. The wounded man fell upon the ground in utter helplessness, and Kennan beheld him tomahawked before he had gone thirty yards. Kennan, relieved from his burden, darted forward with the activity which once more brought him to the van. Here again he was compelled to neglect his own safety to attend to that of others.

The late Governor Madison, of Kentucky, who afterward commanded the corps which defended themselves so honorably at the River Raisin, was at that time a subaltern in St. Clair's army. Being a man of feeble constitution, he was totally exhausted by the exertions of the morning, and was found by Kennan sitting calmly upon a log, awaiting the approach of his enemies. Kennan hastily accosted him, and inquired the cause of his delay. Madison, pointing to a wound which had bled profusely, replied he was unable to walk further, and had no horse. Kennan instantly ran back to the spot where he had seen an exhausted horse grazing, caught him without difficulty, and having assisted

Madison to mount, walked by his side till they were out of danger. Fortunately, the pursuit ceased soon after, as the plunder of the camp presented irresistible attractions to the Indians. The friendship thus formed between these two young men continued through life. Kennan never entirely recovered from the immense exertions he was constrained to make during this unfortunate expedition.

CHAPTER XVIII.

The Three Counties of Kentucky united into One District—
Colonel Boone as a Farmer—He outwits a Party of Indians
who seek to capture him—Emigration to Kentucky—Outrages
by Indians—Failure of General Clark's Expedition.

KENTUCKY now enjoyed a season of repose.
The revolution was ended, the independence of the
colonies recognized, and the cession of the British
posts in the northwest was considered inevitable.
The Indians had not the same incentives to war-
ware and massacre as heretofore, though murder
was so congenial to their nature, and their hatred
of the whites was so intense, that it was unsafe to
trust to any regard of treaties on their part.

The year 1783, although marked by few stirring
incidents, was an important one in the history of
Kentucky.

She still belonged to Virginia, but the subject of
separation was discussed among the people, and it
was apparent to all that the day was not far distant when she would be erected into an independent State; but she organized on a new basis, as
may be said. The three counties were united in
one district, having a court of common law and
chancery, for the whole Territory. The seat of
justice was first established at Harrodsburg, but
was soon after removed to Danville, which con-

tinued the capital and most important town in the State for a number of years.

Upon the cessation of hostilities between England and the Colonies, it was stipulated that the former were to carry away no slaves, were to surrender to the United States her posts in the Northwest, and were permitted to collect the legal debts due her from our citizens.

Each party violated these conditions. Virginia peremptorily forbade the collection of a single debt within her territory until every slave taken away was returned; while England, on her part, refused to surrender a post until all the debts due her subjects had been legally recognized and collected. The result of these complications was that England held her posts in the Northwest for ten years after the close of the war.

Colonel Boone, as was his custom, devoted himself to his farm, and was engaged in the cultivation of considerable tobacco, though he never used the weed himself. As a shelter for curing it, he had built an enclosure of rails which was covered with cane and grass. The raising of tobacco has become so common of late in many States of the Union, that nearly all understand the process. Boone had placed the plants so that they lay in three tiers on the rails, the lowermost one having become very dry. One day, while in the act of removing the lower pile, so as to make room for the rest of his crop, four stalwart Indians entered, carrying guns.

When Boone looked down into the grinning faces of the warriors, he understood what it meant:

they had come to take him away prisoner, as he had been taken before.

"We got you now, Boone," said one of them; "you no get away; we carry you to Chillicothe."

Boone, of course, had no gun at command, as he was not expecting any such visit, while each of the Shawanoes carried a rifle and held it so as to command him.

When Boone looked more narrowly into their faces, he recognized one or two of the Shawanoes who had captured him five years before near the Blue Licks.

He affected to be pleased, and called back, with a laugh,

"How are you, friends? I'm glad to see you."

But they were not disposed to wait, for they had ventured, at considerable risk, to steal thus close to the settlement, in their eagerness to secure such a noted prisoner as Colonel Boone.

They, therefore, pointed their guns at him in a menacing way, and suggested that the best plan for him to induce them not to pull the triggers was to descend immediately.

"I don't see as there is any help for it," was the reply of the pioneer, "but, as I have started to shift this tobacco, I hope you'll wait a few minutes till I can shift it. Just watch the way I do it."

The four warriors were unsuspicious, and, standing directly under the mass of dry pungent stuff, they looked up at the pioneer as he began moving the rails. He continued talking to his old acquaintances, as though they were valued friends, who had just dropped in for a chat, and they turned their black eyes curiously upon him, with no thought of the little stratagem he was arranging with such care and skill.

By and by Boone got a large pile of the tobacco in position directly over their heads, and then suddenly drew the rails apart, so as to allow it to fall.

At the same instant, with his arms full of the suffocating weed, he sprang among them and dashed it into their faces. Distributing it as impartially as he could, in the few seconds he allowed himself, he dashed out of the shed and ran for his house, where he could seize his rifle, and defend himself against twice the number.

Great as was his danger, he could not help stopping, when he had run most of the distance, and looking back to see how his visitors were making out.

The sight was a curious one. The eyes of the four warriors were full of the smarting dust, and they were groping about, unable to see, and resembling a party engaged in blind-man's buff. These warriors were able to speak English quite well, and they used some very emphatic expressions in the efforts to put their feelings into words. If they expected to find Boone in these aimless gropings they were mistaken, for he reached his cabin, where he was safe from them, had they been in the full possession of their faculties.

When the Shawanoes had managed to free their eyes to some extent from the biting, pungent dust, they moved off into the woods and made no more calls upon the pioneer.

Emigration to Kentucky increased, and new settlements were continually forming. Strong, sturdy settlers erected their cabins in every quarter, and the forests were rapidly cleared. Live-stock increased in numbers, and naturally a brisk trade sprang up in many commodities. Trains of pack-horses carried goods from Philadelphia to Pittsburgh, where they were taken down the Ohio in flat-boats and distributed among the various settlements.

As the expression goes, in these later days, every-thing was "booming" in Kentucky during those years, and the Territory made immense strides in material wealth and prosperity. Most of the im-migrants came from North Carolina and Virginia, and they were hospitable, enterprising, vigorous and strongly attached to each other.

The time for "universal peace," along the fron-tier had not yet come; small affrays were con-tinually occurring between the settlers and In-dians, and in the spring of 1784, an incident of a singular nature took place. A Mr. Rowan, with his own and five other families, was descending the Ohio, one flat-boat being occupied by the cattle, while the emigrants were in the other. They had progressed a considerable distance, when, late at night, they were alarmed by the number of Indian fires which were burning for a half mile along the banks. The savages called to the whites and ordered them to come ashore, but, without making any reply, the settlers continued floating silently down the river. Finding their orders disregarded, the savages sprang into their canoes and paddled rapidly toward the boats; but, in this instance, certainly silence proved golden, for the unnatural stillness which continued seemed to awe the Indians, who, after following the craft awhile, drew off without inflicting the slightest injury. Most likely they were fearful of a surprise, in case of an open attack.

In the month of March, 1785, a settler named Elliot was killed and his family broken up, and while Thomas Marshall was descending the Ohio, he was hailed in the fashion often adopted by the decoys employed by the Indians. In this instance, however, the white man said he was a brother of the notorious Simon Girty, and he wished to warn the settlers against their danger. He admonished them to be on the watch every hour of the day and night, and under no circumstances to approach the shore.

He added the remarkable information that his brother repented the hostility he had shown the whites, and intended to return to them, if they would overlook his former enmity. But, as Simon remained a bitter enemy until his death, nearly thirty years later, his repentance could not have been very sincere.

A brief while after this, Captain Ward was attacked on the river and all his horses were killed, his nephew also falling a victim. In October an emigrant party was fired into, and six slain, then another company lost nine; and the desultory warfare was pushed with such persistency by the savages, that the settlers demanded that the Indian country should be invaded and a blow delivered which would prove effectual in keeping them away for a long time to come.

The situation of affairs became so exasperating that General Clark, in accordance with the fashion, issued his call for volunteers, and in a brief space of time a thousand veterans flocked about him at the Falls of the Ohio.

This was an army which, if properly handled, was irresistible and could have marched straight through the Indian country, laying the fields and towns waste and dispersing any force the tribes could combine against them.

But, from the first, it encountered two most serious difficulties: General Clark had lost prestige from his habits of intoxication, which unfitted him to assume the leadership of such an important enterprise, where a man needed to be cool, collected, and with the command of every faculty of his being.

But for this one fatal weakness, which has stricken so many a genius to the dust, Clark would have risen to far greater eminence, and would have reached and held the position through life to which his commanding genius entitled him.

The provisions for the soldiers were sent down the river in keel boats, but the obstructions delayed them, and, when two weeks passed without their arrival, the dissatisfaction of the men broke out in open insubordination. Desertions began, and in one instance, it is said, three hundred soldiers left in a body. General Clark protested, begged and entreated, but all in vain. His force went to pieces, like snow melting in the sun, and he was finally forced to return to Kentucky, humiliated beyond measure.

Whenever any such movement was started by the whites, the Indians kept themselves informed of every step of its progress. Their spies were out and allowed no incident, however slight, to escape their observation. It was natural, therefore, that when they saw the formidable force break up and go to their homes, they should conclude that the settlers were afraid to invade their territory, with the lesson of the former repeated failures before their eyes.

The Indians were stimulated to greater audacity than ever, and it may be said that the whole border became aflame with the most murderous kind of warfare.

CHAPTER XIX.

General Harmar's Expedition against the Indians — Colonel
   Hardin Ambushed—Bravery of the Regulars—Outgeneraled
   by the Indians—Harmar and Hardin Court-martialed—General St. Clair's Expedition and its Defeat.

THE outrages upon the part of the Indians became
so alarming that Congress was forced to see that
the only way to check them and to give anything
like security to the frontier, was to send a regularly-
organized army into the country, which should so
cripple the power of the combined tribes that they
would be compelled to sue for peace.

A force of eleven hundred men was therefore
organized and placed under the command of General Harmar, who was directed to march against the
Indian towns of the Northwest. In the latter part
of September, Harmar, at the head of this large
body, moved against the villages on the Miami.
The savages, as a matter of course, knew of their
coming, and were gone. General Harmar laid
waste their cornfields and applied the torch to their
lodges, making the destruction as complete as possible. Discovering a fresh trail, he detached one
hundred and eighty of his men, and placing them
under the command of Colonel John Hardin and
Ensign Hartshorn, sent them with orders to move
with all speed with a view of overtaking the fugitives.

Pursuit was pushed with great vigor, when the whole force ran directly into ambush and were assailed on all sides by a large force of Indians. At the beginning of the attack, the militia, numbering five-sixths of the whole force, broke and scattered, while the few regulars stood their ground and fought bravely, until nearly every man was shot down.

When night came, the Indians held a jollification dance over the dead and dying soldiers, and the great victory they themselves had again obtained. Among the witnesses of the curious scene were Ensign Hartshorn (who, having stumbled over a log in the tall grass, was prudent enough to lie still where he was unnoticed) and Colonel Hardin, who was sunk to his chin in mud and water, where he stayed until he gained an opportunity of crawling out. He and Hartshorn succeeded in rejoining the main body.

The news of the frightful slaughter so discouraged General Harmar that he broke up his camp and began a retrograde movement toward the settlements. When a few miles from the Indian towns which he had burned, he halted and sent out Colonel Hardin with three hundred militia and sixty regulars.

They were victimized more shamefully than before. It seems unaccountable how men in such circumstances, and with the crimson lessons of the preceding few years before them, could be so deceived as were the leaders of the expeditions in the West.

Colonel Hardin had not advanced far, when a small company of warriors showed themselves and succeeded with little difficulty in drawing off the militia in pursuit of them—the very purpose of the stratagem—and then the main body of savages attacked the regulars in overwhelming force and with tiger-like ferocity.

Although unused to such fighting, the regulars stood their ground like Spartans, and loaded and fired with great accuracy and rapidity. The warriors dropped like autumn leaves, and had there been only a few hundred of them, the soldiers would have routed them very quickly; but re-enforcements continued to swarm forward, the woods were alive, and every tree and bush seemed to conceal a savage who aimed with deadly effect at the brave soldiers.

The latter stood and fought until only ten men were left, including their intrepid commander. These escaped, while fifty were killed—the fight, scarcely heard of in this day, being one of the most remarkable exhibitions of bravery ever given in the history of our country.

Just about the time the little force was practically annihilated, the militia came back, so as to take their turn in offering themselves as victims to Indian treachery and bravery. The warriors were ready for them, and they were attacked with the same fierceness. The horrible massacre went on until two-thirds of the militia were slain, when the others scattered for the main body.

It would seem that mismanagement could not

go further, and the indignation against Harmar and Hardin was so intense that they were court-martialed. Hardin obtained a unanimous acquittal, as did Harmar; but the latter felt the disgrace so keenly that he resigned his commission in the army .

One of the inevitable results of these repeated blunders on the part of the soldiers was the renewal of the Indian outrages, which became bolder than ever. The condition of Kentucky was so critical that Congress appointed St. Clair, Governor of the Northwest Territory, Major-General, and he was instructed to raise a new regiment for the defence of the frontier.

General St. Clair was given command of the expedition, and it was the crowning act of imbecility and disgrace on the part of those who had in charge the protection of the border. Arthur St. Clair was born at Edinburgh, Scotland, and was in the prime of life when he assumed command of the expedition against the western tribes. It was he who in the month of June, 1777, was besieged in Ticonderoga by Burgoyne's troops and compelled to evacuate the fort with great loss. His career in the Revolution had not been creditable to him, and there was no man in whom the Kentuckians had less confidence than he. When it became known that he was to lead the large force against the Indians, the dissatisfaction was universal, and the predictions of failure were heard in every quarter.

The distrust was so deep that his call for volunteers received no response. It was intended that his command should consist of two thousand regular troops, composed of cavalry, infantry and artillery. These rendezvoused at Fort Washington, the site of Cincinnati, in September, 1791. Kentucky finally sent forward a thousand of her militia, but they so disliked service under St. Clair, that the most of them deserted and returned to their homes.

The chief object of this formidable campaign was to establish a series of posts, extending from the Ohio to the Maumee; and by leaving a garrison of a thousand men on the latter river, it was believed that the neighboring tribes could be kept in a state of submission.

Fort Jefferson was established close to the present boundary line between Ohio and Indiana, but the progress of the army was so snail-like that desertions became numerous. A month passed before the march was resumed, and the impatient Kentuckians left by scores. In one instance at least a whole detachment drew off and went home.

The principal guide and scout attached to the expedition was a Chickasaw chief, who saw what was certain to be the result of this wholesale insubordination, and he with his few warriors also left. The wiser course would have been for St. Clair to have done the same, for nothing but irretrievable disaster stared him in the face.

St. Clair, however, pressed forward, and on the 3d of November, he encamped upon a tributary of the Wabash. Indians were seen continually, but they kept beyond reach. The regulars and levies encamped in two lines, covered by the stream, while the militia were a quarter of a mile in advance on the other side of the river. Beyond these, Captain Clough was stationed with a company of regulars, with orders to intercept the advance of the enemy. Colonel Oldham was directed to send out patrols of twenty-five men each, through the woods to prevent the insidious approach of the Indians.

No attack was made, but during the succeeding night, Captain Clough was rendered uneasy by the discovery that the woods were full of savages, who were evidently carrying out some pre-arranged plan, for the tribes had proven long before their ability to outgeneral the whites in fighting battles in the forest.

The captain reported his discovery to General Butler, who failed to notify the commanding general, and, at sunrise, the Indians made a furious charge upon the camp of the militia. The regulars, as usual, fought with the greatest daring, and the militia, as usual, displayed the greatest cowardice, breaking and fleeing in a panic. The regulars were enabled to hold the savages in check for a short time, but the panic of the militia was irretrievable.

There were none quicker to perceive this than the Indians themselves, who immediately massed and poured a terribly destructive fire into the advance, the artillery and the second line.

The surprise was complete, but credit mnst be given St. Clair and his officers, who were personally brave, and who fought with the utmost daring, striving at great personal risk to rally the men,

CHAPTER XX.

The Brilliant Victory of Mad Anthony Wayne brings Peace to
the Frontier—Boone Loses his Farm—He Removes to Missouri—Made Commandant of the Femme Osage District—
Audubon's Account of a Night with Colonel Boone—Hunting
in his Old Age—He Loses the Land granted him by the
Spanish Government—Petitions Congress for a Confirmation
of his Original Claims—The Petition Disregarded.

WHILE the stirring events recorded in the preceding chapter were taking place, Daniel Boone,
like every one else, was advancing in years, and the
prime of his life was passed before a lasting peace
was gained by the American settlers on the frontier.

Disaster followed disaster, until Congress at last
did the thing which it ought to have done long
before. "Mad Anthony" Wayne, the hero of
Stony Point and a dozen Revolutionary battle-
fields, was appointed to assume the military management of affairs in the West.

This appointment was made in April, 1792,
when he became Major-General and Commander-
in-Chief, and he led an expedition against the de-
fiant combination of tribes, encountering them in
August, 1794, when he utterly defeated and over-
threw them. He compelled the treaty of Greenville, which ended all danger from any combination
of the aborigines—nothing of the kind developing

itself, until the great Tecumseh roused his race against the Americans in the war of 1812.

Boone now applied himself with great industry to the cultivation of his farm near Boonesborough. He soon made it one of the finest and most valuable pieces of land in the country; but, like many a man in his position, he fell a victim to the rapacious speculator, who took advantage of the intricacies and elasticity of the law.

Boone felt such a dislike of legal forms, and in fact of everything that pertained to them, that he failed to secure the title of his land locations. Before he suspected his danger, he found himself deprived of all his possessions, the right to which he never dreamed would be questioned.

The great pioneer had reached that period in life when it would be supposed that he was too feeble to begin over again, but, although the misfortune was a great blow to him, he did not lose courage. He removed to Point Pleasant, on the Kanawha River, in Virginia, where he stayed several years, tilling the ground with his usual industry, and indulging also in his favorite pastime of hunting.

One day, when he returned from hunting, he received a call from a number of friends who had been on a tour across the Missouri. They gave such fervid accounts of the richness of the soil and the abundance of game, that the heart of the old pioneer was fired again as it was forty years before. He determined to emigrate to Missouri with the purpose of spending the remainder of his days there. Accordingly, with his household goods and family, he turned his back forever upon the land of his early sufferings and triumphs. This removal was probably made in 1797, though the precise date is unknown.

At the time named, Spain owned the country, then called Upper Louisiana, and the fame of the renowned pioneer had extended to that comparatively remote region. The Lieutenant-Governor, residing at St. Louis, promised him ample portions of land, and Boone took up his residence in the Femme-Osage settlement, some 50 miles west of St. Louis. Don Charles D. Delassus, the Lieutenant-Governor, presented Boone with a commission, in 1800, as Commandant of the Femme-Osage District — an office which included both civil and military duties.

Boone accepted the office, and discharged the duties connected with it with great credit, up to the time when the territory was purchased by the United States in 1804. Boone lived with his son, Daniel M., until the date named, when he changed his residence to that of his son Nathan, with whom he tarried six years, when he became a member of the family of his son-in-law, Flanders Callaway.

It was at this period that the great naturalist Audubon spent a night with Boone, the account of which is so interesting, that we venture to give it the reader:

" Daniel Boone, or as he was usually called in the Western country, Colonel Boone, happened to spend a night with me under the same roof, more than twenty years ago. We had returned from a shooting excursion, in the course of which his extraordinary skill in the management of the rifle had been fully displayed. On retiring to the room appropriated to that remarkable individual and myself, I felt anxious to know more of his exploits and adventures than I did, and accordingly took the liberty of proposing numerous questions to him. The stature and general appearance of this Wanderer of the Western forests approached the gigantic. His chest was broad and prominent; his muscular powers displayed themselves in every limb; his countenance gave indication of his great courage, enterprise, and perseverance ; and when he spoke, the very motion of his lips brought the impression that whatever he uttered could not be otherwise than strictly true. I undressed, whilst he merely took off his hunting-shirt, and arranged a few folds of blankets on the floor, choosing rather to lie there, as he observed, than on the softest bed. When we had both disposed of ourselves, each after his own fashion, he related to me the following account of his powers of memory, which I lay before you, kind reader, in his own words, hoping that the simplicity of the style may prove interesting to you :

" ' I was once,' said he, ' on a hunting expedition on the banks of the Green River, when the lower parts of this State (Kentucky) were still in the hands of nature, and none but the sons of the soil were looked upon as its lawful proprietors. We Virginians had for some time been waging a war of intrusion upon them, and I, amongst the rest, rambled through the woods in pursuit of their race, as I now would follow the tracks of any ravenous animal. The Indians outwitted me one dark night, and I was unexpectedly as suddenly made a prisoner by them. The trick had been managed with great skill, for no sooner had I extinguished the fire of my camp, and laid me down to rest in full security, as I thought, than I felt myself seized by an indistinguishable number of hands, and was immediately pinioned, as if about to be led to the scaffold for execution. To have attempted to be refractory would have proved useless and dangerous to my life; and I suffered myself to be removed from my camp to theirs, a few miles distant, without uttering even a word of complaint. You are aware, I dare say, that to act in this manner was the best policy, as you understand that by so doing I proved to the Indians at once that I was born and bred as fearless of death as any of themselves.

" 'When we reached the camp, great rejoicings were exhibited. Two squaws and a few pappooses appeared particularly delighted at the sight of me, and I was assured by very unequivocal gestures and words, that, on the morrow, the mortal enemy of the Redskins would cease to live. I never opened my lips, but was busy contriving some scheme which might enable me to give the rascals the slip before dawn. The women immediately fell a searching my hunting-shirt for whatever they might think valuable, and, fortunately for me, soon found my flask filled with *Monongahela* (that is, reader, strong whisky). A terrific grin was exhibited on their murderous countenances, while my heart throbbed with joy at the anticipation of their intoxication. The crew immediately began to beat their bellies and sing, as they passed the bottle from mouth to mouth. How often did I wish the flask ten times its size, and filled with aqua fortis! I observed that the squaws drank more freely than the warriors, and again my spirits were about to be depressed, when the report of a gun was heard in the distance. The singing and drinking were both brought to a stand, and I saw, with inexpressible joy, the men walk off to some distance and talk to the squaws. I knew they were consulting about me, and I foresaw that in a few moments the warriors would go to discover the cause of the gun having been fired so near their camp. I expected the squaws would be left to guard me. Well, sir, it was just so. They returned; the men took up their guns and walked away. The squaws sat down again, and in less than five minutes had my bottle up to their dirty mouths, gurgling down their throats the remains of the whisky.

" 'With what pleasure did I see them becoming more and more drunk, until the liquor took such hold of them that it was quite impossible for these women to be of any service. They tumbled down, rolled about, and began to snore ; when I, having no other chance of freeing myself from the cords that fastened me, rolled over and over towards the fire, and, after a short time, burned them asunder. I rose on my feet, stretched my stiffened sinews, snatched up my rifle, and, for once in my life, spared that of Indians. I now recollect how desirous I once or twice felt to lay open the skulls of the wretches with my tomahawk; but, when I again thought upon killing beings unprepared and unable to defend themselves, it looked like murder without need, and I gave up the idea.

" 'But, sir, I felt determined to mark the spot, and, walking to a thrifty ash sapling, I cut out of it three large chips, and ran off. I soon reached the river, soon crossed it, and threw myself deep into the canebrakes, imitating the tracks of an Indian with my feet, so that no chance might be left for those from whom I had escaped to overtake me.

" 'It is now nearly twenty years since this happened, and more than five since I left the whites' settlements, which I might probably never have visited again had I not been called on as a witness in a lawsuit that was pending in Kentucky, and which I really believe would never have been settled, had I not come forward and established the beginning of a certain boundary line. This is the story, sir:

" 'Mr. —— moved from old Virginia into Kentucky, and having a large tract granted him in the new State, laid claim to a certain parcel of land adjoining Green River, and, as chance would have it, took for one of his corners the very ash-tree on which I had made my mark, and finished his survey of some thousands of acres, beginning, as it is expressed in the deed, ' at an ash marked by three distinct notches of the tomahawk of a white man.'

" 'The tree had grown much, and the bark had covered the marks; but, somehow or other, Mr. —— heard from some one all that I have already said to you, and thinking that I might remember the spot alluded to in the deed, but which was no longer discoverable, wrote for me to come and try at least to find the place of the tree. His letter mentioned that all of my expenses should be paid, and, not caring much about once more going back to Kentucky, I started and met Mr. ——. After some conversation, the affair with the Indians came to my recollection. I considered for a while, and began to think that after all, I could find the very spot, as well as the tree, if it was yet standing.

" 'Mr. —— and I mounted our horses, and off we went to the Green River bottoms. After some difficulties—for you must be aware, sir, that great changes have taken place in those woods—I found at last the spot where I had crossed the river, and, waiting for the moon to rise, made for the course in which I thought the ash-tree grew. On approaching the place, I felt as if the Indians were there still, and as if I were still a prisoner among them. Mr. —— and I camped near what I conceived the spot, and waited until the return of day.

" 'At the rising of the sun, I was on foot, and after a good deal of musing, thought that an ash-tree then in sight must be the very one on which I had made my mark. I felt as if there could be

9

no doubt of it, and mentioned my thought to
Mr. ——. 'Well, Colonel Boone,' said he, ' if you
think so, I hope it may prove true, but we must
have some witnesses; do you stay hereabout, and
I will go and bring some of the settlers whom I
know.' I agreed. Mr. —— trotted off, and I, to
pass the time, rambled about to see whether a deer
was still living in the land. But ah! sir, what a
wonderful difference thirty years make in a country!
Why, at the time I was caught by the Indians, you
would not have walked out in any direction for
more than a mile without shooting a buck or a
bear. There were then thousands of buffaloes on
the hills of Kentucky; the land looked as if it never
would become poor; and to hunt in those days
was a pleasure indeed. But when I was left to
myself on the banks of Green River, I dare say for
the last time in my life, a few *signs* only of deer
were to be seen, and, as to a deer itself, I saw
none.

" ' Mr. —— returned, accompanied by three
gentlemen. They looked upon me as if I had been
Washington himself, and walked to the ash-tree,
which I now called my own, as if in quest of a long-
lost treasure. I took an axe from one of them, and
cut a few chips off the bark. Still no signs were to
be seen. So I cut again until I thought it was
time to be cautious, and I scraped and worked
away with my butcher-knife until I *did* come to
where my tomahawk had left an impression in the
wood. We now went regularly to work, and
scraped at the tree with care until three hacks, as

plain as any three notches ever were, could be seen. Mr. —— and the other gentlemen were astonished, and I must allow I was as much surprised as pleased myself. I made affidavit of this remarkable occurrence in presence of these gentlemen. Mr. —— gained the cause. I left Green River forever, and came to where we now are ; and, sir, I wish you a good night.' "

Spain seemed glad to do honor to the great pioneer, Daniel Boone, who was so well known at that time, that no less a poet than Lord Byron rendered tribute to his daring and achievements. Spain gave him a tract of land, numbering 8,500 acres, which was meant as a recognition of his services to the government. The law as it then existed, required, in order to make his title good, that the grant should be confirmed by the representative of the crown at New Orleans, and another condition was that the grantee should reside upon it himself.

As it would have been inconvenient on the part of Boone to comply with the latter provision, the commandant at St Louis, who was his warm friend, assured him that his title could be perfected without acceding to the requirement.

Boone's dear experience in Kentucky should have been remembered, but he left everything to his friends, and when Louisiana came into the possession of the United States, it was found that Boone had not the shadow of a legal title to the lands presented him, and the commissioners had no choice, according to their instructions, but to reject his claim entirely.

This was a serious blow, but the only one who could be censured was Boone himself. However, there was no fear of his coming to want, for he not only had a large number of immediate relatives, all of whom were strongly attached to him, but the States of Kentucky and Missouri would never permit any such disgrace.

Boone liked Missouri, for the people were kind and hospitable and game was plenty. He could never lose his fondness for the woods, and as the beaver were numerous and their furs valuable, he made considerable money by gathering and selling the peltries.

At the end of several years he had amassed enough funds to carry out an intention which does him great credit. When he removed from Kentucky he was obliged to leave several debts behind him, the memory of which disturbed him not a little. He now made a journey to the State, where he paid every creditor in full, and returned to Missouri with just half a dollar in his pocket.

"Now I am ready to die," said he; "I have paid all my debts, and when I am gone, no one shall be able to say I was a dishonest man."

It would scarcely be expected that in his old age, and in the new country to which he had emigrated, he would be subjected to danger from the Indians, and yet he was placed in peril more than once.

His principal companion on his hunting excursions was a black boy about half grown. While thus engaged they were attacked by a small party of Osage Indians, who, however, were not long in learning that the old fire still burned brightly, for they were speedily scattered without having inflicted any injury upon either of the hunters.

On another occasion, while Boone was hunting entirely alone, he discovered that a large encampment of Indians was in the neighborhood, and he had reason to believe that a number of the warriors were hunting for him.

Boone, it will be remembered, was quite an old man, and it must have recalled the scenes of nearly forty years before, when he alternately hunted and hid in the Kentucky wilderness, before the foot of any other white man had penetrated the solitudes.

For nearly three weeks the pioneer lived that life over again, hiding in the deepest recesses of the forest, carefully concealing his trail and cooking his food only at the dead of night, so that the smoke should not be seen by the Indians, who finally took their departure, without being able to catch a glimpse of the old hunter.

His love for the woods knew no abatement with advancing years, and he spent hours, days, and even weeks, in wandering in the grand old forests, breathing the pure fresh air, shooting the timid deer, maneuvering against the Indians, who tracked him many a mile, and returning to his home wearied, but with the same genial good nature, which was one of his distinguishing traits in his early days.

In the year 1812, Colonel Boone petitioned Congress for a confirmation of his original claims, and knowing that such petitions cannot have too great weight, he sent a memorial to the General Assembly of Kentucky, asking their assistance in obtaining the desired confirmation from Congress.

That legislature by a unanimous vote, passed the following preamble and resolutions :

" The Legislature of Kentucky, taking into view the many eminent services rendered by Colonel Boone, in exploring and settling the Western country, from which great advantages have resulted, not only to this State, but to his country in general ; and that, from circumstances over which he had no control, he is now reduced to poverty, not having, so far as appears, an acre of land out of the vast territory he has been a great instrument in peopling ; believing, also, that it is as unjust as impolitic, that useful enterprise and eminent services should go unrewarded by a government where merit confers the only distinction ; and having sufficient reason to believe that a grant of ten thousand acres of land which he claims in Upper Louisiana, would have been confirmed by the Spanish government, had not said territory passed, by cession, into the hands of the general government ; wherefore,

" *Resolved*, By the General Assembly of the Commonwealth of Kentucky, that our senators in Congress be requested to make use of their exertions to procure a grant of land in said Territory to said Boone, either the ten thousand acres to which he appears to have an equitable claim, from the grounds set forth to this Legislature, by way of confirmation, or to such quantity in such place as shall be deemed most advisable, by way of dona-tion."

While his memorial was pending in Congress, the wife of Boone died at the age of seventy-six years. His memorial was strongly supported by the most distinguished members from the West, but no action could be secured upon it until the 24th of December, 1813, when the committee on public lands made a report, in which the justice of Boone's claims was admitted, and Congress was recommended to give him one thousand arpents, or 850 acres of land.

The act for the confirmation of the title passed on the 10th of February, 1814. As every emi-grant to Louisiana was entitled by law to pre-cisely that number of acres, it is difficult to justify the treatment which Boone received at the hands of the law-makers of the country.

The pioneer was never given any other recogni-tion of his services ; and as he was growing old, his relatives, all of whom were tenderly attached to him, saw that no want of his was not fulfilled so far as it was possible for human kindness to fulfill it. He devoted himself mainly to hunting, and, when at home, carved powder-horns and made trinkets for his descendants, some of whom were to the fourth and fifth generation.

These last he frequently gathered around his knees and told of his many thrilling adventures with the Indians, long years before they were born, while he entertained the older friends on the long, dismal wintry evenings, with his narrative of his experiences on the Dark and Bloody Ground, in the days that tried men's souls.

CHAPTER XXI.

Last Days of Colonel Boone—Reinterment of the Remains of Himself and Wife at Frankfort—Conclusion.

THE hunting days of Colonel Boone at last came to an end. He had passed his three score and ten, and the iron limbs and hardy frame were compelled to bend before the infirmities of age, to which Hercules himself must succumb in the end.

So long as he was able, he kept up his hunting expeditions in the wood, but on one occasion, he was taken violently ill, and made his preparations for death, his only companion being the negro boy, who had been with him many times before.

He was brought to recognize at last the danger of going beyond the immediate reach of his friends, and for ten years he did not do so.

He was held in great affection and respect by his numerous friends and relatives, and he was a more than welcome visitor at the hearthstone of each. The harsh treatment received at the hands of the government could not embitter such a sweet nature as his, and he showed no resentment over the fact that the land upon which he had toiled in the vigor of his early manhood, and whose labors had made it exceptionally valuable, passed to the hands of a stranger without cost or claim.

As the stream of life neared the great ocean beyond, it assumed a serene and majestic flow, which comes only from the assurance that no storms are awaiting the bark which has been tossed so long on the waves of suffering, danger and disaster.

In the summer of 1820, the well known American artist, Chester Harding, visited Boone and painted an excellent portrait of him. The old pioneer was so feeble that he had to be supported by a friend while sitting for the likeness.

Boone at this time made his home with his son-in-law, Flanders Callaway, and he was continually visited by distinguished citizens and foreigners, who, having heard of the exploits of the explorer of the wilderness, hastened to look upon him ere the opportunity should pass forever.

Some years before his death he had his coffin made, and kept it in the house. His temperate habits, the active out-door life of his earlier days, and his regard for the laws of health, naturally resulted in a ripe old age, marked by the gradual decay of the vital powers, and unaccompanied by any pain, as should be the case with all mankind.

It was not until the month of September, 1820, that the premonition of his coming end unmistakably showed itself. He was attacked by a species of fever, which did not prove severe, for he soon recovered, and afterward visited his son Major Nathan Boone. He was attacked again, was confined to his bed three days, and peacefully passed away on the 26th of September, in the eighty-sixth year of his age.

The legislature of Missouri was in session at the time, and as soon as the news reached it, adjourned, after passing a resolution that its members should wear the usual badge of mourning for twenty days.

He was laid by the side of his wife, who died a number of years before, an immense concourse attending the funeral. There the remains of the two lay for a quarter of a century, when an interesting ceremony took place.

The consent of the family having been obtained, the coffins were disinterred and removed to Frankfort, Kentucky, and there placed in the new cemetery.

The ceremonies were touching and impressive. Nearly three quarters of a century had passed since the daring hunter and pioneer, in the flush of early manhood, had threaded his way through the trackless forests from the Old Pine State, and, crossing mountain and stream, braving all manner of dangers, had penetrated the solitudes of Kentucky and laid the foundation of one of the grandest States of the Union.

There were a few old men who had known Boone, and they were present from different parts of the State, with hundreds of friends, descendants and relatives. The hearse was hung with lilies and evergreens, and the ceremony was one which can never be forgotten by those who took part in or witnessed it.

A stirring and powerful address was delivered by Senator J. J. Crittenden, in which eloquent tribute was done the daring hunter, the intrepid scout, and matchless pioneer.

In closing the biography of Colonel Daniel Boone, we feel that the reader of these pages, shares with us in our admiration of the stern integrity, the unquestioned bravery, the clear self-possession, and the honest simplicity of the most illustrious type of the American pioneer, who, long before his death, had fixed his place high and enduring in the history of our country.

Toward the close of the latter part of the century, Colonel Boone dictated his autobiography to a friend, and nothing can be more appropriate as an illustration of his character than these few closing words, with which we lay down our pen:

"My footsteps have often been marked with blood; two darling sons and a brother have I lost by savage hands, which have also taken from me forty valuable horses and cattle. Many dark and sleepless nights have I been a companion for owls, separated from the cheerful society of men, scorched by the summer's sun, and pinched by the winter's cold—an instrument ordained to settle the wilderness.

"What thanks, what ardent and ceaseless thanks are due to that all-superintending Providence which has turned a cruel war into peace, brought order out of confusion, made the fierce savages placid, and turned away their hostile weapons from our country.

"May the same almighty goodness banish the accursed monster, war, from all lands, with her hated associates, rapine and insatiable ambition!

" Let peace, descending from her native heaven, bid her olives spring amid the joyful nations; and plenty, in league with commerce, scatter blessings from her copious hand ! "

GENERAL SIMON KENTON.

CHAPTER I.

Birth of Kenton—Desperate Affray with a Rival—Flees to the
Kentucky Wilderness—He and Two Companions attacked by
Indians—One is Killed and the Survivors Escape—Rescued,
after great Suffering—Kenton spends the Summer alone in the
Woods—Serves as a Scout in the Dunmore War—Kenton and
Two Friends settle at Upper Blue Lick—Joined by Hendricks,
who meets with a Terrible Fate.

THE fame of Simon Kenton, hunter and pioneer,
is scarcely second to that of Daniel Boone ; he was
fully as courageous and equally skilled in woodcraft,
while personally more winning in manner. Had the
opportunities of Boone been his, he would have
achieved a fame scarcely less; but such as he was,
no history of the West would be complete without
mention of Boone's intimate friend, Simon Kenton.

Of the early years of Kenton little is known, and
it is not likely that they were marked by anything
worthy of mention. He was born in Fauquier
County, Virginia, May 15th, 1755. His parents
were very poor, and Simon led a life of drudging
toil on a farm, until he was sixteen, at which age
he was unable to read or write his name.

The young man, however, was strong, robust,

very athletic, good looking, and with a pleasing, musical voice. He was just the kind of youth to become popular among the rough spirits of the border, and it was at that time that an incident occurred which marked an era in his life.

Young as Kenton was, he was a rival of another in the esteem of an attractive young lady of the neighborhood ; and, as the lady herself seemed unwilling to decide as to who was her preference, Kenton and his rival agreed to decide it by a bout at fisticuffs.

The conflict took place, but, through the treachery of his rival, Kenton was terribly beaten. He had no choice but to submit to the outrage in silence, but, like Dr. Winship, the modern Samson, he determined to get strong, and then punish the one who had treated him so foully.

Within the year or two succeeding, Kenton reached the stature of six feet, and, confident of his own strength and skill, he called upon his former rival and asked him to try conclusions again with him. The other was also a powerful man and gladly accepted the challenge, for he hated Kenton intensely, and resolved to give him such a terrific punishment that he would never be able to annoy him again.

At first, the rival got the best of Kenton and injured him severely ; but the future scout was full of grit, and he managed to secure the upper hand, when he administered such a chastisement that when he released his man he seemed to be gasping in death.

Kenton looked at him for a moment, and was so certain he could not live a half hour longer, that he was seized with a panic and fled. He did not dare even to return home for a change of clothing, but faced toward the West and ran as though his pursuers were in sight.

Feeling no doubt that his rival was dead, he was sure his avengers would be at his heels, and he scarcely rested during the day. When, however, he reached the neighborhood of the Warm Springs, the settlements were so sparse that he drew a sigh of relief, and felt that he was in no immediate peril from the officers of the law.

Still Kenton did not dare pause for any length of time, and he was walking forward when he came upon a Jerseyman named Johnson, who was journeying in the same direction.

It is at such times that the heart craves companionship, and the two men affiliated at once. Johnson was driving a pack-horse before him, and seemed pretty well tired out; but he was full of pluck, and it took but a few minutes for the two adventurers fully to understand each other.

As a proof of the fear which Kenton felt that his pursuers might overtake him, it may be stated at this point that he changed his name to Simon Butler, with a view of rendering it more difficult to identify him.

The new friends penetrated the wilderness of the Alleghanies, relying under heaven upon their own prowess and bravery. Both were skillful marksmen, and they had no difficulty in securing all the game

they needed, while they kept unceasing watchfulness against the prowling Indians, who, at
that day, were liable to spring upon them at any
time.

They pushed steadily forward until they reached
a small settlement at the forks of the Monongahela;
there they separated, and, so far as known, never
saw each other again.

At the settlement was a small company under
the leadership of John Mahon and Jacob Great-
house, who had just made ready to explore the
country below them. Embarking in a large canoe,
they floated down the river until they reached the
Province's settlement. Here Kenton formed the
acquaintance of two young men, named Yager and
Strader, the former of whom had once been a captive among the Indians.

He fired the heart of Kenton by his glowing accounts of the region of Kentucky, which he declared was a hunter's paradise.

"There is no richer soil in the world," said
Yager; "vegetation is so luxuriant that it will strike
you with wonder, and the herds of buffalo and elk
which roam through those woods are so immense
that you wouldn't believe me if I were to tell you
the numbers."

Kenton was sure there was some foundation for
the positive assertions of Yager, and he listened
eagerly to what he had to add;

"The region has no white men in it; any one
who chooses to hunt there can do so. I have gone
with the Indians many a time on their hunting ex-

cursions, and I could lead you through the same. If you will go with us, I will do so."

Kenton accepted the proposition with great enthusiasm, declaring that he would start at once.

Yager and Strader were equally hopeful, and in a short time the three were drifting down the Ohio in a single canoe.

Yager had lived among the Indians in his childhood, and while he entertained a vivid recollection of the incidents, he could not be positive concerning the distances between certain points. He was unable to say how far down the river they would have to go to find the place where the Indians crossed from Ohio into Kentucky to hunt, but he was sure he would recognize the spot the instant he saw it, for it was very different from any other point on the stream, and was indelibly fixed in his memory.

They were so anxious to reach the promised land, as it seemed to be to them, that the men rowed strongly and continuously, keeping at the oars far into the night.

There can be no question as to Yager's honesty, but he was led astray by his own impressions; the crossing he was seeking was a great deal further away than he believed.

Kenton and Strader began to think they were a long time in arriving at a point so near at hand. When they expressed their dissatisfaction, Yager still insisted, and the lusty arms were plied again with renewed vigor.

But, though the keen eyes scrutinized the shore on either hand with a watchfulness which could not be mistaken, they failed to discover anything resembling the crossing, which Yager had described so often and so vividly that the others saw it distinctly in their mind's eye.

Kenton and Strader were not angered, but they rallied their companion on his error, and suggested that he was describing and they were searching for a place which never had an existence, unless it was in the imagination of the former Indian captive.

Finally, Yager admitted that he didn't understand how it was, unless they had passed the crossing in the night.

"There *is* such a place," he asserted with great positiveness, "for I saw it more than once, when I was a child with the Indians, and I remember it so well, that I would recognize it on the instant. It must be that we went by it in the night.

After awhile, they agreed to return and explore the country more thoroughly. They did so, visiting the land in the neighborhood of Salt Lick, Little and Big Sandy, and Guyandotte. They finally wearied of hunting for that which it seemed impossible to find, and, locating on the Great Kanawha, devoted themselves to hunting and trapping. They found the occupation so congenial, that they pursued it for two years, exchanging their furs and peltries with the traders at Fort Pitt, for such necessaries as hunters require.

The period passed by these three men on the Kanawha will be recognized by the reader as a momentous one; for not only were the fires of the Revolution kindling, but the embers of war along the border were fanning into a blaze that was to sweep over thousands of square miles of settlement and wilderness, and to bring appalling disaster to the West.

Nothing gives a more vivid idea of the insecurity of the pioneers of Kentucky and Ohio, than the bloodhound-like persistency with which the red men hunted down all invaders of their soil. Boone and his party, which might have been considered strong enough to take care of themselves against any ordinary war party, were attacked before they caught more than a glimpse of the fair land; while the settler, who builded his cabin close to the frowning block-house, was shot down on his own threshold.

Kenton and his two companions had spent months enjoying their free, open life in the woods, when the red men came down upon them like the whirlwind.

It was in the month of March, 1773, while they were stretched out in their rude tent, chatting and smoking, that the dark woods around them suddenly flamed with fire, and a volley was poured in upon them, followed by the fierce shouts of the warriors, who seemed to swarm up from the very earth.

Poor Strader was riddled with bullets, and scarcely stirred, so instant was his death. By wonderful good fortune, neither of the others was injured, and, leaping to their feet, they bounded into the woods like frightened deer, the bullets whistling all about them and their ferocious enemies at their heels.

The gathering darkness and their own fleetness enabled them speedily to place themselves beyond reach of the savages; but their plight was a pitiable one.

So desperate was their haste, that neither had time to catch up blanket, gun or a scrap of provisions; an instant's pause would have been fatal. And now they found themselves in the gloomy woods, with the chilling wind cutting them to the bone, and without the means even of starting a fire.

The brave fellows, however, did not despair. They felt that while there was life there was hope, and they determined to make for the Ohio without delay. Had they possessed their guns, it would have been an easy matter to secure such game as they needed, and to kindle a fire, but with undaunted hearts and with their knowledge of woodcraft which enabled them to determine the direction to the Ohio, they started for the river.

During the first two days, they allayed the pangs of gnawing hunger by chewing succulent roots, while the bark on the trees was a sufficient guide to keep them going in the right direction. The miserable nourishment, however, soon told, and the third day found them much weaker, though with their courage undiminished.

They grew feeble very fast, and both were seized with a violent nausea, caused by the unwelcome substances they had taken into their stomachs to satisfy the pangs of hunger. Their condition became so much worse on the fourth day, that, strong men as they were, they felt it was useless to strive longer. They threw themselves on the ground with the intention of waiting for death, but when they assumed the prone position, they seemed to rally both in body and spirits, and, after awhile, they would rise and press forward again.

On the fifth day, death appeared near to them, and they were scarcely able to crawl. They staggered and crept along for about a mile, and, just as the sun was setting, found themselves on the bank of the Ohio, which was a Beautiful River indeed to them.

Almost at the same moment, they came upon a party of traders, and saw they were saved, for the men gave them the provisions they needed, and were anxious to do all in their power for the emaciated and distressed hunters.

But the story told by the latter filled them with such alarm for their own safety, that they prepared to leave such a perilous section without delay. Hastily gathering their effects together, they made all haste to the Little Kanawha, where they encountered another exploring party under the leadership of Dr. Briscoe, who furnished Kenton with a new rifle and ammunition. Yager had had enough of the wilderness, and he stayed with his new-found friends. But Kenton, with his gun and powder, felt like a giant refreshed, and, bidding the others good-bye, plunged alone into the woods.

He spent the following summer in hunting, just as Daniel Boone did under somewhat similar circumstances, and, toward the close of the season, made his way back to the little Kanawha. Here he found an exploring party under the direction of Dr. Wood and Hancock Lee, who were descending the Ohio with the purpose of joining Captain Bullitt, whom they expected to find at the mouth of the Scioto, with a company of pioneers so large that nothing was to be feared from the Indians.

Kenton willingly accepted the invitation to join them, and the descent of the stream was resumed. They moved at a leisurely pace, often stopping on the way to examine the country. They were not disturbed by the Indians until they reached the Three Islands. There, to their dismay, they discovered such a formidable body of warriors, that they were compelled to abandon their canoes precipitately, and they hurried across the country in a diagonal direction for Green Brier county, Virginia.

The journey was a most uncomfortable one, for they were in constant danger from the red men, and were afraid to pause long enough to secure and prepare the necessary food.

To add to their troubles, the leader of the party, Dr. Wood, while tramping along was bitten by a venomous snake, known as the copperhead. The physician applied all the remedies at his command, but, for several days, he lay at the point of death and unable to move. Despite the great danger of pausing on the way, the party were compelled to go into camp for a couple of weeks on account of their leader's condition. At the end of that time, however, he had so far recovered that the journey was resumed, and they reached the settlements without further mishap.

Kenton was so sorely troubled by the recollection of the affray with his rival several years before, whom he supposed to be dead, that he was afraid to remain in Virginia. Accordingly, he built a canoe on the banks of the Monongahela, paddled to the mouth of the Great Kanawha, and resumed his hunting, which he prosecuted with great success until the spring of 1774.

Then it was that a brief but virulent war broke out between the Indians and Colonies, caused, as will be remembered, by the murder of the family of the celebrated Mingo chief, Logan. The part played by Kenton in this campaign was the important one of scout, in the execution of which duties he tramped over the country around Fort Pitt and a great deal of the present State of Ohio.

There still lingered in the mind of the daring Kenton a strong faith in the statements made to him by Yager that there were sections of the surrounding country with a wonderfully rich soil, abundant vegetation, and immense numbers of game. He determined to make search for it, and met with little difficulty in persuading two friends to join in the hunt.

A strong canoe was constructed and stocked with provisions, and the trio paddled down the river to the mouth of Big Bone Creek, on which the famous Big Bone Lick stands. There they landed, and

10

spent several days in exploring the surrounding country; but they were disappointed; nothing answering the representations of Yager was discovered.

Entering their canoe once more, they ascended the river to the entrance of Cabin Creek, a short distance above Maysville. With faith undiminished, they resolved upon a more thorough exploration. In the prosecution of this purpose they came upon May's Lick, where they saw that the surrounding soil possessed unusual richness. Striking the well-known great buffalo track, they followed it for a few hours, when they reached the Lower Blue Lick.

The flats upon each side of the river were swarming with thousands of buffalo that were attracted thither by the salt, while a number of magnificent elk were seen upon the crests of the ridges which surrounded the brackish springs.

"This is the place!" exclaimed the delighted Kenton; "this is the promised land that Yager saw! We need go no further!"

His companions agreed with him, and the delighted pioneers engaged in hunting at once. They could not fail to bring down a great many buffaloes and elk, when the splendid game had scarcely seen enough of their great enemy, man, to learn to fear him.

When they became surfeited with the sport, the three crossed the Licking, and, after a long tramp, came upon another buffalo trace, which led them to the Upper Blue Lick, where they saw the same bewildering abundance of game.

Fully satisfied now that they had discovered the richest and most promising section of all the West, they returned to their canoes, and went up the river as far as Green Bottom, where they had left their peltries, some ammunition, and a few agricultural implements, with the view of cultivating the inviting soil.

They lost no time in hurrying back and beginning the clearing of the land. An acre was denuded of trees in the middle of a large cane-brake, planted with Indian corn, and a cabin erected. This was on the spot where Washington now stands.

The pioneers were in high spirits; for after a long search they had found the land they sighed for, and the future looked promising and bright. They settled down to hard work, and were confident that the fertility of the soil would yield them large returns.

While strolling about the woods one day, with no particular object in view, they were surprised to meet two men, named Hendricks and Fitzpatrick, who were in a sad plight. In descending the Ohio, their canoe had been upset by a sudden squall, and they were forced to swim ashore, without being able to save anything from the wreck. They had been wandering though the woods for several days, and would have perished soon had they not come upon the little party of pioneers.

Kenton had been in a similar predicament, and could not fail to sympathize with them. He urged them to join the diminutive settlement he had started at Washington, and trust to Providence to bring them out right in the end. Hendricks agreed to stay, but Fitzpatrick had had enough of the wilderness, and was so homesick that he only asked to get out of the unfriendly country and back to the Monongahela. Kenton and his companions went with him as far as Maysville, gave him a gun and some ammunition, assisted him across the river, and bade him good-by.

Pity it was that Hendricks did not accompany him, as the sequel will prove.

While Kenton and his two brother pioneers were doing this neighborly kindness for the one, Hendricks was at the cabin which had been erected a few days before. He had been left there without a gun, but with plenty of provisions, and no one dreamed of his being in danger.

The three men, having seen Fitzpatrick off, hastened back to the clearing, pleased at the thought of the companion they had gained, and regretting that the other man had not consented to join them.

When they reached the rough cabin they were somewhat alarmed to see nothing of Hendricks, and the quick eyes of the hunters observed that something unusual had taken place. A number of bullet-holes were noticed in the timbers, which were chipped in other places by the leaden missiles, while some of the articles of Hendricks were scattered around in a way which could leave no doubt he had been visited by Indians.

The fact that he had no weapon with which to defend himself, caused his friends to fear the worst, and with rapidly beating hearts they began an investigation, not knowing how close the peril was to them.

They had not hunted far, when they discovered a thin column of smoke rising from a ravine near at hand. Certain that a large war party of savages was near them, the three men were seized with a panic and fled in the greatest terror.

It was a curious thing for Kenton to do, for he was certainly one of the bravest of men. It would have been expected that he would insist on an investigation before such a precipitate flight, and it was always a source of deep regret to him in after-life that he did not do so.

Having reached a safe point, the trio hid themselves in the cane until the evening of the next day, when they once more ventured back to the clearing, and then approached the ravine from which they had seen the smoke of a camp fire ascending.

Smoke was still visible, and when they ventured closer they were horrified to find only the charred bones of their late companion ! He had been burned at the stake, and in all probability was alive when the others first saw the vapor on the previous day.

Had they not been so terrified by the belief that a large war party was at hand, they might have saved him. As we have said, it was the source of the deepest regret to Kenton that he did not reconnoitre the spot, when such a possibility of rescue existed.

CHAPTER II.

Kenton and his Friends Visit Boonesborough—Desperate En-
counter with Indians—Proceeds with Two Companions to
Reconnoitre an Indian Town on the Little Miami—Captured
while Making Off with a Number of Horses—Brutal Treat-
ment—Bound to the Stake and Runs the Gauntlet—Friendship
of Simon Girty, the Renegade—Finally Saved by an Indian
Trader—Removed to Detroit, and Escapes—Commands a
Company in General Clark's Expedition—Receives Good
News—Visits Virginia—Death of his Father—Reduced to
Poverty—Removes to Urbana, Ohio—Elected Brigadier-
General—His Conversion—His Last Days.

SIMON KENTON and his two friends stayed at
Washington until the following September, undis-
turbed by Indians, though they were never entirely
free from apprehension of a visit from them.

In the month named they visited the Lick, where
they encountered a white man, who told them most
important news. The interior of Kentucky had
been settled in several places, and there was a
thriving pioneer station at Boonesborough.

Kenton and his friends were glad to learn this,
for they had seen enough of the perils of the woods
to long for the society of some of their own race.
They immediately left their dangerous home, and,
visiting the smaller settlements, made a prolonged
stay at Boonesborough, where they were most
gladly welcomed. During the two sieges of the
place which we have described, Kenton was one of

the garrison, and served with great efficiency as a spy and scout until the summer of 1778, when Boone came back from captivity and formed the plan for the attack upon the Indians at Paint Creek.

This expedition, which has already been referred to elsewhere, proved to be a most eventful one to Kenton, who acted as spy. After crossing the Ohio, he kept a considerable distance in advance, on the alert for the first evidence of Indians.

He was suddenly startled by hearing a loud laugh from an adjoining thicket, which he was on the point of entering. Like a flash the scout sprang behind a tree and with cocked rifle awaited the explanation.

He had but a few minutes to wait, when two Indians emerged from the thicket, mounted on a pony. Both were laughing and chatting in high spirits, and with no thought of anything like danger. They had been on some marauding expedition against the whites, and had met with such success that they seemed as elated as a couple of children.

Kenton held his place until they approached within easy distance, when he took careful aim and fired. The well-aimed shot killed the first and badly wounded the second, while the frightened pony whirled about and dashed into the thicket. Kenton instantly ran up to the slain Indian to scalp him, in accordance with the barbarous practice of the border, when a rustling on his right caused him to look up. To his amazement, there were two Indians not twenty yards distant, both of whom were in the act of taking aim at him.

The scout sprang aside at the instant both fired, and though the bullets whizzed close to his eyes he was uninjured. There could be no doubt that the neighborhood was a most undesirable one just then, for other warriors were near by, and Kenton lost no time in taking to the shelter of the woods.

Fleet as he was, he had no more than reached shelter, when a dozen Indians appeared on the margin of the canebrake and the situation of the scout became most serious ; but, at this critical moment, Boone appeared with his party, who opened a brisk fire upon the Indians. The attack was so spirited that they broke and scattered, and Kenton was relieved from his perilous position.

Boone, as we have stated elsewhere, immediately returned to Boonesborough, but the intrepid Kenton determined to learn more of the Indians, and if possible to repay them for the attack they had made upon him.

Accompanied by a friend named Montgomery, they approached the Indian town not far off, and stationed themselves near a cornfield, expecting the red men would enter it for the purpose of roasting the ears. With that characteristic patience of the border scouts, they stayed beside the cornfield the entire day waiting and watching for a shot at some of the warriors. But during the time not a single one appeared, though the whites could hear the voices of the children playing near at hand.

The scouts were greatly disappointed, for they had been confident of seeing some warrior, but night came without such an opportunity having presented itself, and they were forced to ask themselves the question whether they would go back empty handed, so to speak, or whether they would incur some additional risk for the sake of accomplishing something by way of retaliation.

As the best they could do, they stealthily entered the Indian town late at night, picked out four good horses, made all haste to the Ohio, which they crossed in safety, and on the succeeding day reached Logan's fort without disturbance.

This was an extraordinary achievement, for the Indians and settlers were in such open hostility that it may be said the former were constantly on the alert to prevent just such surprises.

Colonel Bowman, at the fort, requested Kenton, Montgomery and a Mr. Clark to undertake a more difficult and dangerous task for him: that was a secret expedition to one of the Indian towns on the Little Miami, against which the Colonel meditated an expedition, and about which, of course, he was desirous of gaining all the information possible.

The duty was a congenial one to the three men, who reached the village without discovery, made a careful reconnoissance by night, and were then ready to return home.

Well would it have been for them had they done so, but the subsequent conduct of Kenton shows that his repeated escapes and continued immunity at the hands of the savages, had rendered him reckless, and caused him to estimate too highly perhaps his own prowess and skill as compared with theirs.

At this time, unfortunately, they discovered an enclosure where the Indians kept their horses. Like all borderers they dearly loved that kind of property, and could not resist the temptation. More than that, instead of selecting the best, they took the whole lot and started for the Ohio.

Such a wholesale proceeding created a good deal of confusion despite the care of the three scouts, and the Indians speedily discovered what was going on.

They poured out of their wigwams and lodges, in great excitement, all eager to prevent the loss of their property, while the whites showed an equal eagerness to get away with it. Instead of abandoning the animals and attempting to save themselves, they foolishly continued their effort to escape with them all.

One rode in front leading the animals, and the other two remained at the rear and lashed them into a gallop, through the woods, while the excited Indians came whooping and shrieking after them.

It was a wild, break-neck proceeding, but the scouts kept it up until they reached the edge of an impenetrable swamp, where, for the first time since starting, they came to a stand-still and listened for their pursuers.

Not a sound was heard to indicate they were anywhere in the neighborhood, and the whites congratulated themselves on what looked like a remarkable achievement. But they were certain to be pursued, and skirting the swamp, they continued their flight in the direction of the Ohio, which was a long way distant.

The horses were pressed to the utmost, the riders frequently changing animals, through the night, the next day, and most of the following night. The next morning they stood on the northern bank of the Ohio.

The wind was blowing strongly, and the river was so boisterous that the crossing was sure to be difficult. At the same time they knew that their pursuers would not delay, and must be close behind them. A hurried consultation was held, and it was agreed that Kenton should swim the animals over while Montgomery and Clark constructed a raft to transport the baggage.

Accordingly Kenton led the animals into the river, while he swam at their side, but the stream had become so rough that he was forced away from them, and all he could do was to save himself from drowning. The horses being left to themselves turned about and swam back to the shore they had left a short time before.

This exasperating performance was repeated until Kenton became so exhausted that he was forced to lie down on the shore until he could recover his strength and wind.

A council of war, as it might be called, was then held and the question considered was whether they should abandon the animals and attend to their own safety, or risk their lives by waiting where they were until the Ohio should become calmer, in the hope of getting them to the other side. Nothing can show the great admiration of the men of the border for the noblest of all animals, than their immediate and unanimous agreement that they would never desert their horses.

The scouts committed the inexplainable blunder of staying where they were, knowing, as they must have known, that the infuriated warriors were rapidly coming up on their trail, and could be at no great distance behind them.

The wind continued churning the water all through the day, and did not abate until the next morning. Then, when they tried to force the steeds into the water, they refused and some of them broke away. The infatuated scouts lost more valuable time in the vain attempt to recapture them and, as was inevitable, the Indians soon made their appearance.

They were in such numbers, and so well armed, that it was useless to fight them, and Clark had sense enough to take to his heels. He succeeded in effecting his own escape. Montgomery was shot down and scalped, while Kenton was seized from behind, when on the very point of assailing a warrior in front, and pinioned. Others speedily gathered, beat and shook the scout, and pulled his hair, until he was tortured almost to death.

"Steal hoss of Indian, eh!" they exclaimed again and again as they beat him over the head with their ramrods.

When they had pounded him until they were tired, Kenton was thrown on his back, and his

arms stretched out at full length. Pieces of saplings were then fastened to his arms and legs in
such a manner that the poor fellow was literally
unable to stir hand or foot.

While thus engaged they continued to beat and
curse him in broken English. When he was strap-
ped in his immovable position he was left until
morning. No pen can picture the utter horror and
misery of such a night, with arm and legs out-
stretched and with body incapable of any motion
excepting a slight turn of the head.

It was a literal crucifixion, without the erection
of the cross. Knowing the Indians so well, he did
not entertain a particle of doubt that he would be
put to death with the most fearful torture that can
be imagined.

The fury of the Indians against Kenton seemed
to increase rather than diminish. It would have
been a very easy matter to tomahawk or slay him
with knife or rifle, when he was so helpless, but that
would have ended the matter and deprived them
of the enjoyment they counted upon at such times.

In the morning they gave a Mazeppa performance, by tying Kenton fast to an unbroken colt
and turning him loose. The horse, however,
seemed to have more pity than his cruel masters,
for after galloping a short distance about the
others, he came back and rejoined them, continuing with the others until nightfall, when Kenton was taken off and fastened by buffalo thongs
to the stakes of saplings as before.

For three days the terrible march continued,

when the Indian town of Chillicothe was reached. The arrival of the prisoner created great excitement, and the chief Blackfish beat Kenton over the naked shoulders with hickory sticks until the blood flowed, and the poor fellow was almost delirious with agony.

All the cries he heard during this fearful punishment were those of fury. These soon changed to a demand that he should be tied to the stake, and it was done. His clothing was torn from his body, his hands fastened above his head, and the Indians danced about him beating and whooping and jeering at the prisoner, who expected every minute that the fire would be kindled at his feet.

Ordinarily this would have been done, but the desire to continue the torture was so great that the savages deferred the last awful tragedy, until they should extract more sport from the victim.

He was kept in this trying position until late at night, when he was released. It seemed as if it were intended that Simon Kenton should go through every form of Indian torture, for, on the morrow, he was led out and forced to run the gauntlet.

The preparations for this were so complete, and the Indians so numerous with their clubs and all sorts of weapons, that it can scarcely be doubted that Kenton would have been beaten to death, had he undertaken to speed the entire distance between the two long rows of Indians.

Instead of doing so, he darted aside and after doubling upon his pursuers, plunged into the council house, receiving only a few blows from the warriors standing near. Within this lodge was held the council to determine what course should be taken with their prisoner. There was no thought or releasing him, but some might prefer to delay the enjoyment of his death by torture no longer, while others were inclined to think it was too pleasant for them to allow the amusement to terminate so soon.

A comparison of views and a ballot showed that the majority were in favor of deferring his taking off a short while longer. His execution, therefore, was suspended for the time, and it was agreed to take him to an Indian town on Mad River, known as Waughcotomoco.

"What is to be done with me after we get there?" asked Kenton of the renegade who interpreted the sentence to him.

"Burn you at the stake," was the reply, accompanied by a brutal oath, as the white savage strode away.

Kenton was given back his clothing, and was not bound while on the road, as it was deemed impossible for him to escape from among his numerous, vigilant captors.

But, as there could be no doubt that his death by torture was fully determined, the prisoner was resolved on one desperate effort to escape, for in no sense could a failure result in making his condition worse than before.

He deferred the attempt until they were so close to Waughcotomoco, that the party exchanged sig-

nal whoops with the warriors of the town who began flocking thither to see the prisoner.

Feeling that it was then or never, Kenton uttered a shout and broke away like a frightened deer,
the Indians following him, some on foot, and some
on horseback. His great fleetness might have enabled him to escape, but while he was running
from those behind, he came directly upon a party
who were riding from the village to meet the
others, and before he was hardly aware of his danger he was recaptured.

After suffering great indignities, they reached
Waughcotomoco, where Kenton was forced to run
the gauntlet again and was badly hurt. He was
then taken to the council-house, where he sat in
despair, while the warriors consulted as to the precise means of his death.

While they were thus engaged, Simon Girty and
three companions came in with a white woman and
seven children as prisoners. Kenton was taken
away to make room for these, and as their fate now
became a matter of debate, the session was protracted
until a late hour. The verdict, however, was inevitable, and on the morrow, Simon Girty, the notorious
renegade, gave himself the extreme pleasure of
communicating the news to the hapless prisoner.

During this interview Girty was astounded to discover in the prisoner his former comrade, who had
served with him as a spy in Dunmore's expedition.
That was before Girty had foresworn his race, and
the two men became warmly attached to each other.

Girty was greatly agitated, and instantly set to

work to secure the release of the prisoner. The difficulty of this task can scarcely be imagined, for such a request was unprecedented ; but Girty persevered, making the most ardent appeals and begging and insisting, until it was put to a vote, when it was agreed that the prayer, coming from one who had served them so faithfully as had the renegade for three years, could not be denied, and it was granted.

Kenton now remained a prisoner among the Indians for three weeks, during which Girty treated him with unvarying kindness. Indeed his conduct in this extraordinary matter is the single bright spot in the career of one of the most terrible wretches that ever lived.

At the end of the time mentioned, however, another council was held, and despite the strenuous efforts of Girty, Kenton was condemned to death at the stake. There now seemed no possible hope, and, telling his friend he had done all he could for him, Girty shook his hand and bade him good-by.

But Kenton's remarkable good fortune did not desert him. The great chief Logan gave him his friendship and did what he could to save him, when Kenton was brought to his village, which was a short distance away. His interference, however, seemed to be unavailing, and he was started for Sandusky under a strong escort, that being the place fixed upon for his final death by torture.

There, however, when Kenton had abandoned all hope, an Indian agent by the name of Drewyer interested himself in his behalf, and by an ingenious statagem secured his removal to Detroit.

He thus became a prisoner-of-war, as Detroit was in the possession of the British, and his situation was immeasurably improved. He was sure to be treated in a civilized manner, and in process of time would be set free.

The situation, however, was anything but agreeable to Kenton, who was continually seeking for some way of escape. None presented itself for a long time, and he remained working for the garrison on half-pay until the summer of 1779.

It was at this time that the longed-for opportunity presented itself, through the kindness of the wife of an Indian trader. Kenton knew well enough that it would never do to plunge into the wilderness without rifles and ammunition, and she agreed to furnish him and two Kentuckians with the indispensable articles.

It was no small task for a lady to secure three guns and ammunition without the assistance of any one, but she succeeded in doing so. In the early summer of that year, the Indians around Detroit engaged in one of their periodical carousals. It was at night, and before giving themselves over to their brutish indulgence they stacked their guns near the house of the lady.

Without difficulty she secured three of the best, and hid them in her garden. Previous to this she had gathered some extra clothing and the required ammunition, which were hidden in a hollow tree outside the town. She managed to communicate with Kenton, who, at the appointed time, appeared at the garden with his friends, got the guns, and thanking his preserver most fervently and receiving her best wishes in return, bade her good-by and hastened away with his companions.

There was no difficulty in stealing out of town, which was full of drunken Indians, but it never would have done to wait ; both they and the guns would be missed in the morning, and search would be immediately made.

The hollow tree was easily found, and hastily equipping themselves with what was stored there, they plunged into the wilderness and started on their long and dangerous journey for Louisville, Kentucky.

Leaving the commonly-traveled route, they first headed for the prairies of the Wabash, and pushed on like veteran pioneers who knew they were continually in danger of pursuit. They lost no time on the road, nor did they cease to use continual vigilance.

They were over a month making their way through the solitudes, but finally reached Louisville, without accident, in the month of July, 1779.

Kenton had become so accustomed to his rough, adventurous life, that he chafed under the quiet and restraint of the town. Slinging his rifle over his shoulder, therefore, he struck into the woods alone and tramped to Vincennes to see his old friend, Major Clark. He was warmly greeted, but he found everything so dull and hum-drum that he re-entered the wilderness, and after a long journey reached Harrodsburg, where he was received with as much delight as though he were Daniel Boone himself.

In the famous expedition of General Clark against the Indians, described elsewhere, Simon Kenton commanded a company of volunteers from Harrod's Station, and was one of the bravest officers of that formidable campaign against the red men, whose outrages were becoming so serious that the blow was determined upon as a means of forcing them to stay within their own lines.

It will be remembered that the command of General Clark numbered over a thousand men, and it will be understood that it was the most effective demonstration that, up to that time, had ever been undertaken on the frontier. Chillicothe, Pickaway, and numerous smaller towns were burnt and all the crops destroyed.

It can well be believed that when they reached Pickaway and the Indians made a stand, the arm of Simon Kenton was nerved with tenfold power, for it was there, two years before, that he had been compelled to run the gauntlet and was beaten almost to death. It was with the memory of the terrible sufferings of that time that he led his company into action, and he fought, as did they, like Richard Cœur de Lion.

The warriors made a brave resistance, but were unable to withstand the furious attack, and soon were scattered like chaff, leaving their dead and wounded on the field. This campaign brought peace and quietness to the frontier during the following two years. Kenton engaged in hunting, or in assisting surveying parties, until 1782, when he received the most startling news of his life.

For eleven years he had been a wanderer in the woods, oftentimes in indescribable peril, suffering almost death over and over again, and never free from the remorse caused by that encounter with his rival so long before in Virginia, whom he believed he left dying upon the ground and from whose presence he fled like Cain from the vengeance of men.

But at the time mentioned Kenton received proof that the man was not killed in that desperate affray, but had recovered, and was then alive and well, as was also the aged father of Kenton.

It can scarcely be conceived how great a burden these tidings lifted from the heart of Simon Kenton, who was no longer afraid to reveal his identity and make inquiries about his friends. It was like entering upon a new and joyous life.

Kenton commanded another company in General Clark's campaign in the autumn of 1782, and, as before, acted as the guide of the army, his knowledge of the country and his consummate woodcraft rendering his services indispensable in that direction.

While this campaign was only one of the numerous similar ones which have marked the settlement of the West, and which, sad to say, were too often accompanied by overwhelming disaster, it was rendered memorable to Kenton by a singular and impressive engagement into which he entered.

It was when the army was on its return, when opposite the mouth of the Licking, Nov. 4th, 1782, that Captain McCracken, who was dying from a wound received in battle, suggested that all the pioneers of the expedition who might be living fifty years from that day, should meet on the spot to celebrate the semi-centennial of the campaign.

It was at the suggestion of the dying soldier that Colonel Floyd drew up the resolution, and the meeting a half century later was agreed upon.

The purpose accomplished, the volunteers were disbanded, and Kenton went back to Harrod's Station, where he was always most gladly welcomed.

He had acquired considerable land, which was rapidly increasing in value. With a few families he began a settlement, which prospered greatly. The soil was very fertile, they were industrious, and they were blessed with abundant crops.

The circumstances being favorable, Kenton made a journey to Virginia to visit his father and friends. Thirteen years had passed since he had fled, believing himself a murderer, and now, among the first to take his hand, after he entered the familiar place, was his former rival in love. He and his wife greeted the handsome pioneer with great cordiality, and all resentment was buried in the happiness of the meeting.

Kenton was thankful indeed to find his aged father in good health, though his mother had been dead a number of years. Accompanied by his parent and the rest of the family, he started for Kentucky, intending that his father should spend the rest of his days with him. Such was the case, indeed, but the days proved fewer than the affectionate son supposed they would be.

The parent was very feeble, and when Red Stone

Fort was reached, he quietly died. He was buried on the banks of the Monongahela, and Kenton, with the remainder of the family, arrived at the settlement in the winter of 1784.

Kentucky was rapidly filling up with emigrants at this time, though, as is well known, the Indians were very troublesome. Kenton saw that the land was certain to become valuable, and he determined to occupy the fertile section around his old camp near Maysville, which he had occasion to remember so well.

He made the venture in the summer of 1784, with a company of pioneers ; but the Indians were so dangerous that they were forced to retire for the time. A few months later Kenton went back with a few friends, built a blockhouse, and soon after was joined by several families.

Settlers continued to flock thither, and the country prospered, despite the hostility of the red men. Kenton, by his foresight, had secured the right and title to a large quantity of valuable land. One thousand acres of this he gave to Arthur Fox and William Wood, and on it they laid out the town of Washington.

Despite the severe blow administered by General Clark, the savages committed so many depredations that a retaliatory campaign was determined upon. Seven hundred volunteers gathered under Colonel Logan and invaded the Indian country, inflicting much damage, and returning with only a trifling loss.

The guide of this expedition was Simon Kenton, who also commanded a company ; but it was scarcely home again when the Indians renewed their depredations with such persistency that Kenton appealed to his old friends to rally once more, and to " carry the war into Africa."

It was promptly done, he assuming the part of captain and of guide as before. Chillicothe was burned, and the expedition returned without losing a man.

By this time Kenton was acknowledged as the leader in the frontier settlement. He possessed a great deal of valuable land, was a master of woodcraft, and in all the troubles with the Indians was looked to for protection and assistance.

During the half-dozen years following, his services in the latter respect were beyond estimate. He demonstrated his skill in the ways of the woods by ambushing a party of dusky marauders who had come down to devastate the border, and by inflicting such severe loss that the others fled in terror and never attempted to molest the settlement again.

But this period will be recognized by the reader as the eventful one of General Anthony Wayne's expedition against the combined Indian tribes of the West. Disaster had followed disaster, until the United States Government saw the necessity of ending the troubles by a campaign which should be resistless, and crushing in its effects.

Simon Kenton, at the time of Wayne's expedition, was a major, and with his battalion he joined the forces at Greenville. It may be said that his reputation at that time was national, and he was recognized as one of the most skillful and intrepid pioneers of the West. His bravery, activity and knowledge of "wood lore," inspired confidence everywhere, and linked his name inseparably with the settlement of the West.

His foresight in taking up the valuable lands was now shown by the results. They appreciated so rapidly in value with the settlement and development of the country, that he became one of the wealthiest settlers in Kentucky.

But singularly (and yet perhaps it was not singular either), the same misfortune overtook him that befell Daniel Boone and so many others of the pioneers.

The rapacious speculators, by their superior cunning, got all his land away from him, until he was not worth a farthing. Worse than that they brought him in debt, and his body was taken upon the covenants in deeds to lands, which he had in point of fact given away. He was imprisoned for a full year on the very spot where he built his cabin in 1775, and planted the first corn planted north of the Kentucky River by a white man, and where for many a time he had braved hunger, death, and undergone suffering in its most frightful forms.

He was literally reduced to beggary by the cruel rapacity of the land sharks, and in 1802 he removed to Ohio and settled in Urbana. Kenton's remarkable sweetness of character, despite the fact that he was one of the most terrible of Indian fighters, was such that he scarcely ever uttered a word of complaint. No man had endured more than he for Kentucky and Ohio, and no one had ever been treated more shabbily; yet he loved the " Dark and Bloody Ground " none the less.

His services and his ability were appreciated to that extent in Ohio that he was elected a brigadier-general of militia, three years after his removal to the State. Five years later, that is, in 1810, he was converted and joined the Methodist Episcopal Church.

Reverend J. B. Finley, the well known missionary of the West, relates that his father and Kenton met at a camp meeting on the Mad River. They were old friends and the interview was a most pleasant one. The meeting was accompanied by a great awakening, during which Kenton took the elder Finley aside and told him how deeply his heart had been touched, how much he was impressed with his own sinfulness, and how desirous he was of obtaining divine pardon.

He bound the minister to keep the whole matter a secret, and the two knelt down in prayer in the woods. Kenton was speedily converted, and springing to his feet, ran shouting back to camp meeting, with the minister panting after him.

The old Indian fighter outran his pastor, and when Mr. Finley reached his congregation, the other had gathered a great crowd about him, and, with a glowing face, was telling the news of his conversion.

" I thought this was to be a secret," called out Mr. Finley, " and here, General, you are proclaiming it to every one."

"It's too glorious to keep," was the reply of Kenton.

He continued a devout and humble Christian for the rest of his life. His voice was remarkably sweet and musical, and he was fond of singing. He took part in many religious exercises and meetings, and entered into the service of his divine Master with the same ardor he had shown in that of his country, during his early and mature manhood.

In 1813, Kenton joined the Kentucky troops under Governor Shelby, with whose family he was a great favorite. He was then nearly threescore years of age, but he was rugged, strong, and as patriotic as ever. He took part in the battle of the Thames, fighting with the same bravery that was natural to him from boyhood.

It was the last engagement in which he bore a hand, and respecting it the following incident is worthy of note:

In the month of May, 1881, Ayres Lefargee, who died at Poplar Plain, Kentucky, was buried at Decatur, Illinois. He was a soldier of the war of 1812, in the fourth regiment of Kentucky troops under Governor Shelby, and was present at the battle of the Thames in which the great Shawanoe chieftain Tecumseh was killed. After the battle he went with Captain Matthews and Simon Kenton to the spot where the chief fell. "Turn the body over," said Kenton, and, upon Lefargee doing so, they found seven bullet-holes in it. Lefargee always claimed that Tecumseh was killed by a soldier named Dave Gealding.

This question has never been satisfactorily settled, though the claim of Colonel Richard M. Johnson seems as good as that of any one. His horse had fallen, and while he was endeavoring to extricate himself, a distinguished looking Indian who, it was claimed by many that knew him, was Tecumseh, made a rush for Colonel Johnson.

" I didn't stop to ask him his name," said Colonel Johnson, when questioned about it afterwards, " for there was no time for explanations, but I fired, when, had I waited five seconds longer, he would have brained me with his upraised tomahawk."

The war of 1812 finished, Kenton returned to the obscurity of his humble cabin, where he lived until 1820, when he removed to the headwaters of Mad River, Logan county, Ohio, near the very spot where, many years before, he had been tied to the stake by the Indians, when they condemned him to death.

It seemed impossible for the old pioneer to escape the annoyance of the land-sharpers. He was still the owner of many large mountain tracts of Kentucky, but he was " land poor," in its fullest sense, and these were forfeited for taxes.

Kenton became so worn out, and so distressed by poverty, that in 1824, when nearly seventy years old, he rode to Frankfort, while the Legislature was in session, to petition that body to release these comparatively worthless lands from the claims upon them for unpaid taxes.

The old hunter was clothed in dilapidated garments, and his rickety horse looked so woe-begone that the wonder was how he could carry such a large man as he was.   But when it became known that Simon Kenton was in town, it caused an excitement like that which the arrival of the menagerie and circus excites.

There was no one in the capital of Kentucky who had not heard of the wonderful exploits of Kenton, and the tall handsome figure of the hunter, with his mild prepossessing features, would have attracted attention anywhere.   It was hard to believe that this old gentleman with his gentle blue eyes, his soft musical voice, and his humble Christian bearing, was the hurricane-like fighter, who had torn the reeking scalp from the head of the fierce savage, who had run the gauntlet more than once, who had trailed the red Indian through the gloomy depths of the forest and who had lived in the wilderness in storm and sunshine, week after week and month after month, when he never closed his eyes with certainty he would not be awakened for an instant by the crash of the tomahawk as it clove his skull in twain.

But this was Simon Kenton, and the crowds began to gather.   General Thomas Fletcher recognized him and donned him in a good respectable suit of clothing.   Then he was taken to the Capitol and placed in the Speaker's chair, where the multitude, in which were the legislators and the most prominent citizens, filed through the building, and were introduced to the great adventurer, who smilingly shook their hands, exchanged a few pleasant words, and blushed like a school boy.

It was the proudest day of Simon Kenton's life, and he had every reason to look back to it with delight, for it resulted in substantial benefit to him.

His presence called up so vividly the great services he had rendered the State, and the burning injustice he had suffered, that the legislators at once released all his lands from the tax claims, and shortly after, through the exertions of Judge Burnet and General Vance, of Congress, a pension of two hundred and forty dollars a year was obtained for the old hero, who was thus secured against want for the remainder of his life.

Kenton now lived a quiet life, serene and hopeful, and quietly contemplating the end which he knew was close at hand. He was held in the greatest respect and the strongest affection by his numerous friends, while Kentucky itself felt a pride in the brave hunter, scout and pioneer.

It will be remembered by the reader, that on the 4th of November, 1782, Simon Kenton became a party to an agreement of singular and romantic interest.

During the expedition of General Clark against the Indian towns, Kenton as usual acted as guide to the army, which numbered fifteen hundred men. On the return of the force, the pioneers which composed it came to a halt, opposite the Licking, and held a conference. Captain McCracken, of the Kentucky Light Horse, had received a slight wound in the arm while fighting, and which caused him little concern at the time. But a virulent mortification had set in, and it became evident to all that he had but a short time to live.   At his suggestion, Colonel Floyd brought forward the resolution by which the pioneers who might survive agreed to meet on that same spot, a half century later, to talk over old times.

The meeting was held in the unbroken wilderness, abounding with its game and with the fierce red man ; and the pioneers were in the flush and vigor of young manhood, with many years of hard, perilous service before them.   They all felt that such as should be spared to see the closing of the half century before them, would witness changes and developments in their beloved country, such as awed the imagination when it attempted to grasp it.

On that lonely spot, where McCracken closed his eyes and was laid mournfully away in his last long rest by his brave brother pioneers, was the heart of the magnificently growing West.   His grave was in sight of the beautiful Queen city, and the howling wilderness now blossomed as the rose.

As the semi-centennial approached, it was looked forward to with a strong interest by the survivors, who were found to be quite numerous.   The lives which these hardy pioneers led were conducive to longevity, provided always the wild Indians afforded the opportunity and failed to cut them off in their prime.

"And tall and strong and swift of foot are they,
   Beyond the dwarfing city's pale abortions,
   Because their thoughts had never been the prey
   Of care or gain ; the green woods were their portions ;
   No sinking spirits told them they grew gray,
   No fashions made them apes of her distortions.

Simple they were, not savage ; and their rifles,
Though very true, were not yet used for trifles.

"Motion was in their days, rest in their slumbers,
   And cheerfulness the handmaid of their toil.
Nor yet too many nor too few their numbers ;
Corruption could not make their hearts her soil ;
The lust which stings, the splendor which encumbers,
With the free foresters divide no spoil ;
Serene, not sullen, were the solitudes
Of this unsighing people of the woods."

As the semi - centennial approached, Simon
Kenton, who had passed his fourscore, was deeply
solicitous lest he should not be able to be present.
He was desirous that every survivor should be at
the gathering, and published an address in which
he said:

"*Fellow Citizens :*—Being one of the first, after Colonel Daniel
Boone, who aided in the conquest of Kentucky and the West, I am
called upon to address you.   My heart melts on such an occasion ; I look forward to the contemplated meeting with melancholy pleasure ; it has caused tears to flow in copious showers.
I wish to see once more before I die, my few surviving friends.
My solemn promise, made fifty years ago, binds me to meet them.
I ask not for myself ; but you may find in our assembly some
who have never received any pay or pension, who have sustained
the cause of their country equal to any other service, and who in
the decline of their life are poor.   Then, you prosperous sons of
the West, forget not those old and gray-headed veterans on this
occasion ; let them return to their families with some little mani-
festations of your kindness to cheer their hearts.

"I may add my prayer : may kind Heaven grant us a clear
sky, fair and pleasant weather, a safe journey, and a happy meeting and a smile upon us and our families, and bless us and our
nation on the approaching occasion.
                                        "SIMON KENTON.

"Urbana, Ohio, 1832."

The year 1832 will be recognized as the terrible cholera season, when the pestilence smote the land and the whole country was in mourning. Men shrank appalled as the multitudes sank on their right and left, and business for the time was paralyzed by the awful scourge which swept from one end of the land to the other.

Cincinnati was shrouded in deepest gloom by the ravages of the fearful disease, yet when the anniversary came round a large number of the old pioneers met, and the Corporation voted them a dinner.

General Simon Kenton, in spite of his anxiety to be present, was unable to appear, owing to his feebleness and indisposition of body. His absence was greatly mourned, for he would have been the prince of all that noble band, could his venerable form have appeared among them.

With Kenton the sunset of life was as quiet and serene as the close of a summer day. In the month of April, 1836, he quietly died in his home, surrounded by his affectionate family, friends and neighbors, and supported by the sublime faith of the meek, devout Christian, who joyfully approaches the dark river and launches out for the other shore.

LEWIS WETZEL.

WHEN one reads of the early days of the great West and of the tornado-like encounters in which the borderers engaged, he finds that there are few more prominent figures than that of Lewis Wetzel, who was born on the Big Wheeling, Virginia, about the year 1764. He had four brothers, Martin, Jacob, John and George, and two sisters, Susan and Christina. Martin was the only brother who exceeded Lewis in age.

The home of the Wetzels exposed them to perils from the Indians, for it will be recognized by the reader as a spot peculiarly open to assaults from the red men.

This was proven by the terrible fate that overtook the family. One day the Indians suddenly appeared and made a fierce attack upon the house.

Several of the smaller children were absent, and during the excitement the mother succeeded in getting away; but the old man was killed and scalped, and Lewis, then thirteen years old, and his brother Jacob, two years younger, were taken away prisoners.

In the fight, Lewis received a slight wound from a bullet, but it did not incapacitate him from traveling, and on the second night after the capture the Indians encamped on the Big Lick, twenty miles distant from the river, in what is now Ohio, and upon the waters of McMahon's Creek.

The prisoners were so young that the captors were justified in considering them of little account, and they did not take the trouble to bind them when they stopped for the night. Lewis, however, was old enough to watch for a chance to get away, and when sure all the Indians were asleep, he touched his brother and whispered to him to make ready to follow him.

They made their way out of the camp without difficulty, but had not proceeded far when they stopped.

" I don't like the idea of going home barefooted," said Lewis, "you stay here while I go back and get a pair of moccasins for you and a pair for me."

The daring lad succeeded in obtaining the necessary articles and soon rejoined his brother ; but as they were about to start on again he expressed his dissatisfaction that they had no weapons.

"We can't get along without a gun ; wait here a little longer and I'll bring one back."

And young Lewis did as he said he would. Now that each had a pair of moccasins, and the elder carried a good rifle, they were prepared for travel, and they plunged into the woods at once.

Lewis Wetzel displayed a knowledge of wood-craft on this occasion which was wonderful in one so young. He discovered the trail and followed it back without difficulty, and knowing he would be pursued, he kept such unremitting watch that he detected the approach of the Indians, and he and his brother hid in the bushes until they passed.

When they were out of sight, the brothers came back to the trail and followed after the Indians. It did not take the latter very long to find they had gone beyond the lads, and they turned about to find them.

But, as before, Lewis was on the watch, and he and his brother eluded them. Shortly after they discovered that two of the warriors were mounted and in hot chase after them ; but Lewis gave them the slip in the same skilful manner, and reaching Wheeling the next day, they constructed a raft and crossed the river.

When they came to the ruins of their home and found that their father had been killed and scalped, they were so infuriated that they took a vow to kill every Indian that was in their power to kill, so long as they should live.

Such is the account as generally given, though a different version is entitled to equal credence. This says that the elder Wetzel was shot, in 1787, while paddling a canoe near Captina, on his return from Middle Island Creek, and that young Lewis received his first wound while standing in the door of his own home. Be that as it may, there can be no doubt that he and his brother took the barbarous oath as stated, and it is equally a matter of history that they carried it out in spirit and letter.

Martin Wetzel acted the part of a wild beast and committed acts for which no law human or divine can find justification. No red Indian ever showed greater perfidy than did he. During Colonel Brodhead's expedition in 1780, Martin Wetzel was a volunteer. An Indian messenger, under promise of protection, came into camp and held an interview with Brodhead. While they were talking in the most friendly manner, Martin Wetzel stole up behind the unsuspecting red man, and quickly drawing a tomahawk, which he had hidden in his hunting-shirt, struck the Indian in the back of the head a blow which stretched him lifeless on the ground.

Colonel Brodhead was exasperated at the atrocious act, yet he dared not punish Wetzel, for three-fourths of the army would have rallied in his defence.

In the life of Daniel Boone we gave an account of the campaign of Colonel Crawford in 1782. Lewis Wetzel served as a volunteer, being no more than eighteen years of age. The campaign was one of the most frightful disasters that ever occurred in the West, Colonel Crawford being captured and burned to death at the stake.

Among the disorganized soldiers who managed to escape the terrible vengeance of the red men, was one named Mills, who reached a spring some nine miles from Wheeling, where he was forced to leave his horse and go the rest of the way on foot. From Wheeling he proceeded to Van Meter's fort, where he fell in with Lewis Wetzel, whom he persuaded to go back with him in quest of his horse.

Wetzel cautioned him against the danger, but Mills was determined, and the two made their way back to the spring, where they saw the horse standing tied to a sapling. The scout knew what this meant, but the sight of his animal drew Mills forward, and running up to the tree, he began untying him. Before he could finish, there was a discharge of rifles from the wood, and Mills fell fatally wounded.

Knowing that the warriors were all around him, the fleet-footed Wetzel bounded off like a deer, with four of the swiftest runners speeding after him. The chase was a terrific one, and after a half mile, one of the Indians came so close that the fugitive, believing he was on the point of throwing his tomahawk, suddenly whirled about and shot him dead, resuming his flight with the same desperate exertion as before.

The art of reloading his gun while on a dead run had been practised by Wetzel, until he could do the difficult feat with ease. Never was there more urgent need of that peculiar skill than on the present occasion, for at the end of another half mile, a second Indian was so close that Wetzel turned to fire.

Before he could do so, the warrior grasped the end of the barrel, and as he was immensely powerful and active, he brought Wetzel to his knees, and came within a hair's-breadth of wrenching the weapon from his grasp. The white man, however, during the fierce struggle, managed to get the muzzle of the gun turned toward the savage, when he pulled the trigger, killing him instantly.

The struggle was very brief, but during its continuance the other two Indians had approached so nigh, that Wetzel bounded away again at the highest bent of his speed and soon had his rifle reloaded. Then he slackened his pace, so as to allow them to come up, but they were suspicious of the white man who always seemed to have a charged rifle at his service, and they held back. Then Wetzel stopped and they did the same. Several times he wheeled about and raised his gun, when they immediately dodged behind trees. One of them did not conceal his body perfectly, and Wetzel fired, wounding him badly. The remaining warrior ran for life, shouting: *"Dat white man's gun am always loaded !"*

Actuated by that intense hate of the Indians which marked the career of Lewis Wetzel and several of his brothers, there was but the single thought of revenge which inspired the muscular arm to deeds as savage as the red man himself ever engaged in. While General Harmar was doing his utmost to establish peace with the Indians, Lewis

Wetzel and a companion hid themselves near the fort, and, in pure wantonness, the former fired upon a warrior who was riding by. He was so badly wounded that he was barely able to reach the fort, where he died that night.

General Harmar was so indignant over the murder, which Wetzel unblushingly avowed, that he sent Captain Kingsbury and a squad of men with orders to take Wetzel dead or alive. All considerations called for the prompt punishment of the murderer, but his capture was an impossibility, inasmuch as he possessed the fullest sympathy of the frontiersmen, who would have rallied to a man in his defence.

When Captain Kingsbury reached the Mingo Bottom, and his errand became known, Lewis Wetzel and a large number of equally reckless companions formed a plan for attacking the party and massacring every one of them. Only by the interference of Major M'Mahan, who persuaded the Captain of his danger and induced him to withdraw, was the crime averted.

Sometime later, however, Wetzel was seized while asleep in a cabin, put in irons and carried to the guard-house. He was greatly humiliated by the shame of being handcuffed, and sent for General Harmar, to whom he made the characteristic proposal that he should release him among the large party of Indians who were around the fort, and allow him to fight it out with them. This of course was declined by the officer, who, however, consented to knock off his irons, but kept on the handcuffs, allowing him to walk about the fort.

After Wetzel had loosened his limbs by some moderate exercise, he suddenly made a break for the woods and was soon among them. He was fired upon by the guards, and General Harmar instantly sent a number of his fleetest runners, including several Indians, in pursuit.

They almost captured him too, for a couple of the warriors sat down on the log, under which he was crouching, and Wetzel afterwards said that his great fear was that his position would be betrayed by the tumultuous throbbing of his heart. The next day he came across a friend who released him from his handcuffs, furnished him with a gun and ammunition, and Wetzel paddled down the river for Kentucky, where he could feel safe from General Harmar.

The latter issued a proclamation offering a large reward for the capture of Wetzel, but no frontiersman ever made the dangerous attempt to take him, and soon after he joined a party of scouts under Major M'Mahan. They numbered twenty men, and were organized to punish the Indians for murdering a family in the Mingo Bottom. One of the inducements for enlisting was the offer of a hundred dollars to the man who should bring in the first Indian scalp.

The scouts had not penetrated far into the hostile country, when they suddenly found themselves in the presence of a large war party. A hasty consultation was held and it was deemed best to withdraw, but Wetzel refused to return until he should accomplish something. He announced that he would never be seen at home until he lost his own scalp or brought that of an Indian with him.

It was a dangerous task he had taken on himself, but he persevered and spent several days in prowling through the woods, hunting for the coveted opportunity. At last he found a couple of warriors encamped by themselves, and he watched by them until the night was far advanced. Finally one of them got up and moved away, taking a torch with him, doubtless with the intention of watching a deer lick. Wetzel was so anxious to kill both savages that he waited until daylight for the return of the other.

He did not show himself, however, and unwilling to wait longer, the merciless white man stole up to where the sleeping warrior lay and slew him with one furious blow of his knife.

Wetzel reached his home without difficulty and received the one hundred dollars reward for the murder.

A singular occurrence took place shortly after this. From the fort at Wheeling, there had been heard on several occasions, cries such as would be made by a wounded turkey, and more than once some of the men had crossed over to ascertain the cause. The fact that several soldiers were never seen again, did not arouse a suspicion of the real explanation in the minds of any one excepting that of Lewis Wetzel.

He concluded to make an investigation for himself. Cautiously stealing around in the direction of the sound, he approached a deep cavern, the mouth of which was some twenty yards above the river. From this crept forth an Indian warrior, who uttered the peculiar call that had lured so many to their death. Wetzel waited until he gained a fair sight of the savage, when he took careful aim and the decoy never uttered his deceptive signal again.

Wetzel supposed that his trouble with General Harmar would gradually die out with the lapse of time, but the commander had issued standing orders to his officers to arrest him wherever and whenever he could be found. On his way down the river toward Kenawha, Wetzel landed at Point Pleasant, where he roamed about the town with perfect unconcern. While doing so he unexpectedly came face to face with Lieutenant Kingsbury, who had set out to capture him once before.

Wetzel expected a desperate encounter with him, and braced himself for the attack; but Kingsbury, who was personally brave, saluted him with the order to get out of his sight, and passed on. Wetzel thought it wise to leave the neighborhood, and, taking to his canoe, he put off for Limestone, which place, and the county town, Washington, he made his headquarters for a considerable time after.

His skill with the rifle, and his reckless bravery, could not fail to render him a great favorite among the rough men of the border. Could his capture have been arranged with perfect safety to those concerned, it is not probable that any one could have been induced to undertake it.

One day Wetzel was sitting in a tavern in Maysville, when Lieutenant Lawler of the regular army, who was going down the Ohio to Fort Washington with a number of soldiers, landed and discovered him. Without a moment's unnecessary delay, he ordered out a file of soldiers, took Wetzel aboard the boat, and before the citizens had time to rally, he was delivered to General Harmar at Cincinnati.

The General placed him in irons again, preparatory to his trial for the killing of the Indian, and then followed a scene of extraordinary excitement. Petitions for the release of Wetzel poured in upon General Harmar from every quarter, and the indignation became so great that mutterings of a general uprising were soon heard. Serious trouble for a time threatened, for passions were roused to a high pitch, and the intensity deepened as the time for the trial approached.

Finally Judge Symmes issued a writ of habeas corpus in the case, and abundant security being furnished, Wetzel was released. He was escorted in triumph to Columbia, where he was treated to a grand supper, including the usual speeches and congratulations, and where no doubt he concluded his friends were right in looking upon him as a model of heroism and chivalry to whom it was an honor to do homage.

Lewis Wetzel hunted Indians as most men hunt the deer and buffalo. He looked upon the red man as legitimate game, and many a time has he slung his rifle over his shoulder and plunged into the woods for the express purpose of bringing down one of the race against which he had vowed eternal vengeance.

Numerous of his barbarous exploits must remain unrecorded, and well would it be could the necessity never arise for a history of any of them, for they do not show the character of an undoubtedly brave man in an attractive light.

Late one autumn he started out on one of his sanguinary hunts and directed his steps toward the Muskingum River. He had not tramped long when he discovered a camp where four Indians had established themselves for the winter. Not dreaming of any danger, the red men, contrary to their custom, had not taken their usual precautions, and kept neither watch nor sentinels.

This was a tempting opportunity, but a single white hunter, no matter how daring and skillful, might well hesitate before attacking four athletic and well-armed warriors; but the hesitation of Lewis Wetzel was caused only by the necessity for reflecting on the best course to be pursued.

He decided to make his attack on the four in the dead of night when all were sound asleep. He therefore waited patiently in the gloom until he saw they were wrapped in profound slumber. Then he stole forward, and with his dreadful knife, dispatched three in quick succession, but the fourth darted into the woods and escaped in the darkness.

It was near Wheeling, while he was engaged on

one of his numerous scouts, that he came upon a deserted cabin. It was raining at the time, and he was glad to use the place as a shelter. A few pieces of boards were gathered together in the loft and used as a bed, but before he fell asleep, six Indians entered and started a fire, with a view of preparing their evening meal.

Had the scout been asleep when they entered they would have been certain to discover him by his heavy breathing, and as it was, Wetzel scarcely saw how he could escape detection. So he grasped his knife and held himself ready for the desperate encounter which was certain to follow such a discovery.

The Indians, however, did not dream of the presence of the human tiger that was glaring down upon them from the loft above, and soon the half dozen were unconscious in sleep. Feeling that his quarters were dangerous, Wetzel cautiously stole out during the darkness and hid himself behind a log which commanded the front of the cabin.

In the morning the first warrior who presented himself at the door was shot dead. Before the others could comprehend what had taken place the murderer was fleeing like a deer through the woods, and was soon safe from all danger of pursuit.

Such exploits as these increased the popularity of Wetzel, while the attempts made by General Harmar to punish him for his crimes deepened the dislike felt toward him for what was regarded as his unjust persecution of a worthy man.

Not long after the Indian-killer accepted the invitation of a relative to visit him on Dunkard Creek. It was some distance away, and the two men pursued their walk through the woods at a leisurely pace, talking of their hunting adventures, chatting like a couple of school-boys, and with no thought of impending trouble.

But when they emerged from the forest into the clearing where the home of the relative stood, a most startling sight met their eyes.

The house was a mass of smoking ruins. The Indians had been there and left this proof of their ferocity. Wetzel carefully examined the trail and found that the party numbered three warriors and one white man, and that they had taken off a single prisoner.

The last was the betrothed of the relative of the scout, and, as may well be supposed, he was wild with excitement and fury and determined to pursue them without an instant's delay. But Wetzel argued him into something like calmness, and he saw the necessity of placing himself under the control of such a wonderfully skillful woodman as was his companion.

The wish of Wetzel was to overtake the party before they reached the Ohio, though there could be no certainty as to how much start the red men had gained. It was soon seen, however, that they anticipated pursuit, for they had taken the greatest pains to hide their trail. They might have succeeded in the case of ordinary pursuers, but it was impossible to conceal the faint but unerring signs from the keen eye of Wetzel, who pushed forward on their path like the bloodhound tracking its victim through thicket and morass.

It soon became certain that the savages were making for the river, and feeling quite sure of the particular crossing they would seek, Wetzel left the trail altogether, and with his friend hastened to the same place.

It was a long distance, but the hunters for the time were tireless, never throwing away a single minute. As it was reasonable to believe that the Indians would take a short route to the stream, it can be understood that the pursuers could not hope to gain much in the race after all.

When night settled over the great wilderness, they were still a good distance from the Ohio. They stopped for a brief while until they could swallow a few mouthfuls of food. Then they hastened on again guided by the stars overhead. But even this help was soon taken from them by the heavy clouds which overspread the sky, and shut out the slightest twinkling orb in the firmament.

It was useless to seek to go any further, when, with all their cunning, they could not prevent themselves from losing their bearings and most likely going directly back upon the true course.

So they halted where they were, until it began to grow light in the East, when they resumed their hurried journey. They had not gone far before they struck the trail again, and one of the first tracks recognized was the imprint of the small shoe worn by the affianced of the young man.

The Indians, however, were still far ahead, and though the two hunters pushed forward with all the energy possible, they caught no sight of the enemy, as hour after hour passed away.

But Wetzel was convinced they were gaining, and both were in high hope, for as the afternoon wore to its close, they recognized from the signs around them that they were in the neighborhood of the Ohio, and undoubtedly were close upon the Indians and their captive.

The night had fairly set in when they reached the river side, and they caught the glimmer of the camp-fire of those on the other shore, just below the mouth of the Captina. Cautiously the two pursuers entered the river and swam across. A few minutes spent in reconnoissance enabled them to locate each member of the party, including the captive.

The sight of the young lady drove her betrothed almost frantic, and he insisted on attacking the marauders at once; but Wetzel, who was as cool and collected as though no enemy was within a dozen miles, would not permit it.

" The first hour of daybreak is the time," said he, " and nothing shall be done until then." His companion had no choice but to obey, though it drove him to madness to remain so near his beloved, without striking a blow in her behalf.

The long wearisome hours passed slowly, and at last it began to grow light in the East. The young man was quivering with excitement, but Wetzel had been engaged in too many terrific encounters to lose his self-possession at such a critical time.

The red men are early risers, when on the march, and as soon as it began to grow light in the East, they were astir. Wetzel directed his friend to take sure aim at the renegade, pledging him that he would attend to the Indians.

They fired simultaneously, and each brought down his man. The lover dashed into camp to his affianced, while the two warriors ran among the trees until they could learn the strength of the attacking party. The dauntless Wetzel followed as impetuously as though he had an entire company at his back.

As was his custom, he reloaded on the run, and after a short pursuit, fired his gun at random, so as to draw out the savages. It produced the effect, for the warriors, supposing him to be defenceless, came rushing forth, with uplifted tomahawks and whooping in triumph; but Wetzel took but a few seconds to reload his gun, when he shot the nearest through the body.

As there could be no doubt that his rifle was now unloaded, the single remaining Indian made for him with the fury of a panther. Wetzel, who was no less active and athletic, dodged from tree to tree and ran here and there, baffling the fatal tomahawk that was on the point of being hurled more than once, until his terrible rifle was ready again, when he wheeled and brought down the Indian, who must have wondered in his last moments at the wonderful gun carried by the white man.

While Lewis Wetzel was engaged in these extraordinary forays, several of his brothers were scarcely less active. As they were inspired by the same intense hate which nerved the arms of the more famous scout, it will be readily conceded that the murder of the elder Wetzel years before by the Indians was repaid with more than interest.

After Lewis had roamed through the wilderness some time longer, he concluded to make a journey to the extreme south, and for that purpose engaged on a flat-boat bound for New Orleans. While in that city he got into some serious difficulty, the precise nature of which is unknown. The result was he suffered imprisonment for two years. It is not improbable that he discovered the difference between breaking the law in the Western wilderness and in the Crescent City.

He finally found his way back to Wheeling, where he resumed his roaming through the woods, and soon became involved in his characteristic adventures with the red men.

He was returning one day from a hunt, when happening to look up, he observed a warrior in the very act of leveling his gun at him. Quick as a flash Wetzel dodged behind a tree, the Indian doing the same, and they stood facing each other for a considerable time.

Growing impatient of waiting, the scout resorted to the oft-described trick of placing his cap on the end of his ramrod and projecting it a short distance beyond the trunk. This brought the fire of the savage, and before he could reload the white man shot him.

Wetzel was known so generally as a daring and

skillful scout, that General Clarke, while organizing his celebrated expedition to the country beyond the Rocky Mountains, used his utmost effort to secure him as a member of the company. Wetzel was not inclined to go, but he was finally persuaded, and when they started, he was one of the most valuable members. He kept with them for three months and then turned about and came home.

Some time later he left on a flat-boat, and went to the house of a relative, near Natchez, where he died in the summer of 1808.

STANDARD AND POPULAR BOOKS

PUBLISHED BY

PORTER & COATES, PHILADELPHIA, PA.

WAVERLEY NOVELS. By SIR WALTER SCOTT.

*Waverley.
*Guy Mannering.
The Antiquary.
Rob Roy.
Black Dwarf; and Old Mortality.
The Heart of Mid-Lothian.
The Bride of Lammermoor; and A
  Legend of Montrose.
*Ivanhoe.
The Monastery.
The Abbott.
Kenilworth.
The Pirate.

The Fortunes of Nigel.
Peveril of the Peak.
Quentin Durward.
St. Ronan's Well.
Redgauntlet.
The Betrothed; and The Talisman.
Woodstock.
The Fair Maid of Perth.
Anne of Geierstein.
Count Robert of Paris; and Castle
  Dangerous.
Chronicles of the Canongate.

Household Edition. 23 vols. Illustrated. 12mo. Cloth, extra, black and gold, per vol., $1.00; sheep, marbled edges, per vol., $1.50; half calf, gilt, marbled edges, per vol., $3.00. Sold separately in cloth binding only.

Universe Edition. 25 vols. Printed on thin paper, and containing one illustration to the volume. 12mo. Cloth, extra, black and gold, per vol., 75 cts.

World Edition. 12 vols. Thick 12mo. (Sold in sets only.) Cloth, extra, black and gold, $18.00; half imt. Russia, marbled edges, $24.00.

This is the best edition for the library or for general use published. Its convenient size, the extreme legibility of the type, which is larger than is used in any other 12mo edition, either English or American.

TALES OF A GRANDFATHER. By SIR WALTER SCOTT, Bart.
4 vols. Uniform with the Waverley Novels.
Household Edition. Illustrated. 12mo. Cloth, extra, black and gold, per vol., $1.00; sheep, marbled edges, per vol., $1 50; half calf, gilt, marbled edges, per vol., $3.00.

This edition contains the Fourth Series—Tales from French history, and is the only complete edition published in this country.

(1)

CHARLES DICKENS' COMPLETE WORKS. Author's Edition.
14 vols., with a portrait of the author on steel, and eight
illustrations by F. O. C. Darley, Cruikshank, Fildes, Eytinge,
and others, in each volume. 12mo. Cloth, extra, black and
gold, per vol., $1.00; sheep, marbled edges, per vol., $1.50; half
imt. Russia, marbled edges, per vol., $1.50: half calf, gilt,
marbled edges, per vol., $2.75.

*Pickwick Papers.
*Oliver Twist, Pictures of Italy, and
　American Notes.
*Nicholas Nickleby.
Old Curiosity Shop, and Reprinted
　Pieces.
Barnaby Rudge, and Hard Times.
*Martin Chuzzlewit.
Dombey and Son.
*David Copperfield.

Christmas Books, Uncommercial
　Traveller, and Additional
　Christmas Stories.
Bleak House.
Little Dorrit.
Tale of Two Cities, and Great Ex-
　pectations.
Our Mutual Friend.
Edwin Drood, Sketches, Master
　Humphrey's Clock, etc., etc.

Sold separately in cloth binding only.
*Also in Alta Edition, one illustration, 75 cents.
The same. Universe Edition. Printed on thin paper and containing one illustration to the volume. 14 vols., 12mo. Cloth,
extra, black and gold, per vol., 75 cents.
The same. World Edition. 7 vols., thick 12mo., $12.25. (Sold
in sets only.)

CHILD'S HISTORY OF ENGLAND. By CHARLES DICKENS.
Popular 12mo. edition; from new electrotype plates. Large
clear type. Beautifully illustrated with 8 engravings on wood.
12mo. Cloth, extra, black and gold, $1.00.
Alta Edition. One illustration, 75 cents.
"Dickens as a novelist and prose poet is to be classed in the front rank of
the noble company to which he belongs. He has revived the novel of genuine practical life, as it existed in the works of Fielding, Smollett, and Gold-
smith; but at the same time has given to his material an individual coloring
and expression peculiarly his own. His characters, like those of his great
exemplars, constitute a world of their own, whose truth to nature every
reader instinctively recognizes in connection with their truth to darkness."
—E. P. Whipple.

MACAULAY'S HISTORY OF ENGLAND. From the accession
of James II. By THOMAS BABINGTON MACAULAY. With a
steel portrait of the author. Printed from new electrotype
plates from the last English Edition. Being by far the most
correct edition in the American market. 5 volumes, 12mo.
Cloth, extra, black and gold, per set, $5.00; sheep, marbled
edges, per set, $7.50; half imitation Russia, $7.50; half calf,
gilt, marbled edges, per set, $15.00.
Popular Edition. 5 vols., cloth, plain, $5.00.
8vo. Edition. 5 volumes in one, with portrait. Cloth, extra,
black and gold, $3.00; sheep, marbled edges, $3.50.

MARTINEAU'S HISTORY OF ENGLAND. From the beginning
of the 19th Century to the Crimean War. By HARRIET MAR-
TINEAU. Complete in 4 vols., with full Index. Cloth, extra,
black and gold, per set, $4.00; sheep, marbled edges, $6.00, half
calf, gilt, marbled edges, $12.00.

HUME'S HISTORY OF ENGLAND. From the invasion of Julius Cæsar to the abdication of James II, 1688. By DAVID HUME. Standard Edition. With the author's last corrections and improvements; to which is prefixed a short account of his life, written by himself. With a portrait on steel. A new edition from entirely new stereotype plates. 5 vols., 12mo. Cloth, extra, black and gold, per set, $5.00; sheep, marbled edges, per set, $7.50; half imitation Russia, $7.50; half calf, gilt, marbled edges, per set, $15.00.

Popular Edition. 5 vols. Cloth, plain, $5.00.

GIBBON'S DECLINE AND FALL OF THE ROMAN EMPIRE. By EDWARD GIBBON. With Notes, by Rev. H. H. MILMAN. Standard Edition. To which is added a complete Index of the work. A new edition from entirely new stereotype plates. With portrait on steel. 5 vols., 12mo. Cloth, extra, black and gold, per set, $5.00; sheep, marbled edges, per set, $7.50; half imitation Russia, $7.50; half calf, gilt, marbled edges, per set, $15.00.

Popular Edition. 5 vols. Cloth, plain, $5.00.

ENGLAND, PICTURESQUE AND DESCRIPTIVE. By JOEL COOK, author of "A Holiday Tour in Europe," etc. With 487 finely engraved illustrations, descriptive of the most famous and attractive places, as well as of the historic scenes and rural life of England and Wales. With Mr. Cook's admirable descriptions of the places and the country, and the splendid illustrations, this is the most valuable and attractive book of the season, and the sale will doubtless be very large. 4to. Cloth, extra, gilt side and edges, $7.50; half calf, gilt, marbled edges, $10.00; half morocco, full gilt edges, $10.00; full Turkey morocco, gilt edges, $15.00; tree calf, gilt edges, $18.00.

This work, which is prepared in elegant style, and profusely illustrated, is a comprehensive description of England and Wales, arranged in convenient form for the tourist, and at the same time providing an illustrated guide-book to a country which Americans always view with interest. There are few satisfactory works about this land which is so generously gifted by Nature and so full of memorials of the past. Such books as there are, either cover a few counties or are devoted to special localities, or are merely guidebooks. The present work is believed to be the first attempt to give in attractive form a description of the stately homes, renowned castles, ivy-clad ruins of abbeys, churches, and ancient fortresses, delicious scenery, rock-bound coasts, and celebrated places of England and Wales. It is written by an author fully competent from travel and reading, and in position to properly describe his very interesting subject; and the artist's pencil has been called into requisition to graphically illustrate its well-written pages. There are 487 illustrations, prepared in the highest style of the engraver's art, while the book itself is one of the most attractive ever presented to the American public.

Its method of construction is systematic, following the most convenient routes taken by tourists, and the letter-press includes enough of the history and legend of each of the places described to make the story highly interesting. Its pages fairly overflow with picture and description, telling of everything attractive that is presented by England and Wales. Executed in the highest style of the printer's and engraver's art, "England, Picturesque and Descriptive," is one of the best American books of the year.

HISTORY OF THE CIVIL WAR IN AMERICA. By the COMTE
DE PARIS. With Maps faithfully Engraved from the Origin-
als, and Printed in Three Colors. 8vo. Cloth, per volume,
$3.50; red cloth, extra, Roxburgh style, uncut edges, $3.50;
sheep, library style, $4.50; half Turkey morocco, $6.00. Vols.
I, II, and III now ready.

The third volume embraces, without abridgment, the fifth and sixth
volumes of the French edition, and covers one of the most interesting as
well as the most anxious periods of the war, describing the operations of the
Army of the Potomac in the East, and the Army of the Cumberland and
Tennessee in the West.
It contains full accounts of the battle of Chancellorsville, the attack of the
monitors on Fort Sumter, the sieges and fall of Vicksburg and Port Hudson;
the battles of Port Gibson and Champion's Hill, and the fullest and most
authentic account of the battle of Gettysburg ever written.

"The head of the Orleans family has put pen to paper with excellent
result. . . . . Our present impression is that it will form by far the best
history of the American war."—*Athenæum, London.*

"We advise all Americans to read it carefully, and judge for themselves
if 'the future historian of our war,' of whom we have heard so much, be not
already arrived in the Comte de Paris."—*Nation, New York.*

"This is incomparably the best account of our great second revolution
that has yet been even attempted. It is so calm, so dispassionate, so accurate
in detail, and at the same time so philosophical in general, that its reader
counts confidently on finding the complete work thoroughly satisfactory."—
Evening Bulletin, Philadelphia.

"The work expresses the calm, deliberate judgment of an experienced
military observer and a highly intelligent man. Many of its statements
will excite discussion, but we much mistake if it does not take high and
permanent rank among the standard histories of the civil. war. Indeed
that place has been assigned it by the most competent critics both of this
country and abroad."—*Times, Cincinnati.*

"Messrs. Porter & Coates, of Philadelphia, will publish in a few days the
authorized translation of the new volume of the Comte de Paris' History of
Our Civil War. The two volumes in French—the fifth and sixth—are bound
together in the translation in one volume. Our readers already know,
through a table of contents of these volumes, published in the cable columns
of the *Herald*, the period covered by this new installment of a work remarkable in several ways. It includes the most important and decisive period of
the war, and the two great campaigns of Gettysburg and Vicksburg.
"The great civil war has had no better, no abler historian than the French
prince who, emulating the example of Lafayette, took part in this new
struggle for freedom, and who now writes of events, in many of which he
participated, as an accomplished officer, and one who, by his independent
position, his high character and eminent talents, was placed in circumstances and relations which gave him almost unequalled opportunities to
gain correct information and form impartial judgments.
"The new installment of a work which has already become a classic will
be read with increased interest by Americans because of the importance of
the period it covers and the stirring events it describes. In advance of a
careful review we present to-day some extracts from the advance sheets sent
us by Messrs. Porter & Coates, which will give our readers a foretaste of
chapters which bring back to memory so many half-forgotten and not a few
hitherto unvalued details of a time which Americans of this generation at
least cannot read of without a fresh thrill of excitement."

HALF-HOURS WITH THE BEST AUTHORS. With short Biographical and Critical Notes. By CHARLES KNIGHT.
New Household Edition. With six portraits on steel. 3 vols., thick 12mo. Cloth, extra, black and gold, per set, $4.50; half imt. Russia, marbled edges, $6.00; half calf, gilt, marbled edges, $12.00.
Library Edition. Printed on fine laid and tinted paper. With twenty-four portraits on steel. 6 vols., 12mo. Cloth, extra, per set, $7.50; half calf, gilt, marbled edges, per set, $18.00; half Russia, gilt top, $21.00; full French morocco, limp, per set, $12.00; full smooth Russia, limp, round corners, in Russia case, per set, $25.00; full seal grained Russia, limp, round corners, in Russia case to match, $25.00.

The excellent idea of the editor of these choice volumes has been most admirably carried out, as will be seen by the list of authors upon all subjects. Selecting some choice passages of the best standard authors, each of sufficient length to occupy half an hour in its perusal, there is here food for thought for every day in the year: so that if the purchaser will devote but one-half hour each day to its appropriate selection he will read through these six volumes in one year, and in such a leisurely manner that the noblest thoughts of many of the greatest minds will be firmly in his mind forever. For every Sunday there is a suitable selection from some of the most eminent writers in sacred literature. We venture to say if the editor's idea is carried out the reader will possess more and better knowledge of the English classics at the end of the year than he would by five years of desultory reading.
They can be commenced at any day in the year. The variety of reading is so great that no one will ever tire of these volumes. It is a library in itself.

THE POETRY OF OTHER LANDS. A Collection of Translations into English Verse of the Poetry of Other Languages, Ancient and Modern. Compiled by N. CLEMMONS HUNT. Containing translations from the Greek, Latin, Persian, Arabian, Japanese, Turkish, Servian, Russian, Bohemian, Polish, Dutch, German, Italian, French, Spanish, and Portuguese languages. 12mo. Cloth, extra, gilt edges, $2.50; half calf, gilt, marbled edges, $4.00; Turkey morocco, gilt edges, $6.00.

"Another of the publications of Porter & Coates, called 'The Poetry of Other Lands,' compiled by N. Clemmons Hunt, we most warmly commend. It is one of the best collections we have seen, containing many exquisite poems and fragments of verse which have not before been put into book form in English words. We find many of the old favorites, which appear in every well-selected collection of sonnets and songs, and we miss others, which seem a necessity to complete the bouquet of grasses and flowers, some of which, from time to time, we hope to republish in the 'Courier.'"— *Cincinnati Courier.*

"A book of rare excellence, because it gives a collection of choice gems in many languages not available to the general lover of poetry. It contains translations from the Greek, Latin, Persian, Arabian, Japanese, Turkish, Servian, Russian, Bohemian, Polish, Dutch, German, Italian, French, Spanish, and Portuguese languages. The book will be an admirable companion volume to any one of the collections of English poetry that are now published. With the full index of authors immediately preceding the collection, and the arrangement of the poems under headings, the reader will find it convenient for reference. It is a gift that will be more valued by very many than some of the transitory ones at these holiday times."— *Philadelphia Methodist.*

THE FIRESIDE ENCYCLOPÆDIA OF POETRY.   Edited by HENRY T. COATES.   This is the latest, and beyond doubt the best collection of poetry published.   Printed on fine paper and illustrated with thirteen steel engravings and fifteen title pages, containing portraits of prominent American poets and fac-similes of their handwriting, made expressly for this book. 8vo.   Cloth, extra, black and gold, gilt edges, $5.00; half calf, gilt, marbled edges, $7.50; half morocco, full gilt edges, $7.50; full Turkey morocco, gilt edges, $10.00; tree calf, gilt edges $12.00; plush, padded side, nickel lettering, $14.00.

"The editor shows a wide acquaintance with the most precious treasures of English verse, and has gathered the most admirable specimens of their ample wealth.   Many pieces which have been passed by in previous collections hold a place of honor in the present volume, and will be heartily welcomed by the lovers of poetry as a delightful addition to their sources of enjoyment.   It is a volume rich in solace, in entertainment, in inspiration, of which the possession may well be coveted by every lover of poetry.   The pictorial illustrations of the work are in keeping with its poetical contents, and the beauty of the typographical execution entitles it to a place among the choicest ornaments of the library."—*New York Tribune.*

"Lovers of good poetry will find this one of the richest collections ever made.   All the best singers in our language are represented, and the selections are generally those which reveal their highest qualities. . . . . The lights and shades, the finer play of thought and imagination belonging to individual authors, are brought out in this way (by the arrangement of poems under subject-headings) as they would not be under any other system. ". . . . We are deeply impressed with the keen appreciation of poetical worth, and also with the good taste manifested by the compiler."—*Churchman.*

"Cyclopædias of poetry are numerous, but for sterling value of its contents for the library, or as a book of reference, no work of the kind will compare with this admirable volume of Mr. Coates   It takes the gems from many volumes, culling with rare skill and judgment."—*Chicago Inter-Ocean.*

THE CHILDREN'S BOOK OF POETRY.   Compiled by HENRY T. COATES.   Containing over 500 poems carefully selected from the works of the best and most popular writers for children; with nearly 200 illustrations.   The most complete collection of poetry for children ever published.   4to.   Cloth, extra, black and gold, gilt side and edges, $3.00; full Turkey morocco, gilt edges, $7.50.

"This seems to us the best book of poetry for children in existence.   We have examined many other collections, but we cannot name another that deserves to be compared with this admirable compilation."—*Worcester Spy.*

"The special value of the book lies in the fact that it nearly or quite covers the entire field.   There is not a great deal of good poetry which has been written for children that cannot be found in this book.   The collection is particularly strong in ballads and tales, which are apt to interest children more than poems of other kinds; and Mr. Coates has shown good judgment in supplementing this department with some of the best poems of that class that have been written for grown people.   A surer method of forming the taste of children for good and pure literature than by reading to them from any portion of this book can hardly be imagined.   The volume is richly illustrated and beautifully bound."—*Philadelphia Evening Bulletin.*

"A more excellent volume cannot be found.   We have found within the covers of this handsome volume, and upon its fair pages, many of the most exquisite poems which our language contains.   It must become a standard volume, and can never grow old or obsolete."—*Episcopal Recorder.*

THE COMPLETE WORKS OF THOS. HOOD. With engravings on steel. 4 vols., 12mo., tinted paper. Poetical Works: Up the Rhine; Miscellanies and Hood's Own; Whimsicalities, Whims, and Oddities. Cloth, extra, black and gold, $6.00; red cloth, paper label, gilt top, uncut edges, $6.00; half calf, gilt, marbled edges, $14.00; half Russia, gilt top, $18.00.

Hood's verse, whether serious or comic—whether serene like a cloudless autumn evening or sparkling with puns like a frosty January midnight with stars—was ever pregnant with materials for the thought. Like every author distinguished for true comic humor, there was a deep vein of melancholy pathos running through his mirth, and even when his sun shone brightly its light seemed often reflected as if only over the rim of a cloud.

Well may we say, in the words of Tennyson, " Would he could have stayed with us," for never could it be more truly recorded of any one—in the words of Hamlet characterizing Yorick—that " he was a fellow of infinite jest, of most excellent fancy." D. M. MOIR.

THE ILIAD OF HOMER RENDERED INTO ENGLISH BLANK VERSE. By EDWARD, EARL OF DERBY. From the latest London edition, with all the author's last revisions and corrections, and with a Biographical Sketch of Lord Derby, by R. SHELTON MACKENZIE, D.C.L. With twelve steel engravings from Flaxman's celebrated designs. 2 vols., 12mo. Cloth, extra, bev. boards, gilt top, $3.50; half calf, gilt, marbled edges, $7.00; half Turkey morocco, gilt top, $7.00.

The same. Popular edition. Two vols. in one. 12mo. Cloth, extra, $1 50.

"It must equally be considered a splendid performance; and for the present we have no hesitation in saying that it is by far the best representation of Homer's Iliad in the English language."—*London Times.*

"The merits of Lord Derby's translation may be summed up in one word, it is eminently attractive; it is instinct with life; it may be read with fervent interest; it is immeasurably nearer than Pope to the text of the original. . . . . Lord Derby has given a version far more closely allied to the original, and superior to any that has yet been attempted in the. blank verse of our language."—*Edinburg Review.*

THE WORKS OF FLAVIUS JOSEPHUS. Comprising the Antiquities of the Jews; a History of the Jewish Wars, and a Life of Flavius Josephus, written by himself. Translated from the original Greek, by WILLIAM WHISTON, A.M. Together with numerous explanatory Notes and seven Dissertations concerning Jesus Christ, John the Baptist, James the Just, God's command to Abraham, etc., with an Introductory Essay by Rev. H. STEBBING, D.D. 8vo. Cloth, extra, black and gold, plain edges, $3.00; cloth, red, black and gold, gilt edges, $4.50; sheep, marbled edges, $3.50; Turkey morocco, gilt edges, $8.00.

This is the largest type one volume edition published.

THE ANCIENT HISTORY OF THE EGYPTIANS, CARTHAGINIANS, ASSYRIANS, BABYLONIANS, MEDES AND PERSIANS, GRECIANS AND MACEDONIANS. Including a History of the Arts and Sciences of the Ancients. By CHARLES ROLLIN. With a Life of the Author, by JAMES BELL. 2 vols., royal 8vo. Sheep, marbled edges, per set, $6.00.

COOKERY FROM EXPERIENCE. A Practical Guide for House-keepers in the Preparation of Every-day Meals, containing more than One Thousand Domestic Recipes, mostly tested by Personal Experience, with Suggestions for Meals, Lists of Meats and Vegetables in Season, etc. By Mrs. SARA T. PAUL. 12mo. Cloth, extra, black and gold, $1.50.
Interleaved Edition. Cloth, extra, black and gold, $1.75.

THE COMPARATIVE EDITION OF THE NEW TESTAMENT. Both Versions in One Book.
The proof readings of our Comparative Edition have been gone over by so many competent proof readers, that we believe the text is absolutely correct.
Large 12mo., 700 pp. Cloth, extra, plain edges, $1.50; cloth, extra, bevelled boards and carmine edges, $1.75; imitation panelled calf, yellow edges, $2.00; arabesque, gilt edges, $2.50; French morocco, limp, gilt edges, $4.00; Turkey morocco, limp, gilt edges, $6.00.

The Comparative New Testament has been published by Porter & Coates. In parallel columns on each page are given the old and new versions of the Testament, divided also as far as practicable into comparative verses, so that it is almost impossible for the slightest new word to escape the notice of either the ordinary reader or the analytical student. It is decidedly the best edition yet published of the most interest-exciting literary production of the day. No more convenient form for comparison could be devised either for economizing time or labor. Another feature is the foot-notes, and there is also given in an appendix the various words and expressions preferred by the American members of the Revising Commission. The work is handsomely printed on excellent paper with clear, legible type. It contains nearly 700 pages.

THE COUNT OF MONTE CRISTO. By ALEXANDRE DUMAS. Complete in one volume, with two illustrations by George G. White. 12mo. Cloth, extra, black and gold, $1.25.

THE THREE GUARDSMEN. By ALEXANDRE DUMAS. Complete in one volume, with two illustrations by George G. White. 12mo. Cloth, extra, black and gold, $1.25.

There is a magic influence in his pen, a magnetic attraction in his descriptions, a fertility in his literary resources which are characteristic of Dumas alone, and the seal of the master of light literature is set upon all his works. Even when not strictly historical, his romances give an insight into the habits and modes of thought and action of the people of the time described, which are not offered in any other author's productions.

THE LAST DAYS OF POMPEII. By Sir EDWARD BULWER LYTTON, Bart. Illustrated. 12mo. Cloth, extra, black and gold, $1.00. Alta edition, one illustration, 75 cts.

JANE EYRE. By CHARLOTTE BRONTÉ (Currer Bell). New Library Edition. With five illustrations by E. M. WIMPERIS. 12mo. Cloth, extra, black and gold, $1.00.

SHIRLEY. By CHARLOTTE BRONTÉ (Currer Bell). New Library Edition. With five illustrations by E. M. WIMPERIS. 12mo. Cloth, extra, black and gold, $1.00.

VILLETTE. By CHARLOTTE BRONTÉ (Currer Bell). New Library Edition. With five illustrations by E. M. WIMPERIS. 12mo. Cloth, extra, black and gold, $1.00.

THE PROFESSOR, EMMA and POEMS. By CHARLOTTE BRONTÉ (Currer Bell). New Library Edition. With five illustrations by E. M. WIMPERIS. 12mo. Cloth, extra, black and gold, $1.00.
Cloth, extra, black and gold, per set, $4.00; red cloth, paper label, gilt top, uncut edges, per set, $5.00; half calf, gilt, per set, $12.00. The four volumes forming the complete works of Charlotte Bronté (Currer Bell).

The wondrous power of Currer Bell's stories consists in their fiery insight into the human heart, their merciless dissection of passion, and their stern analysis of character and motive. The style of these productions possesses incredible force, sometimes almost grim in its bare severity, then relapsing into passages of melting pathos—always direct, natural, and effective in its unpretending strength. They exhibit the identity which always belongs to works of genius by the same author, though without the slightest approach to monotony. The characters portrayed by Currer Bell all have a strongly marked individuality. Once brought before the imagination, they haunt the memory like a strange dream. The sinewy, muscular strength of her writings guarantees their permanent duration, and thus far they have lost nothing of their intensity of interest since the period of their composition.

CAPTAIN JACK THE SCOUT; or, The Indian Wars about Old Fort Duquesne. An Historical Novel, with copious notes. By CHARLES McKNIGHT. Illustrated with eight engravings. 12mo. Cloth, extra, black and gold, $1.50.

A work of such rare merit and thrilling interest as to have been republished both in England and Germany. This genuine American historical work has been received with extraordinary popular favor, and has "won golden opinions from all sorts of people" for its freshness, its forest life, and its fidelity to truth. In many instances it even corrects History and uses the drapery of fiction simply to enliven and illustrate the fact.

It is a universal favorite with both sexes, and with all ages and conditions, and is not only proving a marked and notable success in this country, but has been eagerly taken up abroad and republished in London, England, and issued in two volumes in the far-famed "Tauchnetz Edition" of Leipsic, Germany.

ORANGE BLOSSOMS, FRESH AND FADED. By T. S. ARTHUR. Illustrated. 12mo. Cloth, extra, black and gold, $1.50.

"Orange Blossoms" contains a number of short stories of society. Like all of Mr. Arthur's works, it has a special moral purpose, and is especially addressed to the young who have just entered the marital experience, whom it pleasantly warns against those social and moral pitfalls into which they may almost innocently plunge.

THE BAR ROOMS AT BRANTLEY; or, The Great Hotel Speculation. By T. S. ARTHUR. Illustrated. 12mo. Cloth, extra, black and gold, $1.50.

"One of the best temperance stories recently issued."—*N. Y. Commercial Advertiser.*

"Although it is in the form of a novel, its truthful delineation of characters is such that in every village in the land you meet the broken manhood it pictures upon the streets, and look upon sad, tear-dimmed eyes of women and children. The characters are not overdrawn, but are as truthful as an artist's pencil could make them."—*Inter-Ocean, Chicago.*

EMMA. By JANE AUSTEN. Illustrated. 12mo. Cloth, extra, $1.25.

MANSFIELD PARK. By JANE AUSTEN. Illustrated. 12mo. Cloth, extra, $1.25.

PRIDE AND PREJUDICE; and Northanger Abbey. By JANE AUSTEN. Illustrated. 12mo. Cloth, extra, $1.25.

SENSE AND SENSIBILITY; and Persuasion. By JANE AUSTEN. Illustrated. 12mo. Cloth, extra, $1.25.

The four volumes, forming the complete works of Jane Austen, in a neat box: Cloth, extra, per set, $5.00; red cloth, paper label, gilt top, uncut edges, $5.00; half calf, gilt, per set, $12.00.

"Jane Austen, a woman of whom England is justly proud. In her novels she has given us a multitude of characters, all, in a certain sense, commonplace, all such as we meet every day. Yet they are all as perfectly discriminated from each other as if they were the most eccentric of human beings. . . . . And almost all this is done by touches so delicate that they elude analysis, that they defy the powers of description, and that we know them to exist only by the general effect to which they have contributed."—*Macaulay's Essays.*

ART AT HOME. Containing in one volume House Decoration, by RHODA and AGNES GARRETT; Plea for Art in the House, by W. J. LOFTIE; Music, by JOHN HULLAH; and Dress, by Mrs. OLIPHANT. 12mo. Cloth, extra, black and gold, $1.50.

TOM BROWN'S SCHOOL DAYS AT RUGBY. By THOMAS HUGHES. New Edition, large clear type. With 36 illustrations after Caldecott and others. 12mo., 400 pp. Cloth, extra, black and gold, $1.25; half calf, gilt, $2.75.
Alta Edition. One illustration, 75 cents.

"It is difficult to estimate the amount of good which may be done by 'Tom Brown's School Days.' It gives, in the main, a most faithful and interesting picture of our public schools, the most English institutions of England, and which educate the best and most powerful elements in our upper classes. But it is more than this; it is an attempt, a very noble and successful attempt, to Christianize the society of our youth, through the only practicable channel—hearty and brotherly sympathy with their feelings; a book, in short, which a father might well wish to see in the hands of his son."—*London Times.*

TOM BROWN AT OXFORD. By THOMAS HUGHES. Illustrated. 12mo. Cloth, extra, black and gold, $1.50; half calf, gilt, $3.00.

"Fairly entitled to the rank and dignity of an English classic. Plot, style and truthfulness are of the soundest British character. Racy, idiomatic, mirror-like, always interesting, suggesting thought on the knottiest social and religious questions, now deeply moving by its unconscious pathos, and anon inspiring uproarious laughter, it is a work the world will not willingly let die."—*N. Y. Christian Advocate.*

SENSIBLE ETIQUETTE OF THE BEST SOCIETY. By Mrs. H. O. WARD. Customs, manners, morals, and home culture, with suggestions how to word notes and letters of invitations, acceptances, and regrets, and general instructions as to calls, rules for watering places, lunches, kettle drums, dinners, receptions, weddings, parties, dress, toilet and manners, salutations, introductions, social reforms, etc., etc. Bound in cloth, with gilt edge, and sent by mail, postage paid, on receipt of $2.00.

LADIES' AND GENTLEMEN'S ETIQUETTE: A Complete Manual of the Manners and Dress of American Society. Containing forms of Letters, Invitations, Acceptances, and Regrets. With a copious index. By E. B. DUFFEY. 12mo. Cloth, extra, black and gold, $1.50.

"It is peculiarly an American book, especially adapted to our people, and its greatest beauty is found in the fact that in every line and precept it inculcates the principles of true politeness, instead of those formal rules that serve only to gild the surface without affecting the substance. It is admirably written, the style being clear, terse, and forcible."—*St. Louis Times.*

THE UNDERGROUND CITY; or, The Child of the Cavern. By JULES VERNE. Translated from the French by W. H. KINGSTON. With 43 illustrations. Standard Edition. 12mo. Cloth, extra, black and gold, $1.50.

AROUND THE WORLD IN EIGHTY DAYS. By JULES VERNE. Translated by GEO. M. TOWLE. With 12 full-page illustrations. 12mo. Cloth, extra, black and gold, $1.25.

AT THE NORTH POLE; or, The Voyages and Adventures of Captain Hatteras. By JULES VERNE. With 130 illustrations by RIOU. Standard Edition. 12mo. Cloth, extra, black and gold, $1.25.

THE DESERT OF ICE; or, The Further Adventures of Captain Hatteras. By JULES VERNE. With 126 illustrations by RIOU. Standard Edition. 12mo. Cloth, extra, black and gold, $1.25.

TWENTY THOUSAND LEAGUES UNDER THE SEAS; or, The Marvellous and Exciting Adventures of Pierre Aronnax, Conseil his servant, and Ned Land, a Canadian Harpooner. By JULES VERNE. Standard Edition. Illustrated. 12mo. Cloth, extra, black and gold, $1.25.

THE WRECK OF THE CHANCELLOR, Diary of J. R. Kazallon, Passenger, and Martin Paz. By JULES VERNE. Translated from the French by ELLEN FREWER. With 10 illustrations. Standard Edition. 12mo. Cloth, extra, black and gold, $1.25.

Jules Verne is so well known that the mere announcement of anything from his pen is sufficient to create a demand for it. One of his chief merits is the wonderful art with which he lays under contribution every branch of science and natural history, while he vividly describes with minute exactness all parts of the world and its inhabitants.

THE INGOLDSBY LEGENDS; or, Mirth and Marvels. By RICHARD HARRIS BARHAM (Thomas Ingoldsby, Esq.). New edition, printed from entirely new stereotype plates. Illustrated. 12mo. Cloth, extra, black and gold, $1.50; half calf, gilt, marbled edges, $3.00.

"Of his poetical powers it is not too much to say that, for originality of design and diction, for grand illustration and musical verse, they are not surpassed in the English language. The Witches' Frolic is second only to Tam O'Shanter. But why recapitulate the titles of either prose or verse—since they have been confessed by every judgment to be singularly rich in classic allusion and modern illustration. From the days of Hudibras to our time the drollery invested in rhymes has never been so amply or felicitously exemplified."—*Bentley's Miscellany*.

TEN THOUSAND A YEAR. By SAMUEL C. WARREN, author of "The Diary of a London Physician." A new edition, carefully revised, with three illustrations by GEORGE G. WHITE. 12mo. Cloth, extra, black and gold, $1 50.

"Mr. Warren has taken a lasting place among the imaginative writers of this period of English history. He possesses, in a remarkable manner, the tenderness of heart and vividness of feeling, as well as powers of description, which are essential to the delineation of the pathetic, and which, when existing in the degree in which he enjoys them, fill his pages with scenes which can never be forgotten."—*Sir Archibald Alison*.

THOMPSON'S POLITICAL ECONOMY; With Especial Reference to the Industrial History of Nations. By Prof. R. E. THOMPSON, of the University of Pennsylvania. 12mo. Cloth, extra, $1.50.

This book possesses an especial interest at the present moment. The questions of Free Trade and Protection are before the country more directly than at any earlier period of our history. As a rule the works and text-books used in our American colleges are either of English origin or teach Doctrines of a political economy which, as Walter Bagehot says, was made for England. Prof. Thompson belongs to the Nationalist School of Economists, to which Alexander Hamilton, Tench Coxe, Henry Clay, Matthew Carey, and his greater son, Henry C. Carey, Stephen Colwell, and James Abram Garfield were adherents. He believes in that policy of Protection to American industry which has had the sanction of every great American statesman, not excepting Thomas Jefferson and John C. Calhoun. He makes his appeal to history in defence of that policy, showing that wherever a weaker or less advanced country has practiced Free Trade with one more powerful or richer, the former has lost its industries as well as its money, and has become economically dependent on the latter. Those who wish to learn what is the real source of Irish poverty and discontent will find it here stated fully.

The method of the book is historical. It is therefore no series of dry and abstract reasonings, such as repel readers from books of this class. The writer does not ride the *a priori* nag, and say "this must be so," and "that must be conceded." He shows what has been true, and seeks to elicit the laws of the science from the experience of the world. The book overflows with facts told in an interesting manner.

THE ENGLISH PEOPLE IN ITS THREE HOMES, and the Practical Bearings of general European History. By EDWARD A. FREEMAN, LL.D., Author of the "Norman Conquest of England." 12mo. Cloth, extra, $1.75.

HANDY ANDY. A Tale of Irish Life. By SAMUEL LOVER. New
Library Edition, with two original illustrations by GEORGE G.
WHITE. 12mo. Cloth, extra, black and gold, $1.25.

"Decidedly the best story of the day, full of frolic, genuine fun, and exquisite touches of Irish humor."—*Dublin Monitor.*

CHARLES O'MALLEY, The Irish Dragoon. By CHARLES LEVER.
New Library Edition, with two original illustrations by F. O.
C. DARLEY. 12mo. Cloth, extra, black and gold, $1.25.

HARRY LORREQUER. By CHARLES LEVER. New Library
Edition, with two original illustrations by GEO. G. WHITE.
12mo. Cloth, extra, black and gold, $1.25.

"The intense spirit and frolic of the author's sketches have made him
one of the most successful writers of the day."—*London Literary Gazette.*

"The author is pre-eminent for his mirth-moving powers, for his acute
sense of the ridiculous, for the breadth of his humor, and his powers of
dramatic writing which render his boldest conceptions with the happiest
facility."—*London Athenæum.*

"We hardly know how to convey an adequate notion of the exuberant
whim and drollery by which this writer is characterized. His works are a
perpetual feast of gayety."—*John Bull, London.*

POPULAR NATURAL HISTORY. By the Rev. J. G. WOOD,
M.A. From entirely new electrotype plates, with five hundred illustrations by eminent artists. Crown 8vo. Cloth,
extra, black and gold, $1.75.

Mr. Wood is an amusing, instructive, and sensible writer—always doing
good work in a good way—and his work on Natural History is without
doubt his masterpiece.

THE ODES OF HORACE. Translated into English verse, with
Life and Notes, by THEODORE MARTIN. With a fine portrait
of Horace. 16mo. Cloth, extra, $1.00.

Mr. Martin's translation has been commended as preserving—more than
any other—the spirit and grace of the original. It is the most successful
attempt ever made to render into English the inimitable odes of Horace.
The memoir prefixed to the volume is a most charming piece of biography.

GREEK MYTHOLOGY SYSTEMATIZED. With complete Tables
based on Hesiod's Theogony; Tables showing the relation of
Greek Mythology and History, arranged from Grote's History
of Greece; and Gladstone's Homeric Tables. With a full
Index. By S. A. SCULL. Profusely illustrated. 12mo. Cloth,
black and gold, $1.50.

"A book which will prove very useful to the student and man of letters,
and of incalculable benefit as a hand-book."—*Republic, Washington.*

"A real want is supplied by this book, which is, in fact, a cyclopædia of
Greek Mythology, so far as that is possible in a single volume of reasonable
size and moderate cost."—*Evening Mail, New York.*

"This text-book on Mythology presents the subject in a more practical
and more attractive style than any other work on the subject with which
we are familiar, and we feel assured that it will at once take a leading position among books of its class."—*The Teacher, Philadelphia.*

THE IMITATION OF CHRIST. By THOMAS a KEMPIS. New and best edition, from entirely new electrotype plates, single column, large, clear type. 18mo.

Plain Edition, round corners. Cloth, extra, red edges, 50 cents; French morocco, gilt cross, 75 cents; limp Russia, inlaid cross, red under gold edges, $2.00.

Red Line Edition, round corners. Cloth, black and gold, red edges, 75 cents; cloth, black and gold, gilt edges, $1.00; French morocco, red under gold edges, $1.50; limp Russia, inlaid cross, red under gold edges, $2.50; limp Russia, solid gilt edges, box circuit, $3.00; limp calf, red under gold edges, $2.50; limp calf, solid gilt edges, box circuit, $3.00.

THE WORDS AND MIND OF JESUS AND FAITHFUL PROM-ISER. By Rev. J. R. MACDUFF, D.D., author of "Morning and Night Watches." New and best edition, from entirely new electrotype plates, single column, large, clear type. 18mo.

Plain Edition, round corners. Cloth, extra, red edges, 50 cents; French morocco, gilt cross, 75 cents; limp Russia, inlaid cross, red under gold edges, $2.00.

Red Line Edition, round corners. Cloth, black and gold, red edges, 75 cents; cloth, black and gold, gilt edges, $1.00; limp calf or Russia, red under gold edges, $2.50.

A DICTIONARY OF THE BIBLE. Comprising its Antiquities, Biography, Geography, Natural History, and Literature. Edited by WILLIAM SMITH, LL.D. Revised and adapted to the present use of Sunday-school Teachers and Bible Students by Rev. F. N. and M. A. PELOUBET. With eight colored maps and over 350 engravings on wood. 8vo. Cloth, extra, black and gold, $2.00; sheep, marbled edges, $3.00; half morocco, gilt top, $3.50.

"No similar work in our own or in any other language is for a moment to be compared with Dr. Smith's Dictionary of the Bible. The Christian and the scholar have a treasure-house on every subject connected with the Bible, full to overflowing, and minute even to the telling of mint and cummin."—*London Quarterly Review.*

COMPREHENSIVE BIOGRAPHICAL DICTIONARY. Embracing accounts of the most eminent persons of all ages, nations, and professions. By E. A. THOMAS. Crown 8vo. Cloth, extra, gilt top, $2.50; sheep, marbled edges, $3.00; half morocco, gilt top, $3.50; half Russia, gilt top, $4.50.

The aim of the publishers in issuing this work is to present in convenient size and at moderate price a comprehensive dictionary of biography, embracing accounts of the most eminent personages in all ages, countries, and professions.

During the last quarter of a century so many important events have been enacted, such as the Civil War in America and the Franco-Prussian War of 1870, and such great advances have been made in the line of invention and scientific investigation, that within that period many persons have risen by superior merit to conspicuous positions; and as the plan of this work embraces accounts of the living as well as of the dead, many names are included that are not to be found in other dictionaries of biography.

THE HORSE IN THE STABLE AND THE FIELD. His Management in Health and Disease. By J. H. WALSH, F.R.C.S. (Stonehenge.) From the last London edition. Illustrated with over 80 engravings, and full-page engravings from photographs. 12mo. Cloth, extra, bev. boards, black and gold, $2.00.

" It sustains its claim to be the only work which has brought together in a single volume, and in clear, concise, and comprehensive language, adequate information on the various subjects on which it treats."—*Harper's Magazine.*

"This is the best English book on the horse, revised and improved by competent persons for publication in this country. It is the most complete work on the subject, probably, in the English language, and that, of course, means the most complete in existence. Everything relating to a horse that history, science, observation, or practical knowledge can furnish, has a place in it."— *Worcester Daily Spy.*

THE HORSE. By WILLIAM YOUATT, together with a General History of the Horse; a dissertation on the American Trotting Horse, and an essay on the Ass and the Mule. By J. S. SKINNER. With a beautiful engraving on steel of the famous "West Australian," and 58 illustrations on wood. 8vo. Cloth, extra, black and gold, $1.75.

BOOK OF THE FARM. The Handy-book of Husbandry. Containing Practical Information in Regard to Buying or Leasing a Farm; Fences and Farm Buildings, Farming Implements, Drainage, Plowing, Subsoiling, Manuring, Rotation of Crops, Care and Medical Treatment of the Cattle, Sheep, and Poultry; Management of the Dairy; Useful Tables, etc. By GEORGE E. WARING, JR., of Ogden Farm, author of "Draining for Profit and for Health," etc. New edition, thoroughly revised by the author. With 100 illustrations. 12mo. Cloth, extra, black and gold, $2.00.

AMERICAN ORNITHOLOGY; or, The Natural History of the Birds of the United States. By ALEXANDER WILSON and CHARLES LUCIEN BONAPARTE. Popular Edition, complete in one volume imperial octavo. 1200 pages and nearly 400 illustrations of birds. Formerly published at $100; now published at the low price: Cloth, extra, black and gold, $7.50; half morocco, marbled edges, $12.50.

This large and handsome volume, printed in a superior manner on good paper from the original stereotype plates of the larger edition, contains the Life of Wilson, occupying 132 pages; a full Catalogue of North American Birds, furnished by Professor Spencer F. Baird, of the Smithsonian Institution; Complete Index, with the names of over 900 birds described in the text, and is illustrated with nearly 400 figures of birds engraved on wood. It is exactly the same size as the larger edition, with the exception that the engravings are reduced in size and are not colored, reproducing every line of the original edition. It is one of the best books of permanent value (strictly an American book) ever published, noted for its beauty of diction and power of description, pre-eminent as the ablest work on Ornithology, and now published at a moderate price, that places it within the reach of all. Every lover of birds, every school, public or family library should have this book. We know of no other way in which so much pleasure, so much information, and so much usefulness can be had for the price.

AMERICAN CHESS PLAYER'S HAND-BOOK. Teaching the Rudiments of the Game, and giving an Analysis of all the recognized openings. Exemplified by appropriate Games actually played by Paul Morphy, Harrwitz, Anderssen, Staunton, Paulsen, Montgomery, Meek, and others. From the works of Staunton and others. Illustrated. 16mo. Cloth, extra, $1.25.

AMERICAN GARDENER'S ASSISTANT. Containing complete Practical Directions for the Cultivation of Vegetables, Flowers, Fruit Trees, and Grape Vines. By THOMAS BRIDGMAN. New edition, revised and enlarged, by S. EDWARDS TODD. With 70 illustrations. 12mo. Cloth, extra, black and gold, $2.00.

DISEASES OF THE HORSE, AND HOW TO TREAT THEM. A concise Manual of Special Pathology, for the use of Horsemen, Farmers, Stock Raisers, and Students in Agricultural Colleges. By ROBERT CHAWNER. Illustrated. 12mo. Cloth, extra, black and gold, $1.25.

JERSEY, ALDERNEY, AND GUERNSEY COWS. Their History, Nature, and Management. Edited from the writings of Edward P. Fowler, George E. Waring, Jr., Charles L. Sharpless, Prof. John Gamgee, C. P. Le Cornu, Col. Le Couteur, Prof. Magne, Fr. Guenon, Dr. Twaddell, and others, by WILLIS P. HAZARD. 8vo. Illustrated with about 30 engravings, diagrams, etc. Cloth, extra, black and gold, $1.50.

THE TROTTING HORSE OF AMERICA. How to Train and Drive him, with Reminiscences of the Trotting Turf. By HIRAM WOODRUFF. Edited by CHARLES J. FOSTER. Including an Introductory Notice by GEORGE WILKES, and a Biographical Sketch by the Editor. 20th edition, revised and brought down to 1878, and containing a full account of the famous "Rarus." With a steel portrait of the author, and six engravings on wood of celebrated trotters. 12mo. Cloth, extra, black and gold, $2.50.

PORTER & COATES' INTEREST TABLES. Containing accurate calculations of interest at $\frac{1}{2}$, 1, 2, 3, $3\frac{1}{2}$, 4, $4\frac{1}{2}$, 5, 6, 7, 8 and 10 per cent. per annum, on all sums from $1.00 to $10,000, and from one day to six years. Also some very valuable tables, calculated by John E. Coffin. 8vo. Cloth, extra, $1.00.

READY RECKONER (The Improved,) FORM AND LOGBOOK. The Trader's, Farmer's and Merchant's useful assistant. Containing Tables of Values, Wages, Interest, Scantling, Board, Plank and Log Measurements, Business Forms, etc. 18mo. Boards, cloth back, illustrated cover, 25 cents.

www.ingramcontent.com/pod-product-compliance
Lightning Source LLC
Chambersburg PA
CBHW020846020726
47497CB00005B/1278